ONCE UPON HER HONOR

JESSIE CLEVER

SOMEDAY LADY
PUBLISHING, LLC.

ISBN-13: 978-1-7333262-4-7

For Meagan Marsh.

Thank you for always being the Lizzie to my Emily.
This one is for you.

CHAPTER 1

*T*en years ago, if you had told her that her life would be forever changed from one moment in a bookshop, Lady Emily Black would not have believed you in the slightest.

But it wasn't as if one could schedule the moment when one might overhear the plotting of a murder.

Of the one person she held most dear.

Of the one person who had ever been able to touch her very soul.

The murder of Professor Xavier Mesmer.

In the six years of her self exile, she'd grown very good at not reacting. So as she stood in Barnaby's Books of London, perusing a copy of Hector Lamire's latest treatise on the refraction of light through concave lenses, she did not react in the slightest. Her breath did not hitch, and her gaze did not wander. Any passerby would have thought her thoroughly engrossed in the book open in her hands.

But just then, Emily could not have read a single word of it if her very life depended on it. For she didn't see the book at all. As soon as she'd heard his name—Xavier Mesmer—just the whisper of it, scuttled about in the quiet of a bookshop on Marlborough Street, it was enough to have her mind careening across time to that moment so long ago. A moment that should have faded with the passage of years, but no matter how hard she tried to will it, it cruelly remained as perfect and fresh as a newly laundered gown.

The moment when Professor Xavier Mesmer had saved her life.

The moment when she had fallen to the ground, her hands pressed to the wound in his leg to staunch the flow of blood. The crimson stream that bubbled up through her fingers, spilling over her hands and into the wet grass of morning.

That was all she could see when she heard the name Professor Xavier Mesmer, and so it was that she did not move. For she couldn't. That was the power Xavier had had on her. Even through a fading memory, he could stop her dead.

She forced herself to blink, opened her senses to the space around her, pulling herself back from that long ago memory.

The sound of rain came first, crashing against the front windows of Barnaby's, rushing to her ears like a swarm of startled birds. Then came the ticking clock. A monstrosity Mrs. Barnaby had acquired in Switzerland and which she'd foisted off on Mr. Barnaby for keeping time in his shop.

Then, oddly enough, a smell. A smell came to her next. The strong odor of wet wool and camphor. The wet wool she could explain as it was raining, but it was the mixture of the two that struck a wary cord deep in her memory.

But reality was coming too quickly now, and she couldn't stop to ponder it. For now she heard the men who had been speaking. The men who conversed on the topic of murder.

As her family was plagued with spies for the British

crown and detective inspectors for the Metropolitan Police, the mention of murder had little effect on her. It was as if someone had made a comment on runny eggs. It was only Xavier's name that held the power to render her insensible. So she turned a keen ear to the conversation and waited.

There were two men on the other side of the bookshelf from where she stood. This was the first disappointing aspect of the two men. They were standing in the section dedicated to home management. Quite an obvious blunder as it could be assumed they were hoping their conversation would go unnoticed. But instead, they stood in the one place to appear most suspicious should anyone notice.

And Emily had noticed.

Over the scent of wet wool and camphor came a more telling aroma—pitch and tar and salt. She could only make out their beaver top hats and not much else, but from their accents, she would have guessed they were well bred. This would exclude the profession of dockhand, and therefore, the smell could only mean these gentlemen had recently come off a ship.

But a ship from where?

"I should like the matter settled as quickly as possible," the man on the left said.

He had a marked accent, vaguely European in nature, but every other word or so there was a slip, and the syllable would come out crisply British. How odd. Was the man attempting to hide his British roots or was he attempting to affect a British accent and failing spectacularly at it?

The man to the right responded. "Of course, my good man. His ship is to arrive at the end of the week, and my men plan to meet him at the dock. London is a dangerous town, you know. Wouldn't want our dear professor venturing off the dock without a proper escort." The sneer was audible in his voice.

Emily closed her book, placed it back on the shelf.

The gentleman on the left seemed unaffected by his companion's obvious, sinister delight.

"Just see to it that it's done." The bell above the shop door tinkled as the man left.

Emily turned and swept around the bookshelf with no hesitation. The man she encountered there was frail and weak, the knobs of his elbows clear through his cutaway coat. He had a twitchy mustache and an alarming lack of eyebrows over the gold rims of his spectacles.

She had also clearly startled him as he massaged the head of a walking stick in both hands.

It was the walking stick that threw her.

Xavier carried a walking stick.

Now.

She swallowed, forcing her composure to steady.

"Can you recommend a good resource for the management of the household menu?" she asked, tilting her head the smallest of degrees as if to impart the need for assistance.

The weak man quivered under her gaze, and at her request, touched the brim of his hat and scurried away with little more than a garbled excuse.

She watched the door of the shop close behind him, the feeling of inevitability falling over her like a warm cloak.

It appeared it was now her turn to save Xavier's life.

* * *

"You must tell someone."

Emily lowered the point of her epee so she could peer at her cousin over the end of it.

"And what am I to say? I overheard two men plotting murder in a bookshop."

Lizzie shrugged. "This family has heard far more outlandish things."

"But that's just the point." She put down her sword entirely and considered her cousin. "The family is likely to dismiss it as common talk. We are a rather warped bunch, you know."

Lizzie lowered her epee as well. "You have a point there." She gestured with a nod of her head. "So what is it you plan to do?"

Emily brushed a hand across her forehead, dislodging her fringe from the sheen of sweat that always developed when she sparred with her cousin. Fencing was glorious exercise, but it required a comprehensive toilette following.

"I'm going to save him, of course," she said.

She felt the pressure of Lizzie's gaze on her, studying her as if her plan to save the man who had saved her was utter rubbish. She squared her shoulders, shrugging off the sensation, and walked over to the tea cart left earlier by her housekeeper, Mrs. Merriweather.

They were in the sewing room of her townhouse at 34 Whitaker in Mayfair. The sewing room because it was more likely she would pick up a sword before picking up a needle. The room had been cleared of unnecessary furniture, and the space left was quite accommodating to their fencing endeavors.

She had wallowed at the family seat in Bedford for several months after the incident of 1834, before resolve hardened her self-recriminations into a plan. It wasn't long after that she had convinced her cousin, rather an expert in the matter, to teach her the finer points of sword play. At the time it had seemed like a wise decision when her plan to become an independent recluse of sorts first unfolded.

A plan which would guarantee that what had happened would never happen again.

Hence her current situation.

Society would not recognize her now. She knew that, and she was glad of it. For too long she'd heard the whispers about town. About the poor daughter of the Duke of Lofton. A spinster now, you know.

But there wasn't anything poor about her.

She had caused her downfall herself, and she would spend the rest of her life redeeming her honor if that was what it took.

She eyed Lizzie now. "You think it a foolhardy plan."

Her cousin cocked her head. "Not foolhardy. Cumbersome actually." She set aside her epee before joining Emily at the teacart. "How do you plan to go about it?"

Emily picked up her cup of tea, grown comfortably cool now and drank deeply, quenching the thirst brought on by exercise. "I've already sent a boy to the dockmaster to inquire after ships arriving from America due in this week. Once I've established a target, I'll go down to the docks at their estimated days of arrival and wait."

"Go down to the docks?" Her cousin regarded her. "In London?" She picked up her own cup of tea with an obvious smirk. "You do know you're a lady, right?"

Emily finished her tea before replying. "I plan to go in disguise."

Lizzie's face lit at her words, and she dropped onto the arm of a nearby chair as if settling in for a good tale. "Oh, which costume will you choose this time?"

In order to make self exile successful, Emily had adopted a series of costumes, which allowed her to go about society unseen. It was a terrific scheme and had worked better than any expectations she may have held. No one looked at maids or dust sweeps. No one questioned an elderly matron shuffling down the pavement.

But more, no one questioned a lad in trousers.

"I'll be going as the lad, of course. I'll need the ability to move quickly if I must defend the professor there at the docks." She leaned against the back of the only sofa in the room, crossed her arms. "The man in the bookshop claimed he'd finish the deed there and be done with the matter. It would suggest I should arrive prepared for the worst."

Lizzie's eyes widened ever so slightly before she said, "Do you think you may need assistance?"

Emily had come to understand that bright-eyed, open expression on her cousin's face and felt an instant pain of guilt for having to close it down. Part of her self exile meant never opening up a family member to potential danger. She would never again allow harm to come to her family because of something she'd done. No matter what.

"I'm afraid not," Emily said, keeping her tone soft. "You know I couldn't allow you to do that."

Lizzie sat up. "You wouldn't be *allowing* me to do anything. I am offering my services. The impetus would be on my conscience, not yours."

Emily had to laugh at her cousin's persistence. In the six years since she'd parted ways with her family, Lizzie had been the one person with whom she'd remained in touch. Oh, she'd corresponded with her father, the Duke of Lofton, and she often took tea with her mother, but the extended family had fallen away from her. Just as she preferred it. You couldn't do harm to someone you never encountered.

But she could admit that lately she missed that big, vociferous family. She missed the tight bonds peril had created between them. The work of the Black family was hazardous at best, and the risk involved forged a strong family connection that had taken an excruciatingly long time to sever. She felt its loss now, deep within her as if it reverberated in her bones.

"But I shan't enjoy being on the receiving end of your

mother's wrath should anything happen to you," Emily said now, thinking of Mrs. Eleanora Black, the wife of her father's bastard brother.

Aunt Nora had been a formidable force in her younger years and now ruled her family with quiet, steely authority. Lizzie was a lot like her, a grown woman now, Emily realized with a jolt. It had been a long time they had been playing at swords, and in those years, Lizzie had blossomed. She'd filled out her awkward frame with hard muscle and soft curves.

She should be married with a family by now.

The thought had careened out of the black tumble of her thoughts, and she shoved it away. While others cast the name of spinster at her with obvious derision, she would not be so crass as to mirror such behavior. Lizzie's choices were her own, and if she had not found someone with whom she wished to share her life, that was Lizzie's own doing. Emily clearly had no latitude to judge.

Lizzie frowned. "I cannot fault you that." She took a sip of her tea. "So you shall go as the lad then? You think there may be an encounter?"

The lad was a costume she had developed several years into her exile. The memory of her betrayal burned so hotly, even years after the fact, that it compelled her to seek a way to physically defend her family from attack. While the fencing lessons with Lizzie had been a good start, it wasn't enough. The fire of guilt had driven her forward to shape herself into a sort of creature that was as far from a lady of the ballroom as she could get.

But even that wasn't enough.

She'd had to test the skills she'd honed against real opponents. Not that she'd gone looking for danger per se. It was just that she hadn't avoided it.

"The lad should suit just perfectly." She straightened. "It's what shall happen afterward that I haven't figured yet."

"You mean how to keep him safe and find those plotting his death?" Lizzie asked.

Emily nodded as she paced across the room. "I didn't recognize the man in the bookshop nor the voice of his companion." She recalled the unseen man's odd accent, and just the memory of it along with the mystery odor of wet wool and camphor stirred the hairs on the back of her neck. "I don't know who it is that seeks the professor's death, and until I do I can't very well let him wander around London unprotected."

"Did you ever think perhaps that's not your responsibility?"

Emily pivoted at her cousin's words. "It is *only* my responsibility," she said softly.

Her cousin gave no outward reaction to her swift reply. She simply went on unaffected. "But why is it someone seeks his death? What is it he's done this time?"

The last time Xavier had been the focus of a potentially fatal plot had been when his telescope technology was the focus of attempted treason. A defected agent for the War Office had sought to obtain the technology by force and sell it to the highest bidder, even if that entity was not Britain. The defected agent had been Lord Crawley, a trusted member of the Office, and he'd posed as a duke to trick Emily into revealing the whereabouts of her cousin, Jane, who held the secret that would destroy Crawley. Jane had almost died because of Emily's foolishness.

Emily studied the pattern of carpet at her feet, willing the past to go quietly away and leave her be. "The War Office is certain Lord Crawley died sometime in the last three years in Italy." Even saying the name of the man sent a shiver down her spine.

Once she had believed she would marry him. Lord Crawley. Only she hadn't known he was Lord Crawley. He posed as a duke to snare her attention. How stupid she had been. How naive. The fire flamed inside of her, and she had to swallow against the guilt.

She moved her gaze, focused on her cousin to distract herself from the distaste of her own weaknesses. "We can only assume someone else is after his inventions now."

"The telescope technology again?"

Emily shook her head. "He's been working on something new. Something to do with filtering water from desert wells. It's quite interesting, but a far departure from his earlier work."

She did not miss the smirk on Lizzie's face, nor the accusing eyebrow cocked up in amusement. "You've been following our dear professor."

Emily pursed her lips as she put her hands to her hips in a posture much like her mother's. "Of course, I've been following his research. I like to stay abreast of current affairs and development in the scientific realm, you know."

"Now you do." Lizzie shook her head slowly. "How different you are from the debutante you once we're."

Emily felt her face heat at the reminder of her careless youth. "I find the state of politics in this country has far more bearing than the latest fashion from Paris."

"You didn't always think that." The words were softly spoken, but the tone held no judgment. If anything, her cousin's voice was like a balm against the fire inside of her, and for a moment, her guilt rested.

It was true. She had once been the toast of London, but her cousin's declaration told her she'd changed when she couldn't believe it herself. A beat of silence passed between them, the tones of understanding ringing in the space.

Finally Lizzie straightened. "I still think you should tell someone," she said as she gathered up her epee. "What if something should happen to you?"

Emily shrugged. "I've told you. You're someone."

Lizzie laughed. "I'm hardly someone." She cradled her sword and gloves in her arms. "It's Madeline who draws the attention this season."

Emily felt the twinge of guilt at her little sister's name. She scrambled backwards in her thoughts, calculating the years that had swept by. "She isn't debuting this season, is she?"

Lizzie nodded as she made her way to the door. "She's all the rage. The daughter of a duke? I'm fairly certain it's more of a splash than when you came out."

Emily's throat felt suddenly dry and not from exertion. Her little sister. Coming out. And she wasn't there to see it. What price betrayal carried with it.

Lizzie was nearly out the door when Emily called after her. "Please give her my best."

The words sailed across the room like a spear, and Lizzie swung about as if Emily had succeeded in a direct hit. Lizzie's eyes were round, her lips slightly parted. In the six years of self exile, not once had Emily indicated the other members of her family existed. Her request was an unprecedented departure from her strict rules, and Lizzie knew it just as she did.

Lizzie regained her composure rather quickly and said, "I shall do that." Her cousin hesitated in the door. "Jane and Austin have come into town. For the start of the season."

Once again a single name had the power to end her.

Jane.

Lizzie's sister. The cousin she'd betrayed with her carelessness, with her selfishness. Jane, whose life she'd put into utter jeopardy with the ridiculous quest to snare a duke. How *stupid* she'd been.

"She asked after you. If you'd be joining the family for dinner one evening."

Emily could only watch her cousin, drink her in as the words ricocheted around her head, as the memories invaded in a single wave large enough to drown her.

Jane.

She'd spent six years trying to make up for what she'd done, but she knew now there would never be enough years left in her life to assuage her guilt. To right her wrongs.

She was doomed to be a reclusive spinster for life. That was her penance, and she'd serve it with pride.

She straightened her shoulders, folded her hands in front of her. "If I shan't be here at our appointed fencing time next week, please tell my mother what happened to me."

Lizzie's eyes closed briefly, and the slouch of her shoulders was visible from across the room where Emily stood. Finally, her cousin opened her eyes, but her expression remained blank. "You know Jane has forgiven you. There is no need to atone for sins you believe you have committed. Not like this."

Emily licked her lips, but the words came easily. "But I have not forgiven myself."

CHAPTER 2

*H*e hated London.

Just the smell of it had his heart longing for the sweet breeze from the Charles River in Boston. The voyage across the Atlantic had been lugubrious and for far too much of it, nauseating as well, but he couldn't refuse the heartfelt plea of a dear friend.

After all, it was the death of a dear friend that compelled him these days. Always now, the death of Bobby Egemont drove him. His student and mentee died to save Xavier's life. To prevent Xavier's research from falling into evil hands. The young man had conceived a ploy to distract the men who wanted Xavier by boarding a research vessel bound for the northern most seas. Bobby had been killed when the men caught up to him and realized they had fallen into a trap. Xavier lived with his friend's death, the guilt resting squarely at his feet.

He no longer performed research on telescopes. Such an innocent act, he had once believed, had drawn the attention of far too many interested more in war than in peace, and he wanted nothing to do with it.

Bobby had died because of it, and he would never again put someone in danger. Not because of his silly research.

As the London skyline came into focus, he could admit it wasn't Bobby Egemont he thought of now.

It was a lass.

A hazel eyed, petite blonde with a tongue sharper than a polished lens.

Lady Emily Black.

She had rambled about in his memory like a specter, appearing suddenly, disturbingly, at the most odd moments only to vanish without so much as a whisper.

As an academic, he prided himself on his orderly and disciplined nature, so he couldn't fathom why it was the vibrant and chaotic Lady Emily had captured his conscience. It was so unpredictable, so unexpected.

So unwanted.

For six years, the unfinished memory of her haunted him. She'd retreated the day after he'd saved her life, and something was left undone between them. It plagued him. He never enjoyed an untested hypothesis. He worked in results. Not might have beens.

He had never returned to England since the episode with Bobby, and he'd sworn he never would.

But then the letter had come. It's tone urgent, but it's substance, that was what had him boarding a ship he'd said he'd never get on.

Lord Avery, the chair at the Royal Astronomical Society, had requested his aid in the meeting of top advisors to the Crown regarding the Ottoman matter. Anyone who had picked up a newspaper recently knew of the tensions in the Middle East. Europe feared an Ottoman collapse if the war with Egypt continued, and England and other European powers were gathering to devise a strategy to prevent such a disaster and end the conflict.

An end to any conflict spoke to the thing that rattled his nerves now, and Lord Avery knew it. But to have a hand in such a global attempt at peace, was, well, irresistible. Xavier was not naive enough to believe England's intent was altruistic. He was fairly certain there were other, more compelling reasons for England to get involved, principally economic ones, but that didn't stop him from feeling the pull, the need to contribute what he could.

So maybe then, Bobby had not died in vain.

It still meant a return to London, and with that, his gut had roiled for weeks on end. The battering waves had not helped in the last few days of their sea voyage, and so he was rather physically ill when he stepped off the gangway at the docks. He knew he need only get away from the stank of saltwater and the reel of the deck beneath his feet, and he would feel himself again.

He would think later that it was perhaps because of his physical impairment that the entire occurrence on the docks seemed so exceedingly strange. Perhaps the sea air had finally gotten to him, addled his brain in ways he hadn't predicted. Perhaps it was the shock of being back in England. He couldn't be certain what it was, but he could be sure it was to date the oddest thing that had ever happened to him.

It started innocently enough as he made his way to the wharf, his trunks on a trolley before him as a dockhand helped him to shore. Lord Avery was to meet him, but he feared the boat had arrived rather too early. He scanned the wharf and while many carriages blazoned with colors stood at the ready, Xavier did not see the familiar seal of his colleague.

They had nearly reached shore when the first man stepped in front of him.

"Professor, ain't it?" The man was missing both of his front teeth and smelled curiously of sausage. He stood but two feet in front of Xavier and effectively blocked his retreat to the shore.

"Isn't it what?" Xavier responded because he wasn't sure the gentleman had asked a complete question.

"You. Ain't ye the professor?" The man spit a little when he spoke, white bubbles forming in the corner of his mouth.

"I am Professor Xavier Mesmer. To whom do I have the pleasure of conversing?"

The sun bore down on them, unusually hot for so early in spring in England. The last time he had been here it had been a rainy spring. Soggy enough to fix his joints, but this sun was worse. It rankled with his determination to remain annoyed with having to be in London.

The man didn't answer him. He turned and gestured to someone else down the dock. A man emerged from between stacks of wooden crates. He was far burlier, wider across the shoulders, and his face lay hidden beneath a rat's nest of beard. Xavier tightened his grip on his walking stick, a sigh of frustration slipping between his lips.

He really did hate London.

Before the gentleman could turn about, Xavier had his walking stick at the ready and brought it down just at the angle between neck and shoulder, striking the man with a disabling blow. The thug fell to the dock with a gurgled moan of pain, but it was enough to draw the attention of several onlookers. Dockhands and captains, seamen and passengers. It was a bustling day at London's wharf, and apparently, Xavier was there to give them a show.

The second, burlier man was faster than he appeared, which would prove to be Xavier's undoing. Before he could get another proper grip on his walking stick, the second thug was on him, his beefy hands clamping on Xavier's shoulder until he heard the snap of sinew and groan of joints. His knees hit the boards of the dock before he realized he was going down, and white hot pain sliced through his thigh.

His hand went to it involuntarily, pressing into the mangled flesh in a sort of hypnotic movement that had developed when the knife wound had healed. It did nothing to help ease the ghost pain of an old injury, but it made him feel as if he could do something about it.

There were shouts from the onlookers now. Someone called for a bobby, but Xavier held no hope in that direction. If this burly chap wanted to end him, it would be done. A bobby would never get here in time. And it wasn't as if he could rely on someone else to save him.

The burly chap grunted as he pressed harder on Xavier's shoulder, and for a moment, he thought the man very well might break a bone.

"What's with the cane, old man?" Spittle rained down on Xavier from the man's nest of a beard, but he didn't flinch. What would have been the point?

"I'm a harmless, old cripple," he shot back. "What is it you want with me?"

The man's reply was only a grunt, and then he was lifting Xavier from the dock with a single hand under his arm. The pain in his thigh redoubled its efforts to make him pass out, and he sucked in a breath, his vision tunneling.

Somewhere in the gray that enveloped him the cries of the onlookers began to take shape. They were no longer calling out to him or to a bobby. They were no longer exclaiming over the crass scene before them. They were shouting at someone else.

He forced his eyes open, gritted his teeth against the pain until the world beyond his hurt took shape.

"Look! It's him. It's the boy!"

His gaze darted from one side of the wharf to the other, but he saw nothing beyond the usual melee of a busy waterfront. He took in the same stacks of wooden crates, the same dockhands and passengers. But this must have been an aberration. Something that drew their exclaim. Finally, he noticed something odd about the crowd. They were looking up.

He allowed his gaze to float, his attention skimming the upper most crates, the discarded netting, the beams that made up the supports of the docks.

That's when he saw it.

Or him rather.

A boy, standing atop such a crate not five feet from him.

The lad was small and slight, dressed in unrelenting black including his face. He didn't know why it gave him such a shock to see it, but the boy had his face covered in a black cloth. Only his eyes were visible through a small slit between cloth and the wide brimmed hat he wore.

The boy looked like nothing more than just that, a boy, and he couldn't begin to imagine why he should draw such attention from the crowd. What was a lad like that supposed to do? Be the second one to get crushed by the barbarian who held Xavier's arm in his vise-like grip?

But then the burly man dropped him without ceremony. Xavier crashed to the dock, his leg giving out without a hope of recovery. The appendage throbbed, crumpled beneath him, and he scrambled to straighten it before he could focus once more on the strange tableau before him.

"Mmmmmm," the beastly man groaned up at the lad.

The boy stood with one leg bent atop the rim of the crate, his fisted hands to his hips as he studied the giant beneath him. And then, if Xavier had not witnessed it himself, he would have denied it happened.

The boy jumped. Leaped clear over the thug and landed with a gentle step on the other side of him.

Between Xavier and the thug.

And without waiting to catch his breath, the lad pulled a sword from a scabbard at his waist. The sun glinted off the deadly edge of the blade, and the boy's legs slipped into a stance so artful and strong, it was as if the lad was born to do it.

But that wasn't the oddest thing that happened.

Blade raised, feet steady, the boy flicked the end of his sword in a come hither motion at the giant, and the giant grinned in response.

Xavier pushed himself to one knee, readying himself to flee, but he knelt there, mesmerized by the display before him. The giant lunged, but the boy was ready. He thrust the blade to the right at the same time he dodged to the left, spinning neatly on his feet.

Two things happened then.

The blade connected, and blood blossomed red across the greasy coat of the giant's left arm.

But the more important thing, the thing that caused Xavier's stomach to clench instantly, was the boy. When he spun about, he was close enough for Xavier to see his eyes.

Hazel eyes.

The word *no* screamed through his brain, and he renewed his determination to regain his feet. His fingers closed around the head of his walking stick just as the lad made his next and final move.

His wicked blade sliced through the air, a soft whoosh as it cut the space and with sickening ease, the sword swept along the backs of the giant's legs just at the knee.

Xavier didn't need to be a man of science to know what had just occurred. The boy had cut the tendons that ran along the length of the giant's legs. While blood erupted from the wound, that was not the damaging result. The thug collapsed like a feather falling to the ground, ethereal and without noise. One moment standing and the next not.

The roaring in his ears was overcome by the cheer of the crowd, a gathered noise that sang the same praises. The lad had done it.

Again.

But he didn't have time to think about that because the lad was already moving. He neatly stepped on the back of the fallen thug and used it to springboard over the man and gently fall to the dock beyond in a neat somersault. As he sprang to his feet, he re-sheathed his sword, his free hand already reaching—

For Xavier.

His brain was trying so hard to keep pace, he didn't have time to resist. The lad was already under his arm, lifting him from the ground.

On the side of his bad leg.

There had been a brief moment when doubt had zinged its way through his head. He must be wrong. Surely he was wrong. What were the odds of someone possessing hazel eyes? It couldn't be her.

But then, in that moment, when the lad perched himself as a support under Xavier's injured leg, he knew without a hint of doubt.

They were running before his thoughts cleared, before resignation could fall like a burst of smoke from a faulty flew. They reached the shore and the long line of carriages, the crowd parting for them in a wave of cheers and triumphs.

It all roiled his stomach more than the traitorous waves of weeks past. More than the mere thought of returning to London.

The lad came out from under his shoulder and snatched the door of a waiting carriage. The conveyance was nondescript, jet black and plain. It blended with any number of carriages, and the thought sent a jolt of apprehension through him.

The boy stepped back and yanked on Xavier's arm to get him to enter the carriage. He wanted to hesitate. He wanted to pull back, but now he was far too close to those hazel eyes, and their gaze propelled him to board.

The door shut with a snap as soon as he hit the bench, the darkness of the closed in space shuddering around him. The carriage sprang into motion before the boy had seated himself, but the rocking motion did nothing to upset his balance.

Not as he took his seat.

Not as he removed his hat, releasing a cascade of unforgettable blonde curls. Not as he withdrew the cloth from about his face, revealing far more than hazel eyes.

Xavier was not rendered shocked. Not in the slightest. Because he already knew who his savior was.

"Lady Emily Black," he said out loud for the first time in six years.

* * *

THAT BIT where she'd vaulted over the beast's back was rather overdone, but the crowd had seemed to enjoy it. Her thrust had been a little weak though, and she'd only managed to score his arm. She needed to work on her footing, obtain a proper stance before going on the attack.

This was something she often did after a bout as the lad. Self reflection for improvement of her form. But the depth of her analysis was thwarted by the presence of Professor Xavier Mesmer.

She had spent the week preparing to see him again. Six years was a long time to nurse a wound, and she'd spent plenty of time nurturing the guilt she harbored over what had happened to him.

Because of her.

Because of her silly, worthless, meaningless attempts to gain a coveted husband in society's eyes.

What rot.

She'd caused a man to spend the rest of his life walking with the aid of a cane. She'd seen him go down on the dock, seen his hand go to his thigh so quickly as if drawn to the thundering pain that must still linger there.

She swallowed now, the image unwilling to be banished from her mind.

Even at the pain of seeing him, at the reminder of what she had wrought, there had been another, unexpected reaction to seeing him.

A tightening of her stomach, a clench around her heart, a beckoning, a *yearning* toward him.

The spark of a different flame now. One she had long forgotten and hadn't realized existed between them.

But it was there, and it burned hot now, threatening the fire she had stoked for so long. The one that drove her to redemption.

It also surprised her to realize how good he looked. Healthy and robust. He'd filled out a little since the last time she'd seen him, but that had likely mostly come from age. They were both older now with the effects of time stenciled on their bodies.

It had been favorable to him. Lines bracketed his mouth and eyes, his hair fell carelessly in a straight wave under the brim of his hat. His shoulders filled out his coat in a way she hadn't noticed before but seeing it now, it gave her an overwhelming sense of protection. How odd.

It was several moments before she realized he had said something.

"I beg your pardon?"

"Lady Emily Black," he repeated. "It's really you."

She licked her lips and attempted a smile. "Yes, I'm afraid it is." She gestured out the window at the passing waterfront. "I'm terribly sorry about that, but I couldn't think of what else to do once I heard what was to happen."

He eyed her, his jaw going firm. "Once you'd heard?"

She settled back against the bench and crossed one leg over the other. The way his eyes flew to her legs, she remembered with a jolt how unladylike she must appear. How brazen. She uncrossed her legs and tucked them back against the bench, ensuring she kept her knees together.

"The plotting of your murder."

She hadn't meant the words to shock, but again, she'd forgotten herself. She'd been mulling over the encounter at the bookshop for nearly a week now, and she'd rather forgotten how upsetting it could be to hear the mention of *murder* without preamble.

She raised a hand in supplication. "I beg your pardon. I didn't mean to be so blunt."

He didn't say anything, but this eyes continued to watch her. She was used to being watched from her days as a debutante, but she could admit the feeling had grown stale in her isolation. It was a little unsettling to have eyes upon her again.

Mesmer finally swallowed and leaned back. "Someone's plotting my murder?"

She had the sense he had come to a decision about something and what he had said was not what he had wanted to say. The idea of which gave her a hiccup in her stomach.

"Yes, I'm afraid I overheard two gentlemen speaking of the deed Tuesday last whence, browsing Barnaby's Books on Marlborough."

"And you're certain they spoke of me?"

She tilted her head. "You are still Professor Xavier Mesmer, are you not?"

"Unfortunately, yes." His expression remained cold.

"Then unfortunately, yes, it is you they spoke of." She let her eyes drift a moment to the window of the carriage to ascertain their progress toward 34 Whitaker. "Do you know why anyone would want you dead?" She paused, recalculated. "I mean now, of course."

"It is growing rather tedious to be such a wanted man," he grumbled, and unbidden, a smile came to her lips.

"I can imagine it's rather burdensome."

Once more, Mesmer seemed to decide something and sat forward, elbows to knees as he regarded her.

"What's happened to you, Lady Emily?"

The air caught in her lungs, and she blinked at him. He must have observed her discomfort because he motioned with his hand before clarifying.

"I mean your costume. What is all of this about?"

Relief flowed through her, and she allowed the smile to return to her lips. It was far easier to speak of the things that occupied her time these days rather than of the thing that drove her to it. Emotions were a far messier matter, especially when others did not understand them.

"I've developed an appallingly good skill at costumes." She smiled triumphantly. It was a harmless thing of which to be proud, and she was happy to share it with others. For she was good at costumes. Her former taste in fashion had lent itself to the dubious practice of going about society unrecognized, and she rather enjoyed basking in her triumph.

"Costumes?" His forehead wrinkled with question.

"Yes," she said emphatically. "You should see what I am capable of with a little kohl and powder." She waved a hand. "I could walk into any ballroom in London, and no one would be the wiser." As soon as the words escaped her lips, she regretted them. They tread far too closely to her past life.

"Is that so?" He leaned back again, crossed his arms over his chest.

It was then she remembered his walking stick, and her eyes searched about nervously. She hadn't seen whether or not he'd made it into the carriage with it, and for a moment, she feared she had made him lose it.

But her gaze soon landed on it, tucked neatly in the corner of the carriage, its silver head glinting in the sunlight that passed through window above it. She drew a breath in relief, but then her eyes caught on the shape of the walking stick's head.

"Is that a phoenix?"

She looked up in time to see Mesmer follow the path her eyes had taken.

A slow smile came to his lips. "You recognize it?"

"Of course, the phoenix—" She stopped speaking once she took in the expression on his face, the telling smirk and the wrinkled forehead. "Do you think me unstudied in the Greek myths?"

"The Lady Emily I am acquainted with is studied in nothing but social decorum."

The remark cut, but she could say nothing in return. For although it stung to be reminded of who she once was, the comment was stunningly accurate of the person she had been.

"I trust you will find I am not the lady you remember."

"I am not sure if I find such an occurrence intriguing or saddening."

The words were spoken so softly she feared she had misunderstood, but his gaze pinned her to the bench, forced her to straighten her shoulders and clear her throat.

"I should hope it's a promising concept." She gestured in a

25

rolling motion with her hand. "I think it best we return to the topic at hand. That of your murder."

He sat up. "Oh, yes. I cannot think of a more exciting conversation to have with a woman I have not seen in six years and who returns to my life clad in trousers. Tell me, Lady Emily, does your mother know you go about in such attire?"

"I acquired these trousers *from* my mother. She applauds the versatility of the fabric."

"Is that so?"

"Yes. Now then." She leaned forward, coming dangerously close to his face. "Someone is trying to kill you. I think between the two of our intelligences we should resolve the matter. Should you like to begin by telling me who it is that may want you dead?"

He didn't retreat at her advance, and a lick of fire burned in her stomach. She enjoyed the sparring. Her isolation had prevented a thorough, invigorating tete-a-tete for some time now, and she found she missed it.

"No one has ever wanted me dead."

She pursed her lips before saying, "Have you forgotten the circumstances of our acquaintance?"

He held up a single finger. "Lord Crawley wanted my technology. Not my life."

She frowned. "I suppose you're right. So should someone want you dead now?"

"You are the only human being to have ever threatened me bodily harm." He said this with a degree of sarcasm she could not ignore.

"I never threatened you bodily harm."

Again with the wrinkling of the forehead.

"Perhaps I might have done, but I hardly remember it." It galled her that she could, in fact, not remember such an occasion because back then, her tongue had been wickedly sharp and dangerously uncontrolled. She was lucky more hadn't happened than what had.

She shook her head. "But I shan't wish you dead now. That would negate my intent entirely."

"What intent would that be?"

"Why, to save your life, of course. I thought that was apparent from my actions on the dock." She gestured to the window as if the waterfront still lay beyond them.

His face hardened. "You intend to save my life?"

She shrugged. "As I said, of course, I do. It's my responsibility."

He blinked. "Your what?"

"Responsibility." She sighed and leaned forward as if he were hard of hearing, and she could help their communication through proximity. "You saved my life. Now I must save yours. It's only reasonable."

"It's only reasonable to trade the saving of lives?" She didn't like the way his eyes widened in question.

"Isn't it?"

He only shook his head and relaxed against the bench. "I'd forgotten what an unusual family you have."

She wasn't prepared for that remark, and her face fell before she could catch herself.

"What is it?" he asked.

She knew better than to hope he hadn't seen, but she squared her shoulders and pressed on. "I haven't seen my family actually in quite some time."

He wrinkled his nose now, which was not as pleasant a change than the wrinkled forehead as she would have hoped. "You haven't seen your family? Why ever not?"

She couldn't tell him the truth of it. That she feared seeing them. That she didn't deserve to see them. How could he possibly understand how heavy a burden she carried?

The Black family stood for loyalty and trust. She had

shattered both of those tenets with stunning ability in a single morning. Everything her family stood for, she'd obliterated with one careless encounter.

She didn't deserve the Black name, let alone the bosom of such a commendable family.

"I simply have not."

If she had expected him to leave the matter, she was sorely mistaken, but she was luckily saved from further conversation by their arrival to 34 Whitaker.

Not the front door, of course.

The carriage rolled to a gentle stop before turning acutely into the alley that ran between the block of townhouses. Three doors down on the left, the carriage pulled to the side, and the conveyance rocked as the driver stepped down.

Mesmer leaned toward the window and had a hand on the door before she could stop him. She laid her hand over his, and electricity shot through her at the touch. It had been so long since she'd touched someone. But it was more than that. The clenching in her stomach and around her heart returned with greater force, and she withdrew, licking her lips.

"Wait," she said because she could say little else.

He slowly slid his hand from the door handle but did not relax back into the bench. He watched her, and she refused to allow her gaze to slide away. Her pride forced her eyes to meet his, and she kept them there until the carriage rocked once more as the driver regained his seat. The carriage lurched forward, slowly this time as darkness enveloped them entirely.

"What..." Mesmer's words trailed off as the carriage slowed to a stop.

She reached over him and opened the door, gestured for him to alight.

He peered through the door at the semi-darkness beyond.

"It's only the mews," she said at his look of apprehension.

Still he did not move, so she stood and sidled around him, stepping down from the carriage into the familiar smell of hay and horse. The mews were cool, a relief from the hot sun she'd had to wait in for Mesmer's ship to arrive. While she enjoyed the freedom of movement trousers allowed, they were rather stifling.

She climbed the stairs opposite them and looked back at the carriage where Mesmer had only just stuck his head out the door. She waved about them, her hand up as if to suggest there was nothing to fear.

"See. It's only the mews. Are you coming? I should think you'd like to rest after your voyage."

"Coming?"

She waved the same hand behind her. "Into the house, of course."

She slipped through the door behind her without waiting for him to decide if it was safe to follow her.

CHAPTER 3

*H*e watched her go and yet he couldn't make himself move.

He peered around the edges of the carriage door, taking in the cavernous space around him. They had passed along the rows of mews standing sentinel at the back of a row of townhouses, and reason stood this should be a mews as well as Emily had indicated, but it was far too large. The entire carriage plus the horses still harnessed to the conveyance had fit inside the structure at once with the driver still atop, presumably.

A whinny to his right drew his attention and confirmed his suspicions. The horses were still very much harnessed and shuffling their feet impatiently as if waiting for someone to unhitch them and allow them access to their oats. He turned back toward the door only to startle at the sight of a small man standing before him. Dressed all in black much as Emily had been, the man could not be more than a meter and a half and stood with his shoulders square, arms folded behind his back.

"She's a bit much upon introduction, I'm afraid," the man

said in such a refined accent it had Xavier taking notice. No Cockney or Irish tones here. The man could have come straight out of a drawing room in Mayfair.

Xavier peered about again. They likely *were* in Mayfair come to that.

"I would have cause to agree with you, sir." Xavier made to alight but his thigh cramped up. He massaged it hopelessly, but by the time he returned his gaze to the slight, little man, he found he'd disappeared. He hadn't even made a sound in retreat. But where he had stood, a stool now rested. Xavier eyed it, glanced about once more, before trying his leg again. This time the leg had not as far to stretch thanks to the stool, and he was able to ease his way out of the carriage.

His shoulder pulsed in pain, the memory of the giant's grip still too fresh. He shook it out, thinking movement would help, but it only throbbed more. Snatching up his walking stick, he forged ahead, climbing the stairs he'd watched Emily take earlier and passed through a small door into—

Kitchens.

The space was pristine and scented with lemons and vinegar. A pot bubbled with an unknown substance on the fire to the left, and a basket of greens rested on a worktable in the center. But other than that, one could not believe this was a kitchen. He had thought Emily had brought them to Lofton House, but that couldn't be. The kitchens of Lofton House would have been constantly busy trying to feed a household that large.

So where had she brought him?

He heard footsteps beyond the room and turned in the direction of the sound only to spot a little old woman waddling in. She carried a silver salver and muttered at spots she had apparently deemed ghastly and shook her head. She stopped suddenly, her gaze whipping up to meet his.

He tried an innocent smile. "Good day, ma'am."

He wasn't sure what else to say, and Emily was no where in sight. He didn't want to frighten the old woman. She was the epitome of grandmotherly nature with her rounded belly blanketed in a crisp, white apron overwhelmed in ruffles and perfect gray curls peeking out from an equally as white and ruffled cap. Her eyes were small and kind behind the round lenses of her spectacles, and a smile creased the corner of her lips.

He relaxed slightly, glad to see he'd avoided startling the woman until she pulled a pistol from the pocket of her apron. His hands went up in reflex, his walking stick banging into the door frame behind him as he did so.

"I mean no harm," he blurted out before the woman could say anything.

More footsteps sounded, and he prayed to a god he didn't believe in that it was Emily. His efforts were rewarded when she stepped through a door opposite, a small tin in her hand. The smile came to her face immediately at the display she encountered.

"Oh, I see you've met Mrs. Merriweather." She tossed the tin back and forth between her hands. "Mrs. Merriweather, this is the professor."

The old woman's smile brightened now, showing her teeth, and she tucked her pistol back into the pocket of her apron. "Oh, lud, darling, how wonderful. Your plan was successful then?"

"Oh, quite," Emily said, placing the tin on the worktable and prying the lid from it. "The height the wooden crates afforded was most advantageous, but I'm afraid I didn't quite have the arch I wanted on my first thrust." She made a motion with her arm as if she once more fought the giant on the docks. She screwed up her face in concentration and shook her head. "I'll get it next time."

Next time?

What on earth was going on here?

"Unfortunately, the thugs those men sent did get a good wallop in before I could intervene." She shook the tin and a soft, rattling noise spilled from it. "Would you be so good as to brew a pot of tea with this mix for the professor? I fear he may need it's special qualities."

Mrs. Merriweather put down the silver salver and nodded vigorously, her gray curls not moving in the slightest beneath her cap.

"Of course, my girl." She picked up the tin. "I'll bring it up straightaway."

Emily moved to the door Mrs. Merriweather had come through and gestured for him to follow. He did but only because he was entranced.

When he'd pictured stepping off the boat in London, the course of events he had thought likely to occur looked nothing like what had actually happened. A woman who had plagued his memories for six years appearing in the middle of a melee on the docks, dressed as a boy no less, whisking him away to some odd structure capable of hiding an entire carriage and team only to encounter a pistol-wielding housekeeper.

It was all madness.

Perhaps if he went back to the ship and tried it all again, he wouldn't be feeling so out of place just then.

To say nothing of the news someone was trying to kill him.

He remembered only too clearly what it had been like the first time someone was after him. The feeling of eyes upon you at every turn. The pressure of knowing that if just for a moment you let your guard down that would be the moment that would see your death.

To think he was the target once more. God, he really hated London.

He followed Emily above stairs, entering the main floor of what appeared to be a townhouse, a well appointed townhouse judging by the satin wallpaper and marble floors of the corridor in which he found himself.

But just like the kitchens, the space reeked of disuse. Quiet descended like a heavy blanket, suffocating and cloying, and he wanted nothing more than to shrug it off. Where was the gaiety of Lofton House? The bustle of young children scampering about the halls. The brisk calls of a matron, or matrons at a time, manning the household and directing the servants. The bantering of grown brothers navigating the trials of life.

This place, whatever it was, held none of that.

The corridor transitioned into a foyer with vast rooms spilling to either side. Emily went into the one on the right. She was still dressed in trousers, and it was disconcerting to watch her walk in front of him. He was lucky he had unfamiliar surroundings to pull at his gaze because the sight of Emily in those trousers was enough for a priest to give up the collar.

The room in which he found himself was a drawing room, but it was unlike any drawing room he had seen in London or America. There was no delicate furniture costing more than a month of his salary. No antique pottery or fine China.

There were books. Stacks of books. Heaps of books. And there were but five pieces of furniture. A desk with a straight back chair set directly in front of the windows to his left as he entered the room, which judging by the soft rumble of noise emanating from that direction was the front of the house that faced the street. A sofa and a chair and ottoman set made up the remainder of the room. It wasn't the scarcity of the furniture, but rather its condition.

It was all very well used.

The surface of the desk, at least the parts he could see between the strewn paper and toppled books, was scarred as if the occupant had gotten carried away in writing and accidentally marked the wood itself. The sofa revealed a distinct impression he feared would resemble the length and breadth of Lady Emily, a thought his already strained mind could not entertain at the moment. The chair was much the same, a perfect dent in its center with a corresponding dent in its ottoman.

None of the furniture matched, but rather appeared to be pulled straight from the discard pile. The chair had a mended leg. The cushion of the ottoman had been covered over with a rug, but its stuffing still poked from a corner or two. The sofa's upholstery certainly came from the time of Napoleon, and the desk, well. It was a victim of its owner's thirst for knowledge, which he couldn't quite say he regretted.

But his favorite feature were the side tables.

They were all stacks of books.

A tea cup lay discarded on one such pile by the sofa. A stack by the chair contained a notebook and quills. How the occupant did not spill the ink, he couldn't be sure.

"Would you mind telling me where I am?" he finally asked when the continuing silence got the better of him.

Emily started as if she'd forgotten he was there. She stood across the room, rummaging in a pile of post. She stopped, her hand coming out of the rubbish with a single note between two fingers.

"Oh, I'm sorry," she said, brushing a toss of curls out of her face. "This is 34 Whitaker, Mayfair." She frowned at the note in her hand. "Another invitation to the Brownlow ball. Does the woman not learn?" She tossed the note aside, rummaged through the books before pulling one free. She opened it, not bothering with further explanation as if he should know exactly where 34 Whitaker was.

He opened his mouth to request further explanation and stopped. She had tucked her lower lip into her teeth and concentrated on the script in the journal she held in her hands. Her pale hair tumbled about her shoulders, having been freed from the hat she'd worn to the docks.

She was beautiful.

She *had* been beautiful, he recalled, but there was something different about her now. Softer. Gentler. He very much feared her beauty had turned to something more, ran deeper inside of her, and now her beauty was not only on the outside but on the inside as well.

He swallowed.

"And what might 34 Whitaker be?"

Again, he seemed to startle her as she blinked up at him.

"Well, my home, of course." She snapped the journal shut.

"The last time we met your home was Lofton House."

He couldn't be certain, but something passed over her face then like a shadow. But she shook her head quietly and put the journal aside.

"My father allows me the use of this house as no one seemed to want it. Rather small, I should say. What with the growing family, it didn't suit any of the other children." She moved past him toward the desk at the front of the room. "Please do have a seat. Mrs. Merriweather should be up with the tea shortly."

He sat and stood again immediately as he realized he was simply going along with whatever she said. He rubbed the head of his walking stick.

"Emily, I should very much like to know what's going on here."

She turned only her head as she rummaged through the

pile of books on the desk. "I told you. Someone is plotting your murder. I have brought you here to keep you safe until we can plan our next move."

"Our next move? You can't be serious."

She held another journal in her hands. "Of course, I'm serious. You don't think you can ward off the killer yourself, do you?" Her tone dripped with incredulity, and his manhood tucked its tail between its legs.

He unconsciously rubbed a hand against his thigh. Emily's brow creased in response to his motion, and she stepped to the door.

"Where is Mrs. Merriweather? She's usually not this tardy."

"She's fine, Emily. Listen. I think you'd better explain everything that's going on. Why does your housekeeper carry a pistol?" He pointed to the back of the house where the mews should have been. "And what is that contraption where you keep your carriage? And who is your driver? The man moves as if he's some kind of agent for the Crown."

Emily shook her head, a smirk on her lips. "He's hardly an agent. Anymore, that is."

She paced back to the desk. "Mrs. Merriweather carries a pistol because unfortunately her past employment has taught her it is necessary to keep her person safe. Jackson, my driver, wants nothing more than to care for the horses, and his past is nobody's business but his own." She turned. "But there is Bridgette. I would avoid her whenever possible."

His mind reeled with how casually she relayed the sordid past of her servants, and he feared what Bridgette may entail that she warranted avoidance.

"Bridgette? What the devil is the matter with her?"

"She talks excessively," Emily said with a frown and a shake of her head. "You'll never get away if you get her going, so I find it best to avoid eye contact." She gave a small smile and a shrug and turned away just as Mrs. Merriweather pushed in a loaded teacart.

"Set yourself down, Mr. Professor, and we shall see to what ails you."

"It's Professor Mesmer, ma'am."

"Oh, of course it is." She pushed past him with the cart and began to pour before he could settle himself on the couch again.

She handed him a steaming cup.

"What is it?" he asked, remembering the tin in the kitchen.

"It's her ladyship's own concoction, Mr. Professor." She gestured with the cup until he took it.

"That's what I'm afraid of," he muttered and sniffed at the tea.

"It's white willow bark with turmeric and ginger. I find it helps." Emily regarded him over the journal opened in her hands.

His leg quickened at the words, their tantalizing mixture promising relief.

"Thank you," he said, but he didn't take his eyes from her and drink. He could only watch her, silhouetted by the light from the windows behind her.

Mrs. Merriweather cleared her throat, and when he could pry his eyes away to look at her, a grimace folded her features. Her lips creased into a bitter frown before she turned too Emily.

"Are you sure about saving this one, my lady?"

Emily tucked a piece of hair behind her ear. "I'm afraid I haven't a choice in the matter," she said, still not looking up so she didn't see the glare Mrs. Merriweather passed in his direction as she left.

"You haven't a choice?" he said when the draconian housekeeper had departed.

Emily looked up, her hazel eyes earnest. "Of course, I haven't a choice."

* * *

WHEN SHE HAD THOUGHT about this moment for the past week, she hadn't considered the level of resistance she would face.

The man was permanently injured because of her. Why would he not immediately accept an offer of assistance from the very person who had caused the injury? It was only just that said person should pay for her crimes and what better way than a life for a life?

Why was he being so obstinate?

She crossed the room and dropped onto the ottoman to face him. "There is someone who wants you dead, and I just so happen to be skilled at detection and have the requisite physical capabilities to protect one's person." She settled her hands in her lap, the very picture of practicality. Except for the trousers, of course. "I am absolutely the person you want for this job."

"Except I'm not hiring." His words were toneless and rankled.

She dismissed them. "Now then. You never answered me. Who would want you dead?"

Something passed over his eyes, again as if he made some sort of silent decision, and he leaned back. "As I said, the last person to have any interest in me or my work was Lord Crawley, and if the blokes at your hearty old War Office are to be believed, the man died in Italy some years ago." He took a sip of his tea, stopped, regarded the cup before looking to her. "This is rather good. You say you concocted it yourself?"

She nodded. "White willow bark is a common reliever of ailments, but the ginger and turmeric add a nice zest I found.

To say nothing of their own amenable qualities." She gestured for him to go on. "What is it you're working on now? Some sort of water filter, I understand."

He eyed her over the rim of his cup. "You've been keeping an eye on me. I'm flattered, Lady Emily."

She tossed him a glare. "I keep an eye on many innovators, Professor Mesmer. Be careful what you suggest of my reputation."

He sipped at his tea. "Noted. And I *am* working on a water filter. Desert wells are often contaminated with the careless tending of livestock. The well is lost, and the villagers who once used it as a main source of sustenance are now forced to dig a new one. A reckless waste of resources. But if the water could be filtered—"

"There would be no need to dig a new well," she finished for him. She pointed a finger. "Such a filter could be worth much to someone willing to leverage it as a tool for extortion."

He wrinkled his nose. "Why is it that your mind goes to the most sinister so quickly?"

She shrugged. "A casualty of my upbringing. But it's true, isn't it?" She didn't wait for him to answer. "Someone with influence in an arid region could contaminate wells deliberately and then offer the filter at an exorbitant sum. The people would be forced to pay it because they need the water to live." She clapped her heads together in glee. "What an obvious scheme. How delightful."

She became aware of Xavier's questioning expression and settled, a smile turning up the corners of her mouth.

"Wouldn't that be possible?" she asked with a modicum of reserve.

"It would be, but it's highly unlikely. I've released my research to all the universities and colleges around the world. I used my connections in the astronomical societies to ensure the research went as far and wide as possible. I will not have another telescope situation to contend with." He drank deeply at his tea before returning the cup to the saucer with a sharp ring. "With universal access, the research holds no power for good or for evil. Just as it should be."

"Evil is rather a strong word, Mesmer."

"So is murder."

She leaned forward on crossed arms. "So you truly don't believe someone would want you for your research like last time?

"Again, I must point out that if someone wanted me for my research, why murder me? That would do them no good."

She thrust to her feet, the urge to move giving her no option. She paced to the windows and back along the dormant fireplace. "So if it's not your research then what could it be? There must be a reason someone would wish to cause you harm."

He laid his head along the back of the sofa, his eyes drifting shut. She watched him, concern gnawing at her stomach.

Before he said with a drawl, "I'm afraid the only reason would be my association with you."

She put her hands to her hips. "I beg your pardon?"

He opened a single eye. "You're the only person in the whole of my life that I ever encountered, which resulted in harm to my body."

When said like that, the words stung, but she couldn't blame him because they were true.

She pursed her lips, nodded, and resumed pacing.

"So tell me of your personal endeavors then."

"You wish to be intimate with me, my lady?"

She could hear the sarcasm in his voice and did not need to turn around to know a smirk could be found on his lips.

"To a degree, Professor, but I would ask you to keep your statement decent."

"Where is the fun in that then?"

She did turn now, her mouth lifting on just one side. "Perhaps you're too cowardly to find out."

She had meant it in jest, but Xavier's face closed, his gaze hooded. She had only seen such a stern look on his face once before. When he'd learned the name of his friend's killer. To have him look at her with such intensity now forced her to turn away. "I would like to propose a bargain."

"Is it a bargain or are you going to tell me what it is you'd like us to do?" His voice had grown weary, and she worried she was overtaxing him. A sea voyage and then a dockside scuffle did not do well for one's body.

"I should like to think we would work as a team." She kept her voice even, reasonable, as if she were discussing nothing more than the day's weather.

He lifted his head but only slightly. "Work as a team on what?"

"On unmasking your potential murderer, of course?"

He sat up, his eyes alert. "Unmasking the potential murderer?"

"Yes. What is it you thought we were doing here?"

He blinked and finally scrubbed a hand over his face and through his hair. "I had thought the incident at the dock was the extent of your responsibility." He regarded her. "Didn't you say it was your responsibility to save my life? Well, you've done it, my lady."

She shook her head, took a step toward him. "No, not at all." She stopped. Shook her head again. "No, that isn't it. Yes, I am responsible for your life and that includes finding the man who wants you dead."

He gestured to the world beyond them. "But you've already saved my life."

"Only in that moment." She licked her lips. "Who is to say what the killer will try next?"

"I think you'd better tell me the whole story."

She sighed but dropped once more onto the ottoman. "I was in Barnaby Books on Marlborough last week when I overheard two gentlemen plotting your murder. One gentleman had a strange accent and the other was quite short with far too copious eyebrows. The man with the strange accent demanded the deed be done immediately, and the short man with the eyebrows said it would be completed at the dock." She leaned forward, clapped her hands together. "But it didn't happen because I stopped it. We must tread carefully now. More so than ever."

He narrowed his eyes. "Just why is that?"

She blinked. "Have you ever had a plan not succeed in the way you intended?"

He nodded.

"How did it make you feel?"

"Frustrated." His eyes widened. "Ah, I understand your point then. You believe we've upset the killer, and now he may try something more dangerous."

She clapped her hands together again, pushed to her feet. "That is exactly what I suggest. We should be prepared to get ahead of it, which means a strong defense." She twirled, pointed a finger. "Or perhaps even more than that, we should seek the killer ourselves." She snapped her fingers. "Of course. That makes the most sense. Why wait for him to strike again? Why not root him out before more damage is wrought?"

Xavier struggled to his feet. When he made his way to her, he limped far more than he had when he'd first disembarked from the ship that morning. The pang of guilt pierced more sharply than usual.

"You will do no such thing. Are you mad?" A funny little line had appeared between his eyes.

She remembered how she had often vexed Professor Mesmer in her earlier years. Her selfishness and ignorance were somehow frustratingly amusing to him. But that was not the feeling he emitted now. He was angry now. Almost as if he cared for her well being, which was absurd.

"I am not mad, Professor. I am quite sane." She placed a placating hand on his arm, which he immediately tossed off.

She stared at the hand he had rendered useless and obstinately replaced it on his arm. He threw it off again.

"Xavier, I must—"

He kissed her.

She hadn't been expecting it, yes, but there was something far sadder than that. It was the simple fact that she hadn't been touched in so long. That for so long her body had existed without the life-sustaining connection to another person. And in a single movement, that isolation had been terminated in the most base and visceral way.

It ruptured within her all the loneliness, all the sadness. It exploded at the touch of his lips.

His lips.

They were warm, soft, coaxing and yet unyielding all at once. The heat alone was enough to awaken a part of her she believed was long banished, but there was so much more. There was yearning, desire, want, life, all of it. All of it focused on the single point where their lips connected.

He didn't touch her anywhere else. Didn't lean into her. Didn't put out a hand to cup her face. It was only their lips. The most vulnerable part forced to feel what she had not wanted to for six years.

Alive.

That part of her felt alive. Her whole body felt alive. It sang with a radiance she had exiled that day in the glade when the life she had known had ended. But she hadn't been successful. It wasn't exiled—it had merely gone into hiding, lurking in her subconscious where she couldn't find it. But at the first glimmer of desire, the first sensation burst forth, rising up as one reaching for the surface of a lake, her entire body already tasting that first, quenching draft of air.

She'd been kissed before. Back when she'd been a conceited debutante, flirting with every eligible gentleman as if such behavior would win her a coveted match. But those kisses hadn't felt like this. Those kisses had only been a mere touching of flesh. This. This was heady. This was power. This could be...

Love.

He released her before she was ready, and she stumbled, rocking back on the heels of her feet. Her hand flew to her lips before she could stop it, giving herself away.

He was breathing heavily, his eyes half closed.

"I'm not apologizing for that," he said through a gust of air.

"I didn't ask you to," she whispered.

They stood like that for some moments, each trying to gather their composure. But it wasn't awkward. She had expected tension, awkwardness, a kind of avoidance. But there was none. They faced each other and the truth of what had just happened between them.

Six years of separation. Separation from what? There's had never been an amicable relationship, but then wasn't there some nonsense about the attraction of opposite forces?

Whatever it was she couldn't ignore it now. The clenching in her stomach, the squeezing of her chest when she'd first glimpsed him striding down the docks. She'd believed it a symptom of her disconnected existence, but that kiss had proven her wrong.

Dangerously wrong.

She stepped back, allowing the space between them to grow, buffer her from this intangible thing that called to her.

"I had thought you would see the reason in this plan," she said when she was finally able to gain her breath, pressing on as if nothing had happened.

For she needed to. She needed to pretend it hadn't happened because it had, and it meant far too much.

Right now she must focus and if to do so required a spot of imagination on her part then so be it.

"Reason? In pursuing a killer?"

"In preventing your murder." She wouldn't allow her gaze to drop from his, to look away at a spot that would not challenge her so.

His life meant too much to her to allow a bit of awkwardness to get in the way. She must force him to see reason. She simply must.

"Can't you see I must do this?" Her tone was suddenly wrought with unshed tears.

His breathing stilled, and his eyes grew round at her words. He watched her with lips slightly parted, lips still damp from her kiss.

Blinking as if a spell were broken, he turned away from her, and his shoulders slumped.

"Then what is your plan?" He turned to look at her over his shoulder. "Do you plan to follow me around the conference?"

She regarded him, his cocky grin and amused eyes.

"Conference?"

He sobered, turning to face her completely.

"That is why I'm here."

She shook her head, her thoughts scrambling, tumbling over one another. "You're not here for research? Like the last time?"

His frown was suffocating. "No, I am most certainly not."

He crossed his arms over his chest. "Lord Avery, my colleague from the Royal Astronomical Society, has requested my presence at the conference on the Ottoman affair to be held at Kensington Palace."

A throbbing began at her temples. "You're here to discuss the Ottoman affair?"

He nodded. "Lord Avery was to meet me at the docks." He peered over his shoulder, and she realized he was taking in the time from the grandfather clock behind her. "He's likely there now, growing concerned after my absence. I should like to send him a message if you've an errand boy I may use."

She closed the distance between them in two strong steps, glaring up at him. "You've been asked to attend the conference of Her Majesty's most trusted advisers on the most heated conflict in world politics as we speak, and you failed to mention it *once* in this conversation about your potential *murder*?"

It was all she could do to keep from screaming.

He blinked in rapid succession. "Was that relevant?"

She closed her eyes, the only way she could keep from railing at him. "The entire conference could be in danger."

She heard him shift and opened her eyes. The smirk had returned.

"And just what is it you plan to do? Save everyone?"

CHAPTER 4

"*I* did not suggest it is a dare."

Emily peered at Xavier through the polished lenses of her spectacles. "I'm not so easily coerced into perilous endeavors." She pursed her lips.

He eyed her. "Then what are you doing here?"

She frowned. "Saving your life. Must I keep reminding you of that?"

He didn't answer her. He only cast her a weary glance before turning to face the rest of the room.

The delegates had gathered at Kensington Palace for the first day of the planned eight-day conference. The room was stuffed with an eclectic mix of gentlemen. The usual aristocracy, a couple of dukes and a marquess. Even a baron if she were correct. There were a few noted members of military rank, an admiral and a general. Then there were the odd aficionados. A banker from Zurich. The ambassador of Prussia. A dignitary of some note from Austria. The professor. He was the gentleman least likely to fit a pattern, but it was clear upon their entrance, he was well received and even more, well regarded.

Lord Avery, the marquess as it turned out, was specifically chosen by Queen Victoria to secure a man of letters who could add a scholarly tone to the meeting. There was some grumbling as to his American roots, but once he spoke articulately and exhaustively, most grumbling stopped.

She had made note of it, of course.

She had already mentally cataloged the room, beginning a list of suspects, which would require further investigation or careful surveillance while she was in attendance.

For she would not be so remiss as to believe the threat did not come from within the conference itself. As far as she could gather, Xavier had been the only target thus far, but that suggested nothing. She would not prematurely close any avenues of investigations on mere happenstance.

"You look charming today, my lady."

She shushed Xavier almost immediately.

"It's Miss Quinton, and well, you know it," she hissed. "Do not give up my disguise so quickly. I worked very hard on this."

She adjusted her cap, tucking the dark strands of her wig more securely beneath it. She wore a drab gown of gray damask of no shape whatsoever. It was easier that way to hide necessary accoutrements in the false cage of an overly large corset. She'd darkened her complexion with powder, adding nuance and shape where there was none. And no one looked at a woman with spectacles.

When she was done, she gave the illusion of an overly large nose, sunken cheeks, prominent chin, spectacled eyes, and a ring of pudge about the middle. The perfect, spinster secretary.

It was harder to convince Xavier of her disguise than to actually assemble it.

She had explained how her cousin-in-law, Penelope, had once posed as a secretary to great success, hiding her literary endeavors until she herself decided to reveal them. Her moniker, Miss Quinton, was a nod to her formidable aunt, whose strength she would need to emulate in such an exhaustive, perilous mission.

He studied her now, his mouth folded in a grimace.

"I should hate to be the reason such an elaborate costume was uncloaked."

She would not rise to his sarcasm, but she was not one to ignore such opportunities.

"I knew your mother had instilled some manners in you." She smiled with her teeth. "It appears it only takes some time to witness it."

"My mother will be pleased to hear it."

She looked at him sharply. "I didn't know you had a mother."

"I think my very existence should suggest the fact." His smile was bemused.

"You've never spoken of her," she pressed on.

He looked about the room. "I should hardly think she would come up in natural conversation."

"What is she like?"

He turned fully to her. "You wish to discuss this now?"

A maid entered then, refreshing the buffet where tea, coffee, and sundries had been laid out for the delegates, and Lord Avery suggested the delegates should fortify themselves before they began the morning session.

"Probably not," she muttered. "But we will have this conversation at a later time."

That funny line had appeared between his eyes again. "Why do you care so much about my mother?"

She swallowed. "Shouldn't I show concern for the mother of a dear friend? I should think it only respectful."

"You forget our acquaintance was reestablished whilst both of us wore trousers."

She looked away from him completely now. "Your point is well observed, Professor. Shall we?"

"Yes, Miss Quinton, my private secretary. We shall."

"I would request you refrain from the sarcasm. It's proving rather dull." She moved past him, following the stream of delegates and private secretaries into the main chamber, the Green Salon of Kensington Palace.

With the queen's departure to Buckingham Palace, the royal homestead was largely unoccupied, and the rooms carried a musty air of disuse about them. A few of the apartments on the upper floors had been granted to certain royalty, but the whole place rather shivered with neglect. Not of the physical kind. It was the spirit of the place the hung like a shroud.

She steered herself to the side where small desks had been placed for the delegates' private secretaries. The delegates themselves found seats around a vast table set in the center of the room, surrounded by the green, sage, mint, and emerald trappings of the room. From the wallpaper to the window treatments, she felt as though someone had unrolled an exquisite lawn and at any moment, a game of croquet would break out.

Xavier slipped into the seat before her, and she took note of those who sat next to him. The Prussian ambassador sat to his left and the banker from Zurich to his right. She wasn't sure if this was of import, but she made note of it anyway.

The morning session began with a hearty "God save the Queen!" to which Xavier looked around in blinking confusion. The Prussian ambassador, the Austrian dignitary, and the Zurich banker shared his confusion, so she ignored the behaviors of the others.

The room rapidly grew warm as she had feared, but the expanse of her costume allowed a nice breeze to swirl around her person inside her gown. The gentlemen in the room however began to wilt. Tea was brought in copious amounts, and windows were flung wide. A breeze soon started that had the draperies rushing to and fro in a distracting frenzy. The windows were once more shut by half. The resulting disturbance was deemed bearable so as to keep at least some of the refreshing air circulating the room.

She had nearly nibbled off the nub of her quill in impatience before the gentlemen finally settled down to the business of the conference, the Ottoman conflict. It was nearly eleven o'clock in the morning before they truly commenced, and she wondered at the dearth of efficiency naturally occurring in the male species. She thought it not common to all males, but there was something about gentlemen in positions of authority that lent itself to a deficiency of productivity.

The topic was exceedingly dull.

She tried to take an interest, but the delegates spent nearly a quarter of an hour deciding how best to address their meeting. Should it be *The Conference On the Matter of Ottoman Conflict* or was that far too suggestive of a disturbance? Should they rather say *The Committee on the Ottoman Affair*, which sounded like a gathering of leisure furniture.

It was a good hour before real business was properly conducted, and by then, delegates began to flitter away. With the stuffiness of the room came the teacarts, and those accustomed to the drink had partaken heavily of it. The dukes and the baron had already excused themselves for the necessary, and she wouldn't doubt the Zurich banker was next. He shuffled back and forth from thigh to thigh in his seat, and she wanted nothing more than to demand he sit still.

Lord Avery attempted to keep matters moving ahead, but then the Austrian dignitary requested the floor and began a painfully detailed account of trade in his country and how the Ottoman affair was curtailing critical economic arteries.

She discovered more about Austrian exports in the next forty-five minutes than she ever cared to know in a lifetime.

The dukes and the baron had returned by then, and the Zurich banker was off like a shot.

Silly man. Even she could tell he needed the necessary.

She took the time during the Austrian's speech to observe the other private secretaries. She was pleased to see she was not the only female among them. It had taken a precious amount of arguing with Xavier to convince him a female secretary would not be suspicious. Penelope would be proud. Or she'd write it into one of her novels. It was difficult to tell with her.

The dukes had each brought an elderly gentleman so resembling each other, she wondered if they were of the same family, having been brought up in the profession, while the baron had brought a mere child. She felt no remorse in thinking of him thusly for one of the dukes' secretaries had had to show him how to properly dust his notes to prevent smudging.

The Prussian ambassador's secretary was the other woman among their pool. An older lady with gray hair pulled back tightly from an angular face. A small pair of spectacles sat on the very end of her nose, and she twitched her quill across the paper more than easing it across. The severity of her expression and movements were somewhat softened by the frequency with which she smiled.

The Austrian dignitary's secretary was proving to be a nuisance. A middling chap with a jiggly belly and a penchant for cherry snuff. It was debatable which caused her greater consternation—the constant sniffing or the nauseating smell of cherry. He'd hardly taken any notes, and she added him to her list of suspects.

The Zurich banker had brought no secretary, which was

notable. He had also taken a great deal of time in the necessary. She added two check marks against his name on her list of suspects.

Not that any of these observations served as hard evidence. She was just beginning her investigation, and it helped to make such conclusions in order to understand the players.

They broke for luncheon without hardly any work having been accomplished that she could see, and she followed Xavier into the antechamber where breakfast had commenced only hours before. She wasn't hungry in the slightest, and yet the gentlemen delegates stepped up to the buffet and filled plates with heaping servings of roast, pickled beets, and yellow potatoes swimming in fatty butter, the sight of which had her turning away.

Xavier found them seats at the rear of the room where they could speak with some semblance of privacy. The dukes had taken the stage so to speak and soon had the audience enraptured with a grotesque stalking story.

"Counting on the number of times I nearly fell asleep this morning, do you think the presumed killer is hoping for death by boredom?" Xavier said, leaning in close enough to whisper.

She shook her head. "That would assume you would not be overcome by the stuffiness of the room."

He leaned back, settling into his seat as the duke ramped up his story. Something about being caught on the bluff in a windstorm, knowing his prey lay only feet ahead of him.

"If you found yourself on a bluff in a windstorm, might you not think to seek shelter?" Xavier mused, but she wasn't listening to him.

A footman had entered the room and gone directly to the Zurich banker, slipping him a small, folded piece of paper.

The man had glanced but briefly at the note before standing and slipping from the audience with careful quietness.

She stood without thinking.

"Where are you going?" Xavier's tone held a note of concern.

"Private matters," she mumbled before following the banker.

She had never been to Kensington Palace, and the sweeping corridors were daunting. The butler who had greeted the delegates upon arrival had shown them where the necessary establishments were and the rooms where the conference was to be held, but the rest of the palace lay just out of reach, almost like a mirage. There but not really, melting into one fathomless corridor after another.

But the banker's heeled shoes rang crisply through the echoing space, and based on their retreating sound, he was not headed to the necessary.

She picked up her pace, glad her soft boots left no echoing trace of her pursuit. She turned the corner just in time to see the gentleman take a sharp departure from the corridor to the left. It was darker here in the labyrinth, cut off from the outer parts of the palace that captured the daylight. She slipped a hand into the hidden compartment of her costume, her fingers closing around the handle of a blade she'd secured to the false corset.

She reached the point where the banker had turned off but found nothing except a waterfall of intricate tapestries. She spun about, checking to see if she'd gotten her positioning right. She was sure she had, so where had the banker gone?

She paused, allowing her heartbeat to settle and her breathing to grow shallow. He must have stopped somewhere along this point in the corridor. She'd seen him disappear.

Shuffling noises.

There were distinct shuffling noises coming from the wall on her left, the same place where the banker had disappeared. She pressed forward, reaching with tentative hands, skimming her fingers over the folds of tapestries. She found the crack in the wall hangings at the same moment a muffled groan came from the wall.

She stopped, stared.

The groan was followed by a thud and then eerie silence.

She scrambled to part the tapestries, her hands pulling at layers of fabric until the door they had concealed became visible. Her heart thundering, her breath gasping, she plunged ahead, her hand at the ready to draw her dagger forward and—

She stopped and nearly swallowed her tongue in her gasps for air.

The banker stood in a room that appeared to be some sort of bedchamber, cluttered with ornate trappings and gilded furniture. He stood at the side of a bed, his trousers around his ankles. The maid who had freshened the breakfast sundries bent over the bed, her skirts thrown about her shoulders, and the flabby, white skin of the Zurich banker's butt bounced merrily as he thrust into the writhing maid.

He paused, and both of their heads turned to her, standing there in the doorway, chest heaving, face likely bright with exertion.

The Zurich banker blinked a time or two, but a lopsided smile eventually came to his face.

"Well, if you give me but a moment, miss, I'd be happy to take care of you next."

* * *

LADY MADELINE BLACK had a difficult time finding what it was the members of society found enjoyable about the season.

She had spent most of her formative years admiring her older sister, Emily. The way she practiced walking so as to keep her chin up, her shoulders square, her step light. The fittings for gowns, the outings to choose fabric and lace, shoes and hats. The lessons on etiquette, French, and dancing. It was the dancing she liked best.

But it was such a small part of the rest of the season, which left the rest of it incredibly dull.

Not that she complained. Madeline never complained. In a family the size of hers, complaining did very little except deplete your own reserves. So she didn't complain. She looked for the good instead. It was far easier than attempting to be heard. Especially when you were the younger daughter of a duke.

What did a duke's daughter have to complain about really?

She could find much to complain about in her companion.

Lord Ritchie Sheppard was the son of the Marquess of Ainsley and made tan watercolor seem vibrant. They had passed a good thirty minutes in their walk from Lofton House to Hyde Park speaking of the desirable attributes of the Friesian horse. Ritchie was well versed on the subject, but if you had asked her just then, she couldn't name a single one of them.

It was a beautiful day, and she welcomed the breeze that swept through the overhanging tress of the park and lifted the hair that had escaped under her bonnet, tickling her face in a gentle caress. It felt good to be out of doors. She'd always favored the family's time at their country estate in Bedford where she exercised a great deal more freedom in wandering about the grounds.

But here in London. In London, she was expected to be Lady Madeline Black, daughter to the Duke of Lofton. She often thought it wouldn't be so bad if Emily were here.

Emily, being the eldest, would have drawn some of the attention to herself. Another daughter for sons to covet. Another path to a connection with a ducal family.

How very dull.

"Don't you agree, Lady Madeline?" Ritchie said now.

"Oh, quite," she said, not having a single inkling of what he referred to and also not caring over much.

She embraced the pleasure of physical exercise and the feel of sunshine on her shoulders. They'd only be in town for a fortnight and already she longed for the freedom of the country. For years she had looked forward to her coming out, but that was when Emily was still here. She thought she'd share a season with her sister. Swap stories of the eligible beaus who courted them, share laces and bonnets and flounces, exchanging gowns and helping with one another's hair beads.

It was lonely without her.

Had she really thought properly, Emily would likely not have shared a season with her regardless. She was a good deal older than Madeline and should have been married off by now. But still. Her big sister would be there. In her dreams.

In reality she had Lord Ritchie Sheppard.

She cast a glance back at her chaperone, her maid, Walters, and the woman gave her a knowing look in return. At least that was comforting.

They rounded the path into the first open space of parkland, and she scanned the assembled couples looking for an ally. There were others of an age, but they, too, brought her only disappointment. None were of an ability to distract from Lord Sheppard. But maybe they would be enough to distract him from her.

She nodded in the distance to a gathering of young people, only one of whom she recognized.

"I see darling Lady Portia just there. Might we go and have a chat?"

She'd cut off poor Ritchie in the middle of his recitation of known conditions suffered by Friesian horses, but she didn't really care.

Neither did Ritchie it seemed.

"Oh, I'd be delighted to escort you, my lady." He neatly cut across the path when the sound of hoofbeats reached her.

Her.

Not Ritchie.

For a man so obsessed with horses, she figured he would be more astute to them. He was not.

But the galloping sound of a speeding horse was so familiar to her she could hardly miss it. Especially in the middle of Hyde Park.

She turned in time to see two riders take the turn in the path she and Ritchie had just traveled. Sweat flecked the flanks of the gentlemen's horses, and their lips rippled at their bits as the riders bent over them, urging them faster.

How incredibly careless.

She stopped in the path, hands going involuntarily to her hips as she prepared to scold the two miscreants as soon as they drew near enough. But at the last moment, the second rider, the one farthest from her, veered, knocking into the other rider.

The horse whinnied, tripping on its front hooves as it was sent off balance. The rider scrambled to correct, jerking the reins until the horse righted itself.

But it was too late.

The rider had lost control and come off the path.

Directly at Madeline.

Later she would recall Ritchie still rambling beside her about horses while his very life hung in jeopardy as a result of one and Walters reaching out a useless hand, too far away to save her.

But as she had learned from her mother, no one could save you like you could save yourself.

And so she did.

She turned and leapt, knocking neatly into Ritchie's lower back and sending them both tumbling to the ground just as the out of control rider tore the grass where they had just stood.

"What's this then?" Ritchie came up spurting. "I daresay, my lady. I have never been so affronted in my life."

She rolled over, brushed the grass from her hands as she peered around the edges of her bonnet, searching for the mad horseman.

She found her brother instead.

"Ashley Black, wait until mother hears about this."

Ashley Black slid from his panting horse and dropped to his knees beside her.

"God, Madeline! Are you hurt?"

She pushed to a sitting position. "Hardly thanks to you. Are you out of your mind? What if Father hears about you riding so recklessly? Through the park of all places."

"It wasn't my idea." He grabbed her shoulders, her arms, her head. "I'm so sorry, Mads."

She blinked. "Wasn't your idea?" She looked around. "Was someone else riding your horse then?"

A grumbling noise at her right elbow signaled the return of Ritchie as he fumbled in the grass attempting to obtain a standing position. He muttered something about giving her his precious time, but she paid him no heed.

"It wasn't my idea, Mads," Ashley said again. "A blathering old fool said I wouldn't do it."

"A blathering old fool? Is that how you refer to yourself these days?"

Ashley sat back on his heels, tossing her an aggrieved expression. "Mads," he said patiently.

She pushed her bonnet back into place and sat fully erect, hands in her lap. "All right then. Tell me what's happened. I promise to keep my tongue in check."

Ashley pointed back the way they had come near the Grosvenor gate entrance to the park.

"I was meeting Will at the gate for our usual exercise—"

"You mean daily promenade in front of the eligible young debutantes, yes."

Ashley eyed her.

She swallowed. "I beg your pardon. I shall truly keep my lips shut now. Proceed."

"When a tottering old fool rode up on his gelding to say he could beat me across the park. On a gelding, no less."

"You nearly got us both killed on a wager about a horse race. With an old man?"

Ashley's face folded. "You mustn't tell Mother, Mads. She'll have my head."

"You nearly took mine!" That last bit was likely too much as Ashley's eyes narrowed with further guilt.

She laid a hand on his arm.

"I promise I shan't tell Mum, but you must promise me not to accept any more wagers from tottering old men."

Ashley's expression brightened in the smallest of degrees. "I can safely make that promise." His eyes darted back in the direction they had come as if expecting a phantom to be there.

"What is it?"

He shook his head. "It's just…well, the old man. He was

rather odd. I'd never seen him before, and he didn't give his name. He just rode up and challenged me to a race." Ashley pushed at his hat, scratched his forehead. "It was all around a strange occurrence for a ride in the park."

Madeline shook her head. "I'm sure an old man like that likely doesn't have anything on his agenda, and a horse race in the park with a young chap like you was an exciting prospect."

This had a smile returning to her brother's face. "Eh? I'm an exciting prospect?" He adjusted the lapels of his coat, and she regretted saying anything. Ashley needed no help with his ego.

"I for one am finding this entire charade dull and overtaxing."

She looked up, shielding her eyes from the sun. She'd forgotten Ritchie was there.

She sighed and made to apologize when she felt her mother's influence press at the small of her back. The season was proving so frightfully dull. Why not have a little fun with it?

"If you're finding it so overtaxing, why don't you bugger off then?"

Ritchie's mouth fell open wide enough to insert his own foot as she supremely wished he would. He spluttered once or twice, pulling at the sleeves of his coat while he attempted to say something.

Ashley grinned. "Eh, that's right. I'm sure there's a whist game somewhere and the spinsters wishing you would join them. That seems more to your liking, old chap."

Lord Ritchie Sheppard snapped his mouth shut, spun on his heel in the grass, and strode away.

"I feel rather bad for doing that, but I certainly couldn't listen to any more dribble about horses." She extended her hand so Ashley could help her to her feet. "And then you went and nearly ran me over with one. I'll be happy to have nothing to do with horses for the rest of the day."

Ashley peered over at the path again, the same look of consternation on his face.

"What is it, Ash?" She followed his gaze to the path where Ash's friend, Will, was just coming up the way at a sedate trot. He raised a hand when he spotted them, and Ash returned his friend's salute.

He shook his head before returning back to her. "It's just so odd, that's all. I can't seem to let it go."

She walked with him to where his horse stood munching at the grass, his bridle dragging along the ground.

"That's just the family talking," she said. "Growing up with stories of espionage and treason will do that to a person. You mustn't let it get to you. It was just a silly old man looking to have a thrill."

Ash grabbed up the bridle and pulled his horse's snout in for a scratch. "It's not that, Mads. The old man was so persistent. Like he needed to make sure I went along with it." He peered down at her. "Why would he do such a thing?"

She squeezed her brother's arm. "You'll understand when you're an old fool, Ash. Sometimes old men must try to recapture their youth. You've seen Father and Uncle Nathan."

Ash's face cleared almost instantly, a grin propping up one side of his mouth. "I have seen them. You're right, Mads." He nodded in the direction Ritchie had disappeared. "No good with Lord Horsey then?"

She laughed. "No, not good at all." She shuffled her feet in the grass. "Ash, did you expect the season to be so dull?"

He regarded her for a moment, and she was struck by how much he'd come to look like their father. "I fear it's a lot different for me than it is for you, Mads. I do all I can to avoid finding myself strapped with a wife. I can't imagine what it's like for you. Going through some bizarre audition to play the role of wife."

She let her gaze drift to Will as he trotted up to them.

"I can't help but think it would all be better if only Emily were here." She'd nearly whispered the words and was startled when Ash's arm came around her.

"I know what you mean, Mads. Everything would be better if Emily were here."

CHAPTER 5

"So did you let him have a go?"

He was fortunate, he knew, to only receive a glare and not a bodily injury.

"I did not." She pronounced each word as if she were flinging a dagger at him.

It did nothing to stop his grin.

"So your intrepid sleuthing has unmasked a randy banker from Zurich. What cunning. What fortitude. What would the conference do without your protection?"

She ripped her terrible hat and wig from her head as they entered the foyer of 34 Whitaker. "I must be missing something." She spun about nearly knocking him into the door. "It's likely to be the greatest conflagration of foreign power seen on British soil this decade, and the entire day would lull a rambunctious toddler into a stupor."

He doffed his hat and gloves, placing them on the table in the foyer. "I should hardly think a toddler would be reduced to a nap. Surely he would find a way to escape before succumbing to such a fate."

Mrs. Merriweather's sudden appearance at his elbow did have him backing into the door then. Her gaze penetrated his very skin, and he held up his hat and gloves as if in a peace offering. She took them without comment as well as accepting a bundle of things from Emily. She disappeared as silently as she had appeared. He watched her go, uneasiness prickling the back of his neck.

"It is an interesting staff you have," he muttered as Emily slipped into the front drawing room he had learned was a kind of refuge for her. In the near week he'd made his residence at the house, he'd started to unravel the enigma that was Lady Emily Black. She had surrounded herself with a staff made up of individuals with damaged pasts much like her own. Staff with unthinkable, deadly skills that somehow fit perfectly into her new life as a reclusive, spinster investigator.

For that was what she was.

The journals that lay all over the room were filled with tales of her adventures. He knew because he'd picked up every one he could find, leafed through it, marveled at what she'd done. She *was* a master of disguise. She was educated in the chemical arts thanks to someone she referred to only as Wickshire. She had skills in some Eastern fighting arts as well as ample instruction in swordplay.

And she'd tested the damn skills out. On real people. In real, lethal situations.

He didn't know whether to lock her up and throw away the key or congratulate her.

He knew such atypical behavior could only stem from her roots in a family mired in espionage, but still. It was damned remarkable.

He had written to Lord Avery on that first, revealing only what he must about his current situation. The man had responded immediately with assurance he would share nothing with the other delegates to keep Xavier's position safe.

It was that afternoon his trunks had appeared. After tea, Mrs. Merriweather had announced his room was ready should he wish to freshen up before supper (This was said with such steel, it was obvious it was more than a suggestion.), and he'd climbed the stairs to find his trunks at the ready in his chamber. When he'd asked Emily about them, she'd merely gazed at him quizzically.

Of course, his trunks should arrive. Would she allow them to go missing?

He'd had only a scant few days to prepare for the conference, but Emily easily left him to his own devices. But that didn't mean she wasn't a distraction.

He'd observed her daily routines. As a man of science, it was hard not to. She rose early, and judging by the perspiration she exhibited at breakfast, she conducted some sort of physical exercise first thing. She then disappeared into her rooms for less than one hour on the clock to emerge dressed in a day dress, her hair tied back in a simple ribbon. He knew it to be a day dress because it was such an odd fashion, he'd needed to ascertain what it was called. It was a loose fitting garment with a higher skirt that, he realized quite quickly, gave her greater freedom of movement.

For a recluse, Emily valued freedom a great deal.

She then spent the majority of her day in the front drawing room. At her desk. In the chair by the window. Forever studying and scratching notations. She'd created a profile of every delegate at the conference before he'd scarcely learned all of their names. She knew every exit to Kensington Palace and every layout of corridor and the garden plans as if she'd been raised there.

He had overcome his rambling seasickness and regained his land legs. That was his only worthy accomplishment in the entire time he'd been there, and Emily's efficacy had him feeling not quite up to measure.

When she'd come down that morning for breakfast, he had tried not to be surprised by her costume. He'd known all along she planned to don some affair to mask her identity, but even he had been startled. The illusion she created with only some powder and chalk was astonishing. She'd changed nothing at all about her face and yet he wouldn't have believed it was her. And he *knew* it was she.

He watched her now, pulling hair pins as she paced her refuge.

"There must be something we've missed. Surely there would be a reason to break apart a conference bent on peace."

He dropped onto the sofa, leaning his walking stick against the arm. His hand went to his leg, massaging methodically.

"It's not really a conference for peace though, is it?"

She flashed him a look. "Isn't that why you're here?"

"It's why I'm here, of course. But I can't say the same for the other gents."

She strode over to her desk, rummaged in the piles of papers on top, and pulled out a book in the shape of a clerk's ledger. The profiles, he knew, because she'd shared the damned book with him for days before the start of the conference.

"Then we must have missed something." She sat on the ottoman. "Let's start again."

He held up a finger, knowing it would not be well received. "Before we go down that course again, would it be prudent to suggest another tack?"

She only moved her eyes to look at him, and as she still had on the cosmetics to alter her face but no longer bore the wig that completed the ensemble, the entire effect was unsettling.

He swallowed. "Do you think perhaps your family may be of some help?"

Her look blackened.

He pressed on. "It's only that according to my understanding they may have some connections that could prove to be useful." He gestured to the ledger and the room about them. "We only have two pieces of information on which to operate. Your encounter at Barnaby's and the incident at the docks. It isn't sufficient data on which to calculate—"

"No."

The word was spoken so softly he almost missed it. But her expression had hardened even more, and her grip on the ledger threatened to snap the book in half.

He wanted to hurry on, but the tone of her voice sounded all too familiar because it was the tone he used when asked why he had abandoned his telescope research. It was the tone he used when asked to serve on government committees, ones not committed to peace.

No.

It was a word he'd employed often times himself in the past six years, and he felt it, deep in his gut. Felt what it cost her every time she had to speak it.

But it was his life in jeopardy now, and she was being foolish not to accept the help of a family who had years of experience in this field.

He leaned forward, elbows to knees, hoping to convey his earnestness with his posturing.

"Emily—"

She surged to her feet, the ledger banging against her thighs.

"I will not implicate them in this, Xavier." The tears sounded in her voice, but her eyes remained dry.

He backed off but did not give up.

"It's my life we're discussing, Emily. Have you not thought of that?"

"How could I think of anything else since I heard those men in the bookshop?"

The ledger rattled against her skirts as he realized she was shaking now. He gripped his walking stick and pulled himself up.

"Emily," he said but even as he watched, she transformed before him. Every guard a woman could possess went up. Her jaw firmed, her arms crossed over her chest, the ledger resting like a shield. Her whole body warned him not to come closer.

But he did it anyway.

"Emily, no one is responsible for my life but me. This burden does not and *should* not rest on your shoulders. You must understand that."

Her eyes swept back and forth like an animal cornered. Her reaction was so visceral, so raw. While he still felt the pain of Bobby's death, he never thought what it was like for her. Time had a way of dulling the edges of trauma, if not healing it entirely, making the burden easier to carry.

But it didn't appear to have been that way for Emily.

Emily's face. The piercing, frantic eyes. The flaring nostrils. The heave of her chest. God. It was like it was happening right now. All over again.

He wanted to touch her, to break the trance she was under, but he feared if he touched her, he might break her instead.

She didn't answer him. She only continued to huddle where she was, shielding herself and cowering at the same time.

Strong, resilient Emily. Afraid of the shadows of her past.

"Emily." It was nearly a whisper. He didn't know what else

to say to her. Things he wanted to say would need to be said back at himself, and he wasn't prepared to do that.

So they stood there. Locked in a battle of their own making. One that had no winners.

He was suddenly tired. Very tired.

For six years he had pushed. He had fought. He had tried to do better. For Bobby.

But Bobby wasn't here any longer. Bobby was gone.

Xavier was still here. Emily was still here. And they were both letting something from long ago control them.

Someone was trying to *kill* him.

He could go to the Blacks.

The thought niggled at the back of his mind unexpectedly.

There was nothing to stop him from seeking the duke and his myriad connections to the government, the local authorities, and more. The Duke of Lofton, Alec was his name. He could help Xavier. He could stop his murder.

He looked at Emily again. She still stood frozen, the ledger at her chest, but her expression had softened. No, wilted actually. Her lips were parted now, just the smallest of degrees.

Vulnerable.

That small parting of lips. They displayed her vulnerability like she would not allow the rest of her armor to.

It was that that would be his undoing.

He picked up his walking stick, massaged the head, and turned to face her.

"Then I shall leave you to it, shall I?" He tried to smile, but honestly, he didn't have the feeling to make it real.

She blinked, and he turned to the door before she could say anything else.

"Xavier."

It was just his name, but her tone was breathless, slightly manic. He peered over his shoulder at her.

"Xavier, you must let me try." If there had been any other sound in the room at all, he wouldn't have heard her.

She looked so small standing there. Not the fierce marauder. Not the defiant woman.

Just Emily.

Lady Emily Black.

So unsure of her place in this world and always reaching for the one thing she believed would make it better.

It hurt him to look at her.

Because he saw so much of himself reflected there.

She was right. He must let her try.

"Good night, Emily," he whispered and left.

* * *

SHE WATCHED HIM GO, her heart thundering so hard she could barely draw a full breath. She couldn't chase after him. She couldn't call out to him, debate what was plainly etched into his face.

He didn't believe in her.

She didn't know why the thought sliced through her like a hot knife, but it did, sending jolt waves of anguish through her. When she'd embarked on this endeavor, she'd only been thinking about herself. Her need to protect him. To save him like he'd saved her. She'd never considered how he would feel about it.

She'd been a target once. With her family, there was always the possibility of being the target of some deceitful plot, but she hadn't known at the time she was being targeted. She was in blissful ignorance of the entire affair until it had all come crashing down around her, and she'd committed the ultimate sin. Betraying her family.

She shuddered at the memory and looked to the place where Xavier had disappeared.

He didn't believe she could do it. That she could save him. In fact, she wondered now if he even believed he was in danger. Surely after that incident at the dock...

But that could be explained away. Common street thugs perhaps.

But no. She knew what she'd heard. She knew he was in danger. But she continued, uncertain from whence the danger stemmed.

She closed her eyes, picturing the bookshop that day. In her mind, she could clearly hear the strange voice of the man who wished the deed to be done. She could picture the squat man with the bushy eyebrows she had spotted when she'd turned the corner. And that disturbing smell of wet wool and camphor. It was all as if it had just happened.

But there was nothing more than that.

She opened her eyes in defeat. The empty room stared back at her. Empty of furniture. Empty of warmth. Empty of sound. Empty of people. So unlike Lofton House, her beloved family home. She shuddered again.

She needed air. She needed exercise.

The conference had run late, and the sky was already darkening when she slipped out the rear door of 34 Whitaker. She'd donned the lad's costume again because trousers beckoned fewer questions. Her slouched hat hung low over her face, but she kept the length of cloth tied close over her nose and mouth. A passerby would notice nothing amiss, but it made her feel better. More camouflaged. More discreet. She could ease down the street unnoticed.

And she didn't want to be noticed tonight. She just wanted to push her legs, feel her muscles expand and contract, expand her lungs with exertion. She would feel better in an hour or so, she knew. Exercise had that effect on her.

But her mind continued its tumultuous tumble, running the events of the past few days over and over again in her head.

The bookshop. The dock. The conference.

Xavier's kiss.

She nearly choked when the memory sprang into her mind. She'd tried to suppress it. Ignore it. Pretend it hadn't happened.

The kiss would change everything, and she couldn't let that happen. Not right now. She had to save him. Emotion only complicated the matter. She knew that all too well.

She had to stay objective. No matter how his kiss had sparked electricity inside of her. Or how the nearness of his body was enough to send waves of heat coiling through her body.

She'd never been kissed like that.

Again, she recalled the clumsy encounters with young bachelors in her youth. There had been so much uncomfortable groping and awkward pats in obscure places like her elbow. So much unnecessary moaning and fluttery words of nonsense.

And yet Xavier had only touched his lips to hers. The thought had her fingers going involuntarily to the spot on the cloth where her lips hid as if they could feel the ghost of the kiss there.

That was not good at all.

She couldn't let this happen. She only needed to find the killer and stop him. She had to.

The sun had nearly set now, and the city about her was blanketed in that orange glow that erupted right before the sun disappeared entirely and night took over. She loved this time of day. The possibilities that awaited. So much happened under the cover darkness. So much left unseen by the day dwellers of London. She reveled in it.

It was funny to think once she'd only gone about the city at night in a carriage, going to a ball, a soiree, the theater. Wherever her presence would be most advantageous to securing a good match.

A duke.

She wanted to laugh at her younger self now. At the ridiculousness of her intentions. What did a duke matter when you'd betrayed your family?

She turned the corner and stopped.

She knew where her feet had been carrying her. She knew which direction she inevitably took whenever leaving the house at night.

The park sat before her, quiet in slumber, dark in foreboding.

The site of her downfall.

She liked to come here when her thoughts jumbled, when the longing in her chest grew too tight and threatened to choke her. The longing for the life she once lived, safe in the bosom of her family.

She could admit to the darkness how she longed to return home. How she longed for the bustling of Lofton House. For the banter between her mother and Ashley. For the squabbling between the twins, Madeline and Michael. For the muttering her father always did at his desk in the library when the family gathered in the evenings.

She missed home.

But she couldn't go back there. There was too much at stake. Too much yet to be done. And even then, she didn't know if she could go home. Everything was so different now.

She had let herself fall too deeply into her thoughts, and that was why she didn't hear the approaching footsteps until it was too late. The hand grabbed her shoulder with enough strength to have her buckling. She turned the fall into a spin, sliding down and toward her attacker until it broke his grip.

She kept spinning, coming up under his arms with a bruising push that sent him stumbling backwards. But as he went, his hand brushed at her face, pulling down the handkerchief that concealed her identity.

But it needn't have mattered because her attacker had stumbled into the street where the moon penetrated the darkness, and she could make out his face.

"Samuel," she said just as her attacker announced, "Emily."

They regarded one another in a curious fashion, stunned beyond words to have encountered one another in such an unexpected way. She hadn't been expecting to see her cousin, Lizzie's older brother, on the streets of Mayfair so late in the evening, but as a detective inspector for the Metropolitan Police, it was not an impossible occurrence.

Still.

"Whatever are you doing here?" she asked, backing up and beckoning him to rejoin the pavement with her.

Mayfair was quiet this far into the evening, the ton having already dispersed to whatever crush was happening that night, but one could never be too careful of runaway carriages in the dark.

He stepped up on the curb as she'd motioned him, but he didn't answer her. He considered her, his lips slightly parted.

She hadn't seen Samuel in six years. She'd followed his career in the papers and wasn't at all surprised he'd risen as far and as quickly as he had. She'd always admired him, striking out on a path all of his own making.

To say nothing of his wife, the secretary turned novelist Penelope, whom she'd just implemented as cause for her current subterfuge as Xavier's secretary.

She smiled, hoping to lessen Samuel's shock.

"I should say, how are you, Samuel? It's been so long." She

layered this with a thick smile meant to make him laugh, but he only blinked at her.

It was several breaths before he said, "Emily," once more. He shook his head. "I never suspected I would find you lurking about the streets of Mayfair."

She crossed her arms over her chest. "I could say the same for you."

He glanced down, took in her attire. "And dressed as a man, no less." His gaze traveled back to her face. "I cannot say I am surprised."

For the first time that day, a true smile split her face. "Thank you for not asking me if my mother knew I wore trousers."

Samuel returned her smile, a knowing glint in his eyes. "I would hazard a guess that Aunt Sarah gave you those trousers."

She brightened further. "She did, indeed."

Her expression closed as soon as it had opened. That was the problem with isolation. There was no one about who truly understood you, and standing in the dark on the pavement of Mayfair, she realized yet another cost of her exile.

No one understood what it was like to be a female member of the Black family.

Society was structured with all its rules, rules that gave certain presumptions to its members. Presumptions that had her in crinoline and lace, bell-shaped skirts and tight sleeves.

That wouldn't do at all for a Black in service to the War Office. Of course, Samuel would understand that.

But she wouldn't let him off the hook. "And just what is it that's brought you to the streets this night?"

He looked about him, carefully looking one way and then the other. "Reports of a stalker, I'm afraid." He returned his attention to her. "Some of the upper echelons are complaining of a gentleman lurking in the streets in the evening hours. He seems to be watching the houses."

She tilted her head in question. "Don't you have bobbies who can do canvassing such as that?"

He shook his head. "I'd pass it off to the rank and file, but the police force could use the good publicity it would give us to have an inspector patrolling the streets."

She tried to hide her grin. "An inspector that also happens to be the nephew of the Duke of Lofton?"

He smiled on one side of his mouth. "Something like that."

"Had any success?"

His eyes widened at the question. "I can't say that I have —" He stopped abruptly and pointed at her. "You never answered. What are you doing out here at this hour?" His gaze traveled around them once more, but the soft crinkles at the corners of his eyes suggested his suspicion.

She laughed. "Clearing my head, I'm afraid." She nodded across the street at the park. "I like to walk in this direction when I need to sweep the dust from my mind."

"It's rather dangerous, Em." The way he spoke the words lent an air of questioning so subtle she almost missed it.

But his expression changed now, his jaw firmed, his eyes expectant.

She smiled softly. "I can handle myself, Samuel. I'm sure you've heard as much from Lizzie."

"I was hoping it wasn't true."

She laughed softly. "Would you expect anything else in our family?"

He shook his head, and his mouth relaxed. "I cannot say that I would. Still. Please be careful, Em, all right? Your mother worries about you."

While she still took tea from time to time with her

mother, it was startling to hear someone else speak of her in regards to Emily.

She nodded. "I can assure you I am quite all right. But this stalker—has he only been seen in Mayfair?"

Samuel nodded, again his gaze moving vigilantly up and down the street. "He seems to study homes on this edge of the park. I fear he may be planning a burglary, but as I have yet to spot anyone, I can't be sure. Sometimes eyewitness accounts can be colored." His grin was slightly mocking, and she could understand only too well. The upper tiers of society did have a tendency to over-inflate their preserved value.

"I haven't been out this way in quite some weeks, I'm afraid, so I don't think it's I your witnesses have spotted."

He studied her critically. "I suppose it may have been you. Do you always wear that get up when you're strolling about the streets at night?"

"As you can imagine, it's most advantageous."

He nodded but grew still quickly. "You know Jane and Austin have come into town for the season. They have their boys with them, and I know you've never met—"

"Lizzie told me," she said quickly, breathlessly, to stop the dangerous flow of words.

Samuel was a smart man, and she knew he knew to stop. But she also knew he was stubborn like his mother.

He pressed on. "Jane asked after you. She'd love to see you."

Emily couldn't answer him. She was too afraid of what may spill out if she allowed her lips to part, her tongue to shape words. The pain of longing blossomed in her chest.

Jane had two boys now, she knew that. Two little boys she'd never met. Richard and Nathan, named for two of the Black family's most honored members. Lizzie said they were the most rambunctious boys she'd ever met, a delight to their grandparents, and a joy to their many and varied cousins of which she was one. One who would never witness that joy.

She swallowed. "I'll be sure to keep an eye out if I should see your stalker, Samuel." She gestured about them. "You know how the streets of London are, I'm afraid. Ripe with a dangerous element sometimes. Unfortunately." She shrugged and let her hands drop. "You're doing good work to keep the people of London safe. Thank you."

He licked his lips and cast his gaze down the length of the street. "I've heard rumors you are doing some similar activities." His gaze returned once more. "As the lad."

She couldn't help the smile that came to her lips at the tone in his voice. While there was a spot of frustration, there was also a hint of pride. Pride in her abilities. Pride in what she'd done. It shocked her. While she enjoyed sparring with Lizzie, it was never anything more than that. A skilled partner with whom she could develop her skill.

But to hear a member of the Metropolitan Police, a member of the Black family, one who knew only too well the pressures of a family legacy steeped in War Office work, to hear him convey such a notion...

She didn't know what to say.

The pain of longing intensified until she was forced to press a hand to her chest. She nodded to Samuel.

"I'm only doing what I can when the opportunity presents itself, Inspector. I assure you I do not go seeking trouble." That was almost the truth. While she enjoyed a perilous encounter to work out her experiments, she knew what danger lay there and respected it.

Samuel's mouth tipped into a wide grin now. "If it becomes more than that, I shall ask you to formally join the force."

He'd meant the words in jest, surely, but they zinged their way right to the bloom of pain in her chest, and she faltered.

Surely, he meant it in jest.

Somewhere in the distance a church bell sounded a sour note marking the hour. The tone was faint, but it jostled her like a carriage passing too closely. She cleared her throat and adjusted the cloth to cover her face once more.

"I must be on then," she said and made to turn but something stopped her. She glanced back at Samuel. He stood silent and still, so at ease with the night. "Thank you," she whispered, but she didn't know for what she was thanking him.

CHAPTER 6

*T*he second day of the conference soon melted into the third, which became the fourth before his frustration grew to overwhelming proportions.

He'd returned to England, a country with which he did not have an amicable past, to engage in an endeavor of peace only to find his fellow delegates had other agendas.

The Prussian ambassador wanted to keep trade lines open with Egypt. The two dukes and the baron wanted to ensure their exports would still reach the Middle East. And the Zurich banker...well...Emily had already uncovered his ulterior motives for attending the conference.

Xavier had known all along the conference's intentions could not be so altruistic, that economic endeavors would play a large part in the meeting's outcomes, but he didn't think about what it would be like to sit through it. To watch one pompous duke posture to a gluttonous duke that to place any sanctions on Egypt would be tantamount to economic strangulation.

The Zurich banker—one Nils Bossart, he was happy to say because he was faithfully memorizing Emily's profiles—

was asked to provide evidence of this belief, but he had been absent at the moment. Emily had later confirmed the good banker had moved on to the Prussian ambassador's secretary of all things. It was the most alluring thing to happen at the whole of the conference, much to Emily's dismay.

It was decided she did not enjoy coming upon lovers in flagrante delicto, and she wished to abstain from further encounters.

But as that was the only interesting development of the conference, it left her rather put out. He glanced at her now, slouched in her secretary's seat behind him. The morning after their row he had expected to find her taciturn at breakfast, but he was surprised by how animated she was over her eggs.

She'd asked how he'd slept and if he were prepared for the day's outing. She had a new perspective she wished to act on in regards to the delegates and hoped with further surveillance, something would prove useful.

He pondered what sort of dreams she must have experienced to be filled with such verve that morning.

She was not animated now, but after four days hunched over her writing table with nothing to show for it, he couldn't very well blame her. Her drive to see him saved was insatiable, and he knew the lack of evidence must be killing her.

He was simply grateful it hadn't killed him yet.

While he had agreed to allow her to continue with her investigation, it hadn't sat well with him, and in the back of his mind, he cradled the idea of contacting her family. The Duke of Lofton would surely be able to help, but as nothing had happened since that day on the docks, he hadn't pressed the idea.

But that did not mean he'd relaxed. He knew only too well that criminals liked to lull their potential victims into a false sense of security by leaving them be, and he wouldn't fall for it. He hadn't before, and he wouldn't again. The criminal was only biding his time.

This left him in a room of interesting characters, all of which he suspected of something and none of which were producing even the slightest questionable activity.

Even Bossart was fairly mundane.

He cut a quick glance at the Prussian secretary. There was an unexpected development though. She looked close to something resembling a lamppost, but according to Emily, she was quite adventurous amorously speaking.

He couldn't help sliding his gaze over to Emily. Even in the hideous cosmetics and deplorable wig, she looked magnificent. The memory of their kiss still haunted him. He didn't know why he had done it, what had compelled him, but he didn't regret it. Only he didn't know what to make of it.

In all this time, he'd never thought of her like that. Not directly, anyway. He'd always been aware of her as a woman but not once had he felt the pull of attraction. Not until now. Now when the garb of a high society debutante had been stripped away, leaving only an essentially beautiful woman. He'd always suspected she'd been under there, hadn't he? Even then, he knew she could be so much more if only she'd been able to see past the shallow things society held so dear.

He regretted though, how she had come to have a changed outlook. He wished it hadn't come about that way. He wished none of it had happened.

He turned back to the conference and willed himself to focus until they adjourned for luncheon. Most of the delegates left Kensington Palace, preferring a pint at a local pub with the gossip and womanly flesh that went with it rather than staying within in the restrictive confines of a royal palace.

Xavier had no where to go, and they'd both agreed he may be safer staying within the palace during such breaks. The fare was extravagant anyway, and he held no complaints there. Although, he knew all too well the gentlemen who departed were not seeking a finer pasty than what was served at the palace, but rather a pasty of a different kind.

Emily approached him at the same moment Lord Avery touched his elbow. The two had not been able to speak privately since Xavier had dashed him a cryptic note stating he was safe and that circumstances were changeable at the moment.

Emily nodded at Lord Avery. "I only wished to let you know I shall like a spot of fresh air, my good man. Should you need me during luncheon?"

She had adapted a nasally tone as part of her disguise, and it still unsettled him. He knew very well she liked to step out from the palace to see in which direction each of the departing gentlemen went and waved her away.

"That's very well. Thank you, Miss Quinton."

She smiled, showing much of her front teeth in an awkward and slightly grotesque manner. It was all very off-putting, and he marveled at just how easily she slipped into character. He watched her go, unable to take his eyes off her backside because he could easily imagine what she looked like beneath the lumpy mess of a dress she wore. Knew only too well because he'd seen her clad in trousers.

He purposefully turned to Lord Avery. "I'm very sorry for not speaking to you earlier, my lord."

Lord Avery brushed him off with the wave of one hand. "Think nothing of it, Xavier, and please resist the urge to *my lord* me." He grimaced at the words. "I should only hope that you are all right."

His eyes traveled involuntarily to the place where Emily had disappeared. "I should think I'm in safe hands."

Lord Avery's gaze followed his gaze, his eyes narrowing in concern. "Your secretary, Miss Quinton, is it?"

Xavier nodded. "Yes, she's a fine secretary. Gets the job done, I suppose."

Lord Avery looked no less concerned. "I have never before seen you with a secretary."

Xavier paused, thought quickly. "I inquired at an agency for her. I had hoped a secretary would allow me to remain engaged in the conference without distracting my attention with the painstaking task of taking notes."

Lord Avery nodded, his face clearing slightly. "Ah, yes, of course. That's exactly why I asked you to come, Xavier. I knew you'd keep a clear head about yourself." He looked about them at the emptying room. "I wish I could say the same for the rest of this lot." He shook his head. "That's not why I wish to speak to you now though. Would you like to take luncheon with me?"

The man gestured to the antechamber where a sideboard had been set up with cold meats, potatoes, sausages, and breads. In the four days of the conference, Lord Avery had been disposed during luncheon, assisting foreign delegates in securing one thing or another. Various services around the city, adequate staff while staying in town, and in one case, a residence entirely.

Xavier gestured to the antechamber, suggesting Lord Avery proceed before him. "Of course, Avery. It will be good to catch up."

He felt a twist in his gut even as he said the words. Lord Avery was still active in the Royal Astronomical Society and ardently pursued telescope research in the hopes of improving access to the field for amateur astronomers. Even as he thought of it, an image of Bobby flashed in his mind, and he swallowed.

Avery was already to the sideboard, heaping his plate with cold chicken and cheese.

"Well, I'd like to say the Royal Astronomical Society suffers with your absence, Xavier."

He wavered and reached for a plate to hide his hesitation. "I daresay I hardly have time for society work these days. My research keeps me fairly occupied."

Avery picked up a roll, squeezed it as he considered Xavier. "And just what research is that? I'd heard a rumor you no longer dallied in telescopes."

Xavier eyed his plate of food and knew he was unlikely to eat any of it. "No, I'm afraid I have pressed my intellect into service elsewhere."

Avery made a noise of acknowledgment before finding a seat by the windows at the far side of the room. "I can't see what could be more exhilarating than telescope research. I do hope you'll share with me. At least what you can." The man spread his lips in a knowing grin—knowing Xavier never was one to speak of his research then and when he did, he never shared much. Had the thugs that had taken Bobby known as much, the boy might still be alive today.

Not like now. Now he spread the knowledge of his water filtration work as far and wide as possible if only to prevent what had happened before.

Xavier sat, holding the plate of food awkwardly. "Water." It was the only word he could get out before he had to swallow and try again. "I'm researching ways of filtering water."

"Water filtration, eh?" Avery's eyes widened appreciatively. "Well, I must say that's a rather noble endeavor. Where are you hoping to apply your research?"

"In America, expansion is pushing ever westward, but in the drying climates, it's difficult to secure fresh water. The water pulled from wells can become contaminated with live-stock waste."

Avery speared a piece of chicken and pointed at him with it. "So your research will go to the expansion of your country. Interesting concept." The man chewed at his chicken, his eyes narrowed in thought. He swallowed and said, "But you don't believe your telescope research would be equally as useful."

The muscles at the back of Xavier's neck twitched. "What do you mean?"

Avery leaned back in his chair. "Well, wouldn't it stand to reason that the development of lens quality could have applications in fields beyond telescopes? Consider the varied items which require the use of a good lens." Avery snapped his fingers. "Have you ever looked into the improvement of reading glasses?"

Xavier shifted in his seat. "No, I hadn't thought of my telescope research in that way."

Avery nodded. "I'd wondered as much when I heard you'd abandoned the field entirely. There are many applications for the research you've conducted already, Xavier, that do not apply to telescopes specifically."

"You knew I abandoned my telescope research?"

Avery stopped chewing, knowing he'd been caught in a lie.

"You wish me to return to the society, don't you, Avery?"

Avery laughed. "I wouldn't be against it if that's what you're suggesting." He sat up, set his plate aside. "I just don't like seeing a talented scientist such as yourself abandon such a promising innovation over that messy business with that Crawley chap so many years ago."

"What do you know of the affair?" The War Office had been pretty keen to seal the matter of Lord Crawley, and

Xavier wasn't aware Avery knew of it. The muscles at the back of his neck tightened more.

Avery waved off the suggestion and gestured to the space around them at the same time. "I have connections in such matters as you may have guessed." He leaned back in conspiratorially. "Not that I enjoy such connections all the time." He grinned. "They can be a rather damned nuisance, am I right?"

"I should think being asked to chair a conference on the Ottoman affair is an honorable endeavor."

Avery scoffed. "Not likely. Britain doesn't want to lose their trade routes in the Middle East, and that's likely to happen if the region falters in this conflict." He gestured about him. "This is all for show, I'm afraid."

Xavier regarded his friend. "For show?"

Avery at least had the decency to appear contrite. "I'm afraid I lured you here with the only means I had, Xavier. The society needs you. The world needs you to continue your research. To do some good in this world through your own abilities."

Xavier stood, the plate forgotten in his hands. "I'm sorry you've wasted your time, Avery. My research only led to the death of a very good friend, and that will be the end of it. I will not allow it to cause any more harm."

Avery stood as well, his face folded in concern. "But can't you see how backward that is? Bobby died so your research could stay free to the people who would do good with it, and instead of honoring his death by ensuring your research continues, you cut the world off from it."

The words pierced the dark veil behind which he'd hidden for the past six years. It was so much easier to avoid it, pretend that by abandoning his research, he could move on. But he hadn't moved on at all, had he? He'd only avoided it.

"Your friend died so you could continue to make this world better. Why would you give up on him like that?" Avery's tone sounded far too much like pleading.

Xavier set his plate aside. "I should think I'll take in some air before we re-adjourn. Thank you, Avery, for this most informative conversation." He strode from the room in search of anything that did not remind him of his past.

* * *

THE DAY WAS CLOUDY, which worked in her favor if she were to watch the delegates depart for the luncheon hour. No one took notice of a drab secretary taking in the air around the Kensington gardens. She could even cross the park directly to Buckingham Palace without anyone taking note. She couldn't help her smile at how far she'd come in her costuming abilities.

The last of the delegates had departed, and she made to move inside only to run directly into Xavier. A fuming Xavier.

"Whatever is the matter with you?"

His expression soured at the sight of her, and she wanted to scold him for such treatment as she was no cause for such a grimace. But then his eyes drifted away from her, and the grimace remained.

"It appears I was brought here under false pretenses." He wasn't looking at her while he said it, and she followed the direction of his gaze to the departing delegates' carriages along the drive.

"False pretenses? What are you talking about?" While this sounded ominous, it also sounded very good for her intention to find Xavier's potential murderer.

She hated thinking of it that way, but she must stay on top of the matter or he'd end up dead.

She shuddered at the thought and gave herself a mental shake. She couldn't think in absolutes like that. Xavier was well and whole before her, and that was all that mattered.

"I think we'd better take a walk." Without thinking she placed her arm on his as if they were courting, and he was about to take her for a turn around the garden.

They both stopped and stared at her arm on his. She snatched it back.

"Well, that was rather odd, wasn't it?" she mumbled.

She looked up to find him watching her.

"Old habits have a way of resurfacing, don't they?" she asked with a smile, hoping to ease the tension that sprouted along his jaw.

At her question though, the shadows returned to his eyes.

She frowned. "Oh bother." She grabbed his arm and pulled him toward the park.

The cloudy day meant it was cool beneath the canopy of trees in the park, and she wrapped her arms about her middle. The fresh air was welcomed though, and she pressed her face into it, eyes closed to better enjoy it.

When she opened her eyes, she found Xavier watching her. She ignored the warm sensation low in her belly his gaze caused and raised her chin.

"Why do you think you were misguided into coming here?" She asked the question even as she looked about them, scanning their surroundings for potential threats. The park was rather empty, but that was no cause to relax. She slipped her hand into the false corset of her dress, her fingers closing around the handle of her dagger. It wasn't a sabre, but it would do.

"Lord Avery told me so."

She looked sharply at him.

"Lord Avery? But isn't he your friend?"

He glanced away from her as he replied. "He was a

colleague from the astronomical society. Apparently he thought if he could speak to me in person, I would reconsider my decision to leave behind my telescope research."

"Well, I shouldn't think that is any of his business."

He stopped walking so quickly she was three steps ahead of him before she realized it. She turned, looked back at him.

She couldn't decide if he was dumbfounded or unexpectedly pleased with her.

"Is it?" she asked. "Any of his business, I mean?"

He shook his head slowly. "But I'm not sure he realizes that."

She shrugged. "It's hard for people to understand how others feel. If empathy came easily, there would be a lot less conflict in this world."

He started toward her, but she could tell he didn't mean to walk any farther along the path, so she stayed where she was. When he got close enough, she saw the small line of worry had appeared between his eyes again. She had a sudden urge to smooth it away. She shifted her gaze, drew in a deep breath.

"I'm afraid you're right." The words were whispered, and she was forced to bring her attention back to him lest she miss something. "Why is it that no one seems to understand what it was like? What happened six years ago."

She studied his eyes. She hadn't realized how varied they were. The browns and golds. She could look into them forever. Her breath quickened at the thought, and she licked her lips.

"I think everyone experienced it differently. You and I..." She let the thought trail away.

He was just too close. Her thoughts were all muddled. She needed air. She needed space. If she just backed up—

She should have known better than to let her guard down. The rider was on them before she even processed the sound of approaching hoofbeats. In fact, it was Xavier's shifting gaze that even alerted her to danger.

Her fingers tightened on her dagger, pulled it from its hiding place. But it didn't matter. Xavier shoved her, hard, and she fell away from the path and into the grass along the thoroughfare. She scrambled to push her bonnet back, to see the inevitable horror she pictured in her mind.

But instead of a trampled Xavier, she saw something far worse.

He was reaching, reaching up and toward the rider who was now upon them, crushing the ground where she had stood only seconds before. And Xavier was going for the rider atop the horse, reaching, snatching, gaining hold.

But the rider didn't stop. The horse never slowed.

Xavier's grip tightened, and suddenly he was swept from his feet, his walking stick arching through the air in a terrible fall as it crashed, useless on the ground.

And then he was being dragged. His legs went out from under him, but his grip was strong. He pulled himself up the rider's leg, grabbed the saddle horn.

And then he was gone.

Her hat and wig had come loose in the fall, and she shoved them from her face, not caring how flawed her costume would appear. She pushed to her feet, tripped over the hem of her skirt, and tried again. Finally, she was on her feet. The sound of hoofbeats had faded. They were too far now for her to hear it.

Oh God, Xavier. She had to get to him. His life was her responsibility. She choked on a sudden rush of tears and grabbed for his walking stick only to miss. Wiping the tears from her eyes, tears she hadn't realized had materialized, she gained her feet once more and flew to the path, her legs pumping against the skirts that clawed at them. She heard ripping, and something gave, but it didn't stop her. The need to get to Xavier was too great.

She flew around the bend in the path, Kensington Palace looming up in the distance like a hulking sentinel. Fat lot of good it had done them. She barreled down the length of the path, but still, Xavier and the horseman were nowhere. Her lungs burned, the blood thundered in her ears.

One more corner and then—

Nothing.

The empty path back to Kensington Palace stared back at her.

She swung around, her chest heaving as she peered back the way they had gone.

Where had they gone? What had happened?

And then she heard it.

Complaining.

Very American complaining.

She turned about, peering off the edge of the path into a copse of trees that stood artfully to the side. A horse's head just poked through the tips of them, and she dove inside of it. Branches scratched at her, and twigs pulled at her lopsided wig.

Finally, she broke free into a glade to find something that did not surprise her in the least.

The rider had been pulled from his horse, one leg trapped in the stirrup that now held him prisoner. And Xavier. Oh God, Xavier was alive. Fuming, disheveled, and likely hurt, but alive.

And complaining.

"Don't be throwing your pandering English words at me, you English swine!"

He looked up as she broke through the trees, pointing down at the prisoner he held under his boot.

"He called me a wanker. I assume the term is less than flattering."

She blinked. "It's quite uncomplimentary."

He pressed his boot, making the horseman twitch and moan on the ground. "And you Englishmen are supposed to be so refined. I knew you were being rude." He pointed back at the horse who munched lazily at the grass now. "How many other Yanks have you tried to run over with your horse?"

The rider mumbled something, but she was too far away to make it out.

Xavier shook the man with his foot again.

"Oh, it's your first time at it, eh? Well, you're awfully good for only having one go at it." He bent over and with little fanfare, lifted the man to his feet in a single, effortless motion. He gripped the man by the lapels of his coat and continued to shake him. "Why is it you want me dead? And I'll have no more of this wanker business!"

Seeming to come to life, Emily stepped forward until she could make out the horseman's face. She wasn't sure what she had been expecting. One of the delegates, perhaps? But this man's face was unknown to her.

"Yes, precisely why is it you want to see Professor Mesmer dead?" She peered up at the man.

It wasn't until she observed his neat appearance that she realized she had been expecting a hired thug like the ones at the docks. But while this man's clothes were rather worn, his toilette seemed carefully done and his hair was neatly cropped, chin clean. How curious.

"It's not me, miss. It's only that—" His words were cut off as he struggled for air.

She tapped Xavier on the arm. "Maybe ease up a bit. We don't want him to suffocate before we've had a chance to question him."

He seemed to realize his mistake and loosened his grip, allowing the man's feet to touch the ground again.

"If it's not you, then who is it?" Xavier demanded.

The man gulped like a fish wanting air before finally saying, "I don't know who it is. But he...he knows things. Things that can't be known or else..."

"Or else what?" This was getting far more complicated than she'd expected.

"It will ruin my family." The words were wet with remorse and tears, and understanding shot through her.

Xavier must have felt the same way because he let go of the man entirely, tapping an open palm against the man's coat in some kind of sign of fraternity.

"Eh, there now, it's all right. No one died." He peered down at her. "No thanks to you, I might add. What about all that nonsense about saving my life?"

Her face heated. "You're one to talk." She gestured to the horse. "Jumping on a stampeding rider like that. You could have gotten yourself killed *without* the help of the murderer."

"Oh, that's rich. Blaming the victim, are you?"

"Victim?" She scoffed, looking him up and down. "You don't look much like a victim. You were stepping on the poor man when I got here."

"You—"

They both stopped, abruptly aware of the rider in question watching them avidly. The man swallowed uncomfortably when their gazes fell on him.

Xavier leaned down. "Perhaps we shouldn't conduct this argument in front of one of my potential murderers, eh?"

"Quite," she agreed. "But you still must explain yourself," she added to the horseman.

He shook his head, his mouth open in acquiescence. "I'm no murderer, miss. Please, I beg of you. No one must know."

"We've heard that bit." Xavier made a rolling motion with

his hand. "We'll need you to get on a little from there. Who is it and what is it he knows?"

The man shook his head. "That's it. I don't know who he is. I never saw his face, and he never told me his name. It's just—"

"He knows things about your family he shouldn't, and this information would be damning if it were to be revealed."

The man relaxed at her words, his eyes closing in relief. "Yes, that's it exactly, miss."

She crossed her arms over her chest, and the motion had her wig sliding into her face. She shoved it back out of the way.

"But who are you exactly?" Xavier asked.

The man swallowed and adjusted his jacket. "The name's Campbell, sir. I'm naught but the son of a country judge from Surrey. I'm of no consequence, but my father—"

"Your father is Sir Henry Campbell, isn't he?"

The man looked at her, eyes startled. "How do you know that?"

She pursed her lips, filed the information away for later. "That doesn't matter. You said someone approached you and knew this damning information."

Campbell nodded. "He said he'd take out an advert in the papers with it if I didn't do what he asked."

"And he asked you to run this bloke down, did he?" Emily pointed a thumb at Xavier who eyed it with a frown.

"Well, not that exactly. He said I should get rid of him, but he didn't say how."

"Get rid of Professor Xavier Mesmer? Did he use that name specifically?"

Campbell nodded. "That he did." He pointed a shaky hand at Xavier. "And he had a likeness of you. Some kind of sketch. I don't know how he had it."

Xavier's features froze as a slice of dread tripped down her spine. "A sketch?" The word only came out a whisper.

"Oh, yes. Like this." He made a squaring motion with his hands as if to indicate the size and shape of the sketch. "It's like what you'd see in the papers or something. Can't imagine why he would have it."

She tucked that away as well.

"Mr. Campbell, I thank you for your cooperation. Might you have plans to meet this mystery gentleman again?"

He shook his head. "No. He said he'd know if I attempted it."

Xavier straightened. "Did he say you must be successful in your attempts?"

Campbell's gaze drifted upward as if he were thinking before he said, "Come to think of it, he didn't. He only said that I must try to get rid of you."

"How odd." She gestured to the horse lingering behind him. "I think you should ride out of here on your own, and it's probably best if you look sufficiently hurt."

The man rubbed a hand against his left shoulder. "That shouldn't be much of a problem." He turned and picked up the bridle of his horse but turned back. "I'm terribly sorry, Professor," he said, his forehead wrinkled with guilt. "I'm not a violent man, it's just—"

Xavier cut him off with a raised hand. "You mustn't apologize for another's evil deeds."

The man looked relieved and pulled the bridle back over his horse's head.

He was mounted before he called back to Emily. "One other thing, miss."

She paused on her way to the edge of the glade, looked up expectantly.

"Yes?"

"The man who confronted me. He had the oddest voice. I couldn't be sure if he was English or not. So confounding."

CHAPTER 7

*H*e sent his regrets to Avery that he would not be attending the afternoon session of the conference. If he were honest, he wasn't sure if he would be attending any more of the conference at all.

His mind rattled with unprocessed thoughts as he collapsed on the sofa in Emily's drawing room at 34 Whitaker a little more than an hour after he'd jumped a stampeding horseman in Hyde Park.

He supposed it was technically Kensington Gardens where he'd done the jumping, but that hardly seemed relevant.

He'd never tried such a feat before, and his leg throbbed in protest. He rubbed it absently.

The sound of Emily's wig and hat hitting the floor announced her entrance. She was halfway across the room and nearly out of her gown when she stopped, peered at him over her shoulder.

"Do you mind terribly if I get out of this thing? I promise I'm quite descent underneath. At least by my standards. I daresay society would be appalled."

He let his eyes drift shut. He most certainly had no room for the image of a trouser-clad Emily in his beleaguered mind just then.

He waved at where he thought she still lingered in the room. "Carry on," he muttered.

"Thank you."

He heard the rustling of cloth and the snap of bands being untied, but nothing panged him more than the heartfelt sigh of relief when she likely came free of the dress. He couldn't help it. He pictured her in trousers and lawn shirt, bandying about as if it were perfectly normal for a lady to go about with her legs so exposed.

Well, it needn't matter now whether he enjoyed the image in his head or the real thing. He opened his eyes, regretted it, and closed them again.

Until Mrs. Merriweather clattered into the room with a teacart. He opened his eyes again, sat up expectantly.

"Your tea, Professor." There was no more kindness to her tone than the first day of their meeting, but her expression had at least softened since then.

He smiled as he pulled the cart close enough to serve. "I thank you most heartily, Mrs. Merriweather."

"As you should," she murmured and strode from the room.

He watched her go before fixing a cup for Emily. She accepted it as she strode by, her steps long as she paced from one end of the room to the other.

"Campbell only confirms our suspicions," she said as she passed him by.

"That someone is trying to kill me?" He blinked at the tea service. "I wasn't aware that needed to be confirmed."

She swung about, came back the way she had gone. "Confirmed, no. But it's good to have a second source bearing similar information."

"Oh, goody," he muttered, spooning sugar into his tea.

He held the cup between both hands and drank deeply, the warmth soothing as he waited for the tea's miraculous properties to take effect.

He slouched back on the sofa so as to better observe the whirling pace of Lady Emily Black.

She sipped her tea as she walked, a feat he'd never tried before, but as he'd never drunk so much tea as he did whilst in England, he couldn't say he'd ever had the occasion to truly test it. Still, it was amusing to watch Emily.

"You knew Campbell's father." He interrupted her pacing. "How?"

She cast him a quick glance as she made her way by. "I remember my father speaking of him some years ago. The judge had done something the War Office needed to cover up for the sake of foreign relations." She shrugged. "Of course, at the time, I hadn't been paying it much mind, so I remember his name. Not what he did."

"Do you think it's that which this mysterious gentleman has to blackmail young Campbell with?"

She finally stopped at the windows at the front of the room.

"We can only assume." She sipped her tea. "But you know how I dislike making assumptions."

"Still the logic holds. Should this judge have committed some crime and the War Office covered it up, it would suggest that whatever the deed was the Campbells would not care to have it leaked."

She studied the carpet at her feet. "But would that be enough to commit murder?"

"We could always ask your father about it."

The look she sent him would have killed lesser men.

He acknowledged it with a raised teacup. "I stand corrected. I beg your pardon, my lady."

"We have far greater problems to wrestle with than what it was Sir Campbell did."

He tilted his head in question.

"If the mysterious gentleman knows of the deed, he was either somehow directly involved—"

"Which would make him a criminal in truth."

She nodded. "Or he has some connection with the War Office."

He stilled. "Surely that can't be it."

"As I said, I don't enjoy making assumptions, but we haven't much else to work on."

"And the evidence is rather damning, as they say." He held the teacup cradled in his palms. Already he felt the fingers of medicine seep from the tea into his aching muscles.

"I'm afraid it is." She shook her head and sat on the ottoman. "I don't like how messy this whole thing is."

"I'm terribly sorry my potential murder is not tidier for you." He said it with a grin.

She laughed softly and pulled herself deeper into the chair. She reclined, her feet crossed at the ankles, a picture of domesticity he had never before seen.

For one thing, he'd never seen a lady outside of a gown. Well, of course, he had in *that* sense, but not like this. This was far more intimate—to see a woman in the safety of her sanctuary, stripped of her outer accruements, which served to protect her from an unforgiving world.

He realized she'd likely had moments like that innumerable times over the past six years, but no one had been there to witness it. To see her like this, softened, at ease.

Beautiful.

"You can't live like this forever." He hadn't meant to say anything and yet the words had spilled from his lips as if they could not be stopped.

She peered up at him, and the spill of daylight from the

window behind her cocooned her in an ethereal glow. In that moment, he could not at all picture the debutante she had once been. Her hair fell softly about her shoulders, completely unkempt, tied back in a single ribbon, but the entire thing framed her face in a way to make her appear so innocent and pure. Most of her cosmetics had worn off in the melee, and he could see her face again. Her real face with its high cheekbones, delicately arched eyebrows, and supple mouth.

He wanted to kiss her again, and he hated it. His growing attraction to her was unexpected and most certainly inconvenient. He didn't want to be in England to begin with, and to have someone wanting him dead...it was enough to have him on the next ship. Especially after the betrayal of his trusted friend and colleague, Lord Avery.

How laughable that was.

Leveraging something Xavier held so precious to get something he wanted. Telescope research. What did it matter now that a man was dead for it?

He set his teacup aside, ran both of his hands over his face. When he looked up again, Emily's expression had changed, her eyes narrowing as she regarded him.

"I rather think now is not the time to speak of my choice of lifestyle. You had mentioned something about Lord Avery before you attempted to dislodge a rider from a speeding horse."

He held up a single finger. "I was successful in that, so attempt is not really the right word, is it? And you're avoiding speaking of your own problems by pushing the attention onto someone else. You can't avoid the topic forever."

"As I see no problem with my current living situation, there's nothing to avoid." He didn't miss how tightly she gripped her teacup. "What is this about Lord Avery?"

He shrugged. "I've told you everything. Lord Avery lured me here with the tantalizing offer of participating in a peace conference knowing full well the delegates held their economic interests dearer than peace."

"Lured you? That's quite a strong word."

"I'm having strong feelings at the moment."

She blinked. "Just about Lord Avery or the part where someone is trying to murder you?"

"I'm having strong feelings about you actually."

He enjoyed watching her face go blank, her shoulders square, and her eyes search about the room for something other than him on which to land.

"I don't think that's necessary. I'm simply fulfilling a responsibility—"

"There's no responsibility, and I needn't tell you that again."

"No, of course not, because you're wrong. I do have a responsibility, and I will not neglect it."

The throbbing in his leg had subsided to a dull ache, and he knew standing on it now would send him into a spiral of pain. He stood anyway. He had to, the need to move his muscles, the frustration that propelled him to do something else with his energy, had him gripping his walking stick and pulling himself to his feet.

"Then I guess there isn't anything further to discuss."

She looked up at him, her lips parted just far enough that she appeared as if she waited for his kiss. "Have I upset you?"

He raked a hand through his hair. "How could you not? You seem to excel at it."

A shadow passed over her face, and she put aside her teacup and stood. "It seems upsetting people is something I am destined to do. Excuse me."

She made to move past him, and he didn't know why he didn't just let her go. He should have. Too much had happened that day to trust his instincts, to believe he would act rationally. But when she drew that close, when her soft curves and warm body were within reach, he couldn't stop himself.

He pulled her against him, his walking stick falling to the floor with an ominous thud. "I don't remember you being one to run away."

She stared up at him, her eyes wide in surprise. "I'm not running away."

He grinned. "Denying your flaws will not make them go away."

She tugged at his grip. "I am not denying my flaws, and I would ask that you cease disparaging my character."

"I shall cease when you stop giving me cause to do so."

She opened her mouth, and he readied himself for her attack.

But not her kiss.

Instead of railing at him, she reached up, tugged his head down to hers until her lips were pressed against his.

It was not an untutored kiss. He'd realized that the first time he'd taken her lips, but it was not a refined one. While she had been kissed somewhere along the way, and having witnessed her abilities as a debutante he could not be surprised by this, she had never had the chance to develop her skill.

But that didn't mean she neglected to try.

Her arms looped around his neck, pulling him closer until her breasts were pressed against his chest. He reached for her, splaying his hands along her back.

Oh dear God, he could feel all of her.

There was no corset, there was no chemise or shift or whatever nonsense women wore beneath their gowns. She wore only a lawn shirt and trousers, and his hands could not be stopped from exploring.

They trailed down the muscles of her back to the curve of her hip to the roundness of her buttocks. She was...warm. God, she was warm and alive and in his arms.

It had been so long since he'd been with a woman, but this was different. He'd never been with a woman like this. This was primal and fiery and base, and he couldn't have stopped if he'd wanted to.

She angled her head, allowing him to deepen the kiss, and he fell into it.

He forgot all about her ridiculous quest to save him, about her equally ridiculous determination to remain isolated. He forgot someone was trying to kill him. That was how powerful her kiss was.

She vanquished all his worries with just her touch.

He didn't know when it had happened, but suddenly he was sitting, tugging her down with him onto the sofa. The trousers—praise Jesus for a woman in trousers—allowed her to straddle him, bringing her closer to him as she pivoted above him, separating his lips with her own.

God, unskilled but not shy.

She was fire in his hands, and the need to have more was irresistible. He cupped her buttocks, pulled her against his growing desire, ran his hands along the muscles of her thighs, the curve of her calves.

Trousers were suddenly his most favorite thing.

Her fingers spiked through his hair, fingernails running along his scalp, and he groaned.

He wasn't sure what made him do it, why he was compelled, but it was as if being trapped underwater and the urge to breathe was insurmountable.

He had to touch her.

He had to feel her skin under his fingertips, feel her warmth in the palm of his hand.

He tugged at her shirt where it disappeared in the back of

the trousers. It was damp with sweat and unyielding. He tugged harder, heard a wrenching sound, and finally, the damned thing pulled free.

He slipped one hand underneath the edge of it. Just one. Slowly as if to savor that first initial contact.

He'd expected something sexual, something instinctual when he touched her. He wasn't sure he could be more aroused than he already was, and he feared touching her would be his undoing.

But he never expected the way his heart would squeeze, the way his stomach would clench, at the way the need to protect would surge through him.

Protect her.

Save her.

Love her.

It should have scared him and for a moment it did, but he couldn't have let go of her. The only thing that could stop this now was her.

And she did.

She wrenched away from him, falling backwards off the sofa, stumbling to her feet as she pushed her hair out of her face.

He was too stunned to move. He could only watch, drink in the stark expression of her face.

She opened her mouth, once, twice without words, her swollen lips closing over air.

Finally, he heard it. Only a whisper. "I can't do this to you."

And then she fled.

* * *

HE WAS PASSING through the foyer on his way to breakfast the next morning when the front door opened.

Had he had a full grasp of his faculties, he would have noticed the visitor immediately, but he could admit he just wasn't himself that morning. He could brush it off with the usual romantic dribble of having Emily's kiss still lingering on his lips, but that was just nonsense.

A kiss was trifle compared to what addled him.

How his heart had leaped when he'd touched her bare skin, the way it had *yearned* toward her. As if it were trying to go home.

He was still startled by it, still frightened by it, so explosive, unexpected, and potentially dangerous a feeling.

So that was why he didn't see the visitor until he was upon him.

It was a small man, dressed in plain trousers and a loose coat, a scarf tied around his neck, and copious hat slouched on his head.

And then he looked up, and he was not a he at all. "Elizabeth Black," Xavier said incredulously.

He hadn't seen Elizabeth Black, Lizzie by her family, since he'd departed England six years ago.

"Miss Black, you look splendid." He smiled at her, but she appeared frozen in the doorway.

Until she threw herself at him.

Her long limbs wrapped themselves around him.

All of him.

Her trouser-clad legs went directly about his waist as her arms swept around his neck in a vise-like grip. And then she squeezed. She squeezed very hard for such a skinny little thing. It all but knocked him backwards, and he was lucky to snatch the newel post to hold him up.

She released him just as quickly as she had smothered him, dropping to the floor with the agility of a cat.

"I've never been happier to see anyone in my entire life."

While he had anticipated a heartfelt greeting after being

so long separated from a family he hoped to call dear, he hadn't been expecting quite so strong of a reception.

But with all of the Black women, he had learned to set aside societal expectations.

"Well, it is lovely to see you again as well, Miss Elizabeth." The words were stilted as his mind scrambled to find cause for such a joyous greeting. Surely, Lizzie didn't think...she wasn't...that is to say, she didn't want something...

She laughed, running a hand over her face. "Seeing you alive means I shan't have to tell my uncle Emily was killed in some foolish scheme." She sighed. "This is such a tremendous relief, Professor." She patted him on the arm as if he were a small child. "Thank you for that."

She turned and left him standing in the foyer as she took the stairs to the upper floors two at a time.

He watched her go, confusion drawing his brow together. So he followed her.

He was slower than she was, what with his walking stick, and she with her long, agile limbs. But he could hear the progress she made through the house and soon found himself on the upper floor. She disappeared into a room down the way and voices drifted toward him.

He knew it would be rude of him to eavesdrop, but his leg slowed him down so terribly much, he was still a good five feet from the door when the words began to take shape.

"So you were successful then. Well, that's a boon, isn't it?" Lizzie asked.

There was some scuffling noises.

"A boon only so far in that he's still alive." Emily's voice was more muffled as if she were doing something that required her attention elsewhere.

"I would think the professor wouldn't be so limiting on that point."

Emily's voice was clearer now. "I should hope not. But..."

"What is it?" Lizzie prompted when Emily didn't continue.

"It's just that…"

He had never known Emily to be so indecisive in her life, and to hear her now, one would think her incapable of stringing an entire sentence together.

Truth be told, he was in much the same condition, and in a flash, he realized he might have inadvertently stumbled upon an intimate congress of two women. Would Emily wish to speak to her cousin of what had transpired between them the previous night? If she did, he would not wish to be in the vicinity.

But what if he were?

What if he just happened to overhear her? Overhear Emily's version of events, or more, if he heard how she felt about it—no, him. How she felt about him.

God, he sounded like a schoolboy still wet behind the ears. And yet he strained forward listening.

"It's just what?" Lizzie's voice was stronger now as she coaxed her cousin along.

"It's all proving a damn sight harder to unravel than I could imagine."

Xavier stilled. This was not at all where he'd hoped the conversation would go, and it stirred in him the thing he kept trying to ignore. His desire to seek out Emily's family, to enlist their aid in finding the mysterious gentleman with the strange voice.

But he knew doing so would betray Emily, and he couldn't do that.

"Did you think it was going to be easy? You are rooting out a killer, you know," Lizzie said.

"Of course, I realize the gravity of the situation. I just hadn't…well, I guess I didn't understand the enormity of it. Of exactly what it would take to figure this out."

"You mean to solve the case?"

There was a deflating noise as if one of them sat down. "Is that how Samuel speaks of it?"

He recalled Samuel, Lizzie's older brother, as being a member of the police force in London.

Lizzie's laugh was light. "It's not as if one can avoid it with the way he talks about his work."

Emily made a noncommittal noise before saying, "It's a great deal easier in my experiments than it is in reality."

There was a matching deflating noise as if the other joined the first in sitting. "Of course, it's more difficult. In truth, you have no control over the other players. You have no ability to set up the scheme to achieve the best results for you."

There was a moment of silence, and Xavier realized he held his breath.

The other players.

He hadn't thought about it like that. It was true though. They didn't know what the other players in the game would do. In fact, they didn't know who the other players *were*. They seemed to keep coming out of the darkness at them, catching them unprepared.

But what if they were to stage an offensive maneuver?

The other players.

He pushed forward, burst into the room before he could think better of it.

"Yes, the other players. We should follow them."

Two pairs of startled eyes focused on him, unblinking, lips slightly parted. The fact the women were related was of no question in that moment as each shared identical expressions on similar features. But it was the tableau he interrupted that intrigued him most.

"Do you do this regularly?" He gestured with his hand to encompass the room.

There was no furniture to speak of in there except for two single chairs pushed to each side of the room and a small table set to one side. The rest of the room had been stripped bare of trappings with the exception of a worn rug and draperies heavy enough to block the gaze of snoops. Snoops who may glimpse two young women of society going at each other with swords.

It was Lizzie who responded. "Weekly, I'm afraid." She grinned at him from the place where she lounged in the chair on the right.

Emily straightened from her spot on the left. "Were you eavesdropping?"

"Yes," he said baldly, patting his leg. "I'm sometimes slowed in my progression to a place and can inadvertently tend to the rude. I do beg your pardon."

Emily's lips tightened, but he continued.

"I've overheard many interesting things and yet cannot be blamed for my discourteous behavior." He propped up one side of his mouth. "Rather an advantage, I should say."

His quip did nothing to lessen Emily's severe expression. He wondered if he would ever be able to rid her of her ridiculous notion his injury was her responsibility. He'd been bent on avenging Bobby, not saving a spoiled debutante. He was just as much to blame for what had happened.

"Like what?" Lizzie asked, coming to attention.

He tossed his walking stick back and forth in his hands, embracing the game at hand. "I once heard a chap at the college speak of his nightly escapades in women's clothing."

Emily sat up now. "Nightly escapades?"

"It seems the gentleman enjoyed the feel of a corset constraining his ribs."

"How odd," Lizzie breathed. "Tell us more."

He scratched at his forehead. "I should hardly think this kind of talk is suitable for young ladies."

"We're wearing trousers and getting ready for our weekly sparring session. I cannot imagine a topic that is not suitable for our ears."

He frowned. "Nevertheless I shan't be the cause of it. Your mother—" He paused, looked at both of them. "Your *mothers* would have my head."

"He's right, you know," Lizzie murmured to Emily.

"What is this about following them?" Emily stood, ignoring her cousin's comment.

"We should follow the other delegates of the conference." He pointed to Lizzie. "Your cousin is right. We don't know what the other players of the game are up to. We have your profiles on the subjects, but that is only facts. We do not know what their tendencies are here in London. You said yourself you can only watch them depart at the luncheon hour, but what if we were to follow them?"

Lizzie tapped her epee against her leg. "How curious. I think you're right, Professor." She looked to Emily. "You completed profiles for each of the delegates?"

Emily's shoulders twitched. "Of course, I did. It's necessary to understand whom one is coming up against."

"But the profiles are just that. Mere sketches of living beings." Again, he gestured to Lizzie. "But we can't control what those living beings do. We can read about them again and again on paper, but wouldn't it be more valuable to see what it is they do in person?"

Emily frowned. "We all know what happened the last time I attempted to pursue one of the delegates."

Lizzie perked up. "All of us do not know what happened, but we shan't mind hearing about it."

Emily waved her away. "I shall tell you at another time for it's most embarrassing."

Xavier placed his walking stick back on the floor. "But that's just it. They're in Kensington Palace. The palace is so heavily guarded, so secure, there couldn't be a possibility of them conducting anything in residence."

"But that's not to stop them outside of the palace," Emily whispered, but finally, the disquiet had disappeared from her face.

"Who is to say what they are up to once the conference adjourns for the day? God, they could even be conducting their business at the luncheon hour," Xavier went on.

"Do you suggest one of the delegates is meeting his accomplices outside of the meetings?" Emily's eyes were bright now. "It would stand to reason as the encounter in Barnaby's suggests he's inclined to hiring outside help to complete his intentions."

Lizzie stood, swinging her epee idly by her side. "You're going to need help if you're to follow all of the delegates."

"No."

Xavier looked at Emily, startled to find his vehemence as forceful as hers as they objected in unison to Lizzie's suggestion.

Emily closed her eyes briefly before turning to her cousin. "Lizzie, I'm very sorry, but I've already told you. I cannot allow you to get involved."

The skin at the back of his neck tightened, and he nearly held his breath, eyeing the pair of cousins. Here it was again. He regarded Emily, studied the tightness of muscles along her arms, the set of her jaw. The wound rendered six years ago was still very raw with her, and he was coming to realize its effects bled into every aspect of her life.

The drive to solve this matter herself without aid of a family unusually skilled in such endeavors. Her objection to her cousin's help, her desire—no, her need to keep her cousin safe.

What else did her misguided sense of recrimination

cause? How limited was her life because of the guilt she still carried?

He looked about him. The house empty of furniture because it was empty of people. The quiet that trailed about her like a manacle. The isolation she had erected so perfectly, so lovingly against the world.

His chest squeezed, and he tried to focus on the conversation at hand. If he went too far in that direction, he'd only end up looking at himself.

Bobby.

He had to remember Bobby. He was nothing like Emily. He hadn't cut himself off from the world. He hadn't subjected himself to some kind of cruel punishment like the exile she seemed to enjoy. He'd dedicated himself to peace and prosperity.

But even as he thought it, his mind drifted to his abandoned telescope research, and his gut recoiled recalling his conversation with Lord Avery. He swallowed. None of it mattered. Someone was trying to kill him, and he'd never be able to avenge Bobby's death if he should join him in eternity.

No, he was nothing like Emily, but he feared he could do nothing to save her, either.

"We should start our surveillance tonight. As soon as the conference finishes for the day."

He listened to Emily, but this eyes were on Lizzie. Knowing the Black family the way he did, he worried at Lizzie's quiet acceptance of her cousin's demands.

"We'll put together a plan now." Emily looked at the clock in the corner. "We have little more than an hour before we must depart for Kensington Palace. We mustn't tarry." With that, she strode from the room, muttering under her breath.

He waited until the footsteps faded down the corridor

before turning to Lizzie. "You're not going to acquiesce, are you?"

She stepped up to him, and he realized just how tall she was. But it was the look on her face that had him stepping back. He'd seen fire in a person's eyes before. Fire that suggested determination. Fire that suggested strength. But this. This was something else entirely.

This was unbreakable

"I don't care what she thinks." She said the words with a deliberate space between them as if to allow him time to understand just how serious she was. "We still love her. Her family still loves her, and we will not let anything happen to her."

"I will not allow anything to happen to her either." He knew the truth of his words even as he knew he hadn't thought about them before that moment.

"I'm counting on that." The words were nearly a whisper as she swept past him and out the door.

CHAPTER 8

"*Y*our man Jackson…"

She turned from where she'd been watching the park whip by the outside of the carriage window. "…Is an accomplished driver. We have nothing to worry about."

Xavier watched her carefully. "I didn't say we had cause to worry, but do you feel there is?"

"Of course there isn't. Jackson is incredibly skilled at the art of pursuit. We shan't be noticed."

As if to refute her words in truth, the carriage rolled to an unpleasant stop almost immediately. She peered to her right only to find Buckingham Palace looming not far in the distance. They'd hardly traveled far at all from Kensington. Surely, the Prussian ambassador did not mean to stop already.

"Excuse me," she said and ducked out of the carriage.

The day had turned into a beautiful example of spring weather, and the sun beat down on her shoulders as she stepped from the conveyance. She had to cover her eyes in order to see Jackson under the glare of the sun.

"Why ever have we stopped?" she called lightly up to him, hoping none heard her.

This part of London was all bustling with traffic, and thank God, it wasn't traffic that was stopping. People entered and exited the parks here. Either crossing over into St. James's Park or moving through the gates toward the Serpentine, which was a great deal closer on this side.

"It's the ambassador, miss," Jackson called down, being careful to stick to her disguise. "He's stopped."

She turned quickly, peering into the crisscrossing traffic. Jackson was only too right. The ambassador had stopped. His carriage was pulled to the gates at Hyde Park, and the man's obnoxious peach-colored coat stood out in the throng. He looked like a wandering citrus fruit.

"Oh, very good," she said without thinking, plunging back into the carriage long enough to tell Xavier to get out.

He sprang from the carriage in such a way as had her believing he had no leg handicap at all.

She gestured in the ambassador's direction. "The park is lovely on a day such as this, Professor. Shouldn't you like to take in some fresh air?"

He followed her gesture, and she knew the moment he understand. That funny little line appeared between his brows.

"Why, yes, Miss Quinton, I should like to take in the air."

He didn't wait for her and started immediately across the street when a break in the traffic allowed it. She scurried after him, her skirts swallowing her legs defiantly.

She picked them up indelicately—now was no time for propriety—and went after him.

The warm spring air had drawn people to the park in unseemly numbers for so late in the afternoon. She had thought the gentler society folk would be preparing for their evening schedules by this time of day. But it was a frightfully nice day, and she could hardly blame them.

Except when they came between her and her prey.

She was thankful the Prussian ambassador favored such hideous colors as his peach-infused coat, and it was easier to follow him through the crush of strolling debutantes and their beaus, the families spread along the Serpentine, hoping to catch a fresh breeze from the water.

They had chosen the Prussian ambassador, a Mr. Thorsten Haas, for the simple fact that he was foreign. Based on her own experience with the mystery gentleman and Campbell's recollection, it stood to reason that English may not be the first language of the man in question. Haas had spoken very little at the conference and then only in heavily-accented English, the German so thick it was like plucking words from clotted cream.

But it was also so thick it may have been a disguise, just as she believed the mystery gentleman's lilting English accent was also a disguise. It was just too strange to ignore. Especially considering how Campbell had noted it as well.

They pressed along the path, keeping Haas just within their sight as they dodged matrons and spinsters, debutantes and gentlemen. When Haas stopped abruptly, she put a hand to Xavier's arm, turning them to observe the trees along the path.

"You will find the weather in England to be most deplorable, I should say." She made the nasal quality of her voice thick, hiding the polished overtones her governess had drilled into her.

"I should agree with you, Miss Quinton. England is full of deplorable things, I should say."

"Oh, most deplorable. All of it."

"Yes, incredibly deplorable. Shouldn't you say?"

"Oh, I believe I did just say."

"Well, then why didn't you just say it?"

She pulled her gaze from where Haas lingered at the edge of the path, his fingers busy filling a pipe with tobacco.

Xavier was not hesitant to return her glare with one of his own. "It's incredibly difficult to concentrate on two things at once, and it's not as if you were giving me a spectacular and witty conversation on which to act."

She pursed her lips and turned back to the Prussian ambassador.

"But you might find our Hyde Park to be of interest. Do you have any parks in—"

She blinked. She had no idea where the professor lived. She knew he conducted research at a university in Boston, but he also traveled a great deal on the lecture circuit.

"Cambridge."

The word was said so softly it startled her, and she looked up at him. His gaze was heavy, as if it drank her in deeply and completely. Her stomach clenched, and she swallowed against the sudden stricture in her throat.

At some point, she would need to acknowledge what had happened between them. She'd been so stupid to allow it, of course, and it wasn't as if she would allow it again. But it had happened.

She'd felt the heat of his kiss, the strength in his chest and shoulders, the tenderness of his caress—

No.

She couldn't allow herself to feel that. It would only lead to danger.

"Cambridge," she repeated, pulling her gaze from his in order to watch the ambassador.

Haas meandered off the path, striking across the lawn toward the Serpentine where he took a seat on one of the benches along the water. He sat, puffing at his pipe, the epitome of a tourist enjoying the local atmosphere on a sunny day.

"Well, he appears to be most terribly threatening," Xavier muttered beside her.

She frowned. "Perhaps someone is coming."

"Like a clandestine rendezvous in the park?"

"Shhh." She looked about them, but there was no one close enough to have overheard.

"Do you think anyone who can hear us is taking us seriously?"

She pitched her voice louder, a sickly sweet smile on her lips. "I should think no one would do that, what with you being American and all."

"Very funny." He turned his gaze along the water and back up the path. "Do you think he's come here before?"

She shook her head, her wig jostling under her hat. "In the days I've watched him depart for luncheon, he always goes away from the park not toward it. But that's not to say he doesn't come here in the evenings. Perhaps this is a ritual of sorts for him."

"What, like something to help him unwind?" Xavier snorted. "It's not as if he's overtaxing himself during the conference."

She looked at that, at the furrow between his brows. "I'm sorry," she whispered.

He looked sharply at her.

"I'm sorry you were lured here by someone you thought a friend."

He studied her for several seconds before saying, "Thank you." He spread his lips in a false smile. "But never fear, the trip is turning out better than I could have hoped for."

She did not reward his sarcasm with a response.

The shores of the Serpentine grew more crowded with strollers and even a picnicker or two. Families gathered, children played on the expanse of lawn. It was like something from a painting, all sketched out in soft watercolors.

She must have made a noise because Xavier touched her arm, his gaze concerned.

She shook her head. "It's nothing. I just wish something had come of this."

That wasn't it at all, and his expression suggested he knew that as well. For the truth was she longed to be one of those families, encamped on the shores of the Serpentine, doing nothing more than soaking in the warmth of a late spring afternoon.

Instead she was hunting a killer.

Her eyes drifted once more only to stop, arrested, the air catching in her throat so she choked.

"What is it?" Xavier asked, bending ever so slightly to follow the line of her gaze.

But she needn't speak. She didn't have to because Xavier would know what her gaze had found.

"Jane," he breathed beside her.

Jane and her *family*. Her beautiful, little family. Austin Peregrine, the Marquess of Evanshire, dutiful husband to Miss Jane Black, now his marchioness. And their two children. Two little boys she'd never met.

They should have been about four and five years of age now. The older boy was Richard, and she watched him now. He made faces at his little brother, making him laugh. It was the kind of moment one would read about in a novel, and it would squeeze your heart with the perfectness of it.

But standing there in Hyde Park that day, it only brought tears raging to her eyes, a sickness swamping her belly that had no cure. She couldn't watch this. She couldn't watch Jane and Austin, reclined on a blanket, laughing at their children's antics as they tumbled in the grass.

They looked so happy.

And free.

She turned away, bumping into Xavier as she hadn't realized how close he was.

"I think we should return to the carriage and wait for Haas to depart."

Xavier wasn't listening to her. He watched over her head at the spot where the boys were playing, but that little line was between his eyes. She spun about, her gaze locking on her little cousins.

A man had approached them. He was of average height, slender, dressed in a plain suit of navy or black, and his beaver hat was pushed low on his head, so she couldn't see his face from where she stood. But she took an unconscious step forward, the muscles tightening along her shoulders and arms as if she were preparing for a fight.

Her eyes swept over to Jane and Austin. Were they seeing this? Were they going to do something? But they didn't, and they weren't. A couple had approached them, all smiles and nodding greetings, distracting the parents from their children.

Emily moved another step closer, her eyes sweeping back to the boys.

The man had bent now and was addressing each boy in turn as if he were some grandfatherly figure, but it didn't sit right. The boys were not smiling and laughing as they had been doing just moments ago. The older boy, Richard, stood stiffly and eventually slipped an arm around his little brother. Emily could see him tug at the boy from where she stood, trying to pull him back to their parents.

That's when it happened.

The man grabbed each of them by the arm so quickly their small bodies jerked in response. She thought she heard a call from behind her, Xavier telling her to stop, but she was already moving. Her hands slipped into the concealed compartment of her bodice, grasped the hidden tapes that held her skirts in place and with a single tug she released them, her skirts dropping to the ground.

Once freed from their traitorous confines, her legs stretched into a full stride, eating up the distance between her and her little cousins. She didn't see the onlookers staring at her, the exclamations of surprise, the cries of disgust when her skirts fell away revealing trousers. She didn't hear any of it.

She saw only Richard and Nathan, struggling against the grip the man had on their small arms, crying out in pain.

Likely warned by the cries around him, the man looked up, but his face was in shadow beneath his hat. She knew he saw her though, saw her coming for him. He pulled harder on the boys' arms. Richard yelled, tears filling his voice. Somewhere she realized Austin had gained his feet, but he was too far away.

And she was too primed to stop.

She hit the man at full speed, striking him with a blow across his neck that sent him reeling backwards. But in so doing, his arm raised up, dropping little Nathan. The arm hit her though, and it knocked her off balance. She fell to the ground, hard, dirt and grass pushing into her open mouth. She spit, scrambled to regain her feet.

But like the sudden clearing of fog, her senses registered something.

A smell.

Wet wool and camphor.

As soon as the thought was there, it vanished, and she turned just in time to see the man had grabbed little Nathan again with both hands and lifted—lift him so high, pivoted, and let go. She watched as little Nathan's body fell as if time had slowed to a crawl. Little Nathan hit the water of the

Serpentine, his small body sinking, the dark water closing over his head.

She couldn't make her body move. It was like some invisible force held her down, clawed at her limbs so she couldn't get them to cooperate. She couldn't get to her feet. They kept slipping along the grass.

But she must have moved. She must have made it because suddenly she was standing.

The man bent, seized Richard by the arms, and it was happening all over again. Richard's small body going through the air, crashing through the water, disappearing from sight.

And it was like her body was released from whatever held it back. She surged forward her arms pumping, her legs sweeping. The man fled as soon as the small body left his hands, but a part of her longed to give chase, to find him, and hurt him for hurting her family.

But something else zinged through her, something hotter, something primal.

She had to save the boys.

She was sailing through the air before she realized what she was doing. The water of the Serpentine was cold and dark, but she plunged through it, sweeping her arms in wide arcs through the inky black. Her lungs burned for air, but she couldn't rise up to the surface. Her legs pumped, pushing her deeper.

She couldn't find them.

The thought cut through her like a knife, hot and deadly, and despair gripped her.

So she swam harder, pushed deeper.

Her hand struck the first body on her left, and her grip clenched without thinking. Her mind split in two. She had to get the boy to the surface, to air, but the other boy. She didn't even know which one she gripped. No, she could save him, drag him to the surface and come back for the other.

But even as she thought it, fear crippled her. What if she wasn't fast enough? What if she couldn't make it back in time?

She couldn't let the thought stop her, and she thrust with her legs, hoping she was headed to the surface. That was when the second body crashed into her, soft and yielding, unmoving.

Terror drove her now. The feel of the small body curved into her chest without movement, the lack of resistance, so still, so deathly still. Panic fueled her muscles, and she broke through the surface before she expected to.

Air rushed into her lungs, but her arms struggled to lift the small bodies she held, to bring them to the life-giving air, to rip them from the clutches of a watery death.

Hands.

Hands reached from them. Cries of disbelief and anguish, exclamations of relief and subsiding alarm. The small bodies were lifted away from her, out of her arms, and she opened her eyes, the water dripping down her face, water pulling off the cosmetics that hid her identity. It streamed into her eyes, stinging, but she blinked it away.

She had to see them alive.

There was Austin, cradling the boys in his arms as they cried healthy tears of fright. Austin, rocking them, soothing them.

Hands reached for her, and she wanted to push them away, but she was too mesmerized by the sight of her small cousins, alive and wailing.

So she was on her knees on the bank before she realized what was happening.

Before she realized who it was that had pulled her from the water.

"Emily." Her name spoken like an oath. Whispered in shock.

The one thing that could pull her gaze from the boys.

Jane.

Jane gripped her arms. Jane knelt in the grass, the water pooling around both of them.

Jane who stared into her eyes. Jane who demanded she be seen.

The water had washed away her make up, and now Jane saw her.

She opened her mouth, but the pain was too great. It seized her voice and hid it away.

"Oh God, Emily." Jane's beloved face, wrinkled with concern, with worry, with…gratitude.

She couldn't. She couldn't face this. She couldn't *endure* this. Isolation was so much more bearable than facing gratitude from the person you had betrayed.

But she didn't have to face it for long, because suddenly the lights went out.

* * *

SHE WAS NEARLY ten feet away by the time he realized she planned to intervene. The sight of her running, galloping toward the water and the small boys, held in the grip of that man.

It drove a stake through his heart.

To see her. To witness her compassion, to witness the power of her love.

And to know she refused to share that with anyone.

It undid him.

Like a kaleidoscope tearing through his mind, every memory of Emily crashed through his conscience, and he saw it all in a flash. From stunning debutante to heart crushing recluse, it swam before him until it vanished at the same moment she disappeared into the Serpentine.

That was when he realized it.

No matter what, no matter how, he would drag her from her exile, pull her into the light, make her see that life was still worth living.

That she *deserved* to be a part of it.

With him.

That last part whispered through his brain unknowingly, but he felt its echo pulse in his bones.

With him.

He hadn't thought to share his life with anyone. His research had always been his great love affair, but...

Now he had seen so much more.

Emily, her hair tumbled about her shoulders as she lost herself in her journals. Emily, her trouser-clad legs crossed in repose in her worn out chair. Emily, worrying her lower lip as she figured through a problem.

Emily.

She plundered his mind, a battle of feelings that rendered him motionless.

Until she surged through the surface of the water.

His body uncoiled like a spring, and he took off across the grass, heedless of the pain that exploded through his leg. He was still too far away when she came up on shore, water sluicing about her.

Oh God, her disguise.

It melted before his eyes, streaming off her face in rivulets of brown water.

Jane.

Jane had pulled her from the water, held her now in a grip he could see from here was stronger than anything he'd witnessed. Jane who rattled her, the disbelief clear in her hunched shoulders, open mouth.

It was a split second before he tore his coat off, stuck his walking stick under one arm to free his hands, and he plunged awkwardly ahead until he could swoop down on Emily, his coat enveloping her, guarding her from prying eyes.

Jane sprang back in surprise, and he plastered a wide smile to his face.

"Hello, Miss Black," he nearly shouted, a troubled laugh trickling from his lips. "Oh ho, it's Lady Peregrine now, isn't it?" More awkward laughter as he pulled Emily to her feet, wrapped his free arm around her.

He stood there, a soggy Emily stuck under his coat in one arm, his walking stick under the other.

"Fine weather we're having." He was speaking too loudly.

Jane had gained her feet when he'd pulled Emily up, and now she stared at him, transfixed. Austin stood behind her, the boys quieted in his embrace, but he shared the equally astonished expression of his wife.

"Professor?" The marquess whispered.

He pulled Emily closer.

"Terribly sorry about all this, but we must be going."

Emily struggled under his arm, and he loosened his grip. Her face, smudged with ruined makeup, appeared between the edges of his coat.

"Can't talk now," she hissed. "Must be going before anyone notices us."

Jane and Austin both peered about them, but it was Jane who leaned in and whispered, "I'm not sure anyone could miss that, Em."

Emily's eyes darted back and forth. "Still. Must be going."

Xavier laughed awkwardly...loudly...again, tightened his grip on Emily and began to shuffle them to the side. He dropped his walking stick into his hand, used it to propel them toward the path.

"Cherry oh!" he called to a still confused Jane and Austin on the banks of the Serpentine.

They were in the carriage when Emily shook off his coat and said, "Cherry oh?"

He ran a hand over his face. "Isn't that what you Brits say?"

She shoved the coat into his hands, reached up to assess the damage to her wig and hat. It had miraculously stayed on, but it oozed with slimy water. She tugged it from her head.

"If we want to announce we're up to no good, certainly." She wiped more water from her face.

"I think you may have done that when you dropped your skirts in the middle of Hyde Park."

Her hands went to her legs, her eyes growing wide. "Bullocks," she muttered.

He gestured with a finger to her half-dressed state. "Did you manufacture that gown yourself? Rather a neat trick with the bottom part."

Her expression soured, and he had to hold back a laugh.

"It took me ages to get the tapes in the right places. I'll never have time to fashion a new one now."

He tilted his head. "Doesn't Mrs. Merriweather help you with that sort of thing?"

"Does Mrs. Merriweather strike you as the sewing type?"

He thought of the pistol she had pulled on him on their very first encounter. "I suppose not."

"But we have far greater problems than my skirts."

His mind went to a devilish place when she said it like that, but he forced himself to focus. "And that would be?"

She leaned in, droplets of water falling from her chin.

"Our mystery gentleman isn't only after you."

CHAPTER 9

*L*izzie had enjoyed growing up with Jane as her older sister. She had always admired Jane's quiet aptitude, her compassion, her gentle empathy.

So when she watched her sister charge into the Duke of Lofton's library, march up to his desk, and pound her fists on said desk to startle the man from his ledgers, she couldn't help but sit up and admire the whole thing.

"Something is wrong," her sister announced, her jaw hard, her nostrils flared.

Jane had been a quiet young lady up until six years ago when a vow to their grandfather sent her on a wild quest to rescue a doctor from Bedlam and take on the War Office itself. That was rather much, but when she'd become a mother, well, tigers cowered in fear of her now.

"It is?" The duke peered up at the rampaging Amazon in front of him.

"What's going on?" This was from their grandmother, Lady Jane.

Lizzie often played poker with their grandmother in the afternoons. It was nice to have a spot of fun before she was subjected to the rigors of their nightly social calendar. So they sat at the small table in the corner of the library as they did most afternoons.

This was the first afternoon to be accompanied with a show. Lizzie nestled in, draped one arm over the back of her chair. This must be good, whatever it was.

"I saw Emily."

Oh. Bullocks.

Lizzie dropped her arm, her back coming up so straight a ruler would be envious.

Uncle Alec raised a single eyebrow. "You did? Where?"

"Hyde Park." Austin Peregrine, the Marquess of Evanshire, and now her brother-in-law strode in with a great deal more force than his wife, but that was likely only because he outweighed her, not from lack of trying on his wife's part.

"What is so unusual about that?" Uncle Alec asked.

"Someone tried to snatch the boys and Emily...well, she —" Jane cut off, shook her head in frustration. "She...well..."

"Intervened," Austin finally finished his wife's sentence.

Lizzie felt a pang of empathy. It was rather hard to understand Emily's endeavors if one had not witnessed their development. Exile was one thing, but her attempts at disguise and subterfuge were unconventional.

"Intervened how?" Uncle Alec came up out of his chair, leaned forward, fisted hands pushing into his desk.

"She disabled the attempted kidnapper." Austin's tone was steely, and Lizzie's stomach clenched.

Attempted kidnapper.

Well, that didn't fit at all with the potential murder of the professor. What was going on here?

"Emily stopped him?" Lady Jane asked, setting down her hand of cards.

Jane turned to face her namesake. "Yes." It was only a single word, and she shook her head, visibly gathering her thoughts. "She hit him." Pause, more head shaking. "I don't understand how. She came out of nowhere, and she struck him. He let go of the boys and—"

"She was wearing trousers," Austin interrupted his wife, incredulity clear in his tone.

Lady Jane let out a bark of laughter. "Emily? In trousers? I doubt that very much."

Lizzie said nothing, her eyes darting back and forth between the various players.

"She was wearing trousers, and she—" Jane's voice strangled on tears.

Lizzie leaned forward.

"She saved the boys." These words were spoken softly, and Austin placed a hand on his wife's arm.

"Saved them?" Lady Jane's voice was equally as soft.

"The attempted kidnapper threw them in the Serpentine. They don't know how to swim yet." Austin relayed the facts clearly, concisely, and with a lack of feeling that suggested he was trying very hard not to rail at all of London.

Lizzie swallowed.

None of this was right. The murderer was after the professor. Not the boys. Not Richard and Nathan. Her mind swam with the possibilities. If Richard and Nathan were targeted then—

"Why, the whole family's here."

Lizzie looked up in time to see her aunt Sarah enter the room, pulling her gloves from her hands. She'd gone out shopping with Madeline earlier in the day and had likely just returned. This thought was confirmed when Madeline swept in behind her, a smile of greeting on her face.

Sarah stilled almost immediately. "What's happened?"

"Someone tried to kidnap the boys, and apparently Emily saved them," Uncle Alec intoned.

Sarah's eyes widened, and Lizzie knew she would not

have been more surprised had Lizzie stood up in that moment and announced she was joining a nunnery.

"No," Sarah breathed at the same time Madeline let out a gasp of shock.

No, not shock really. Understanding perhaps. Lizzie watched her cousin, watched her eyes dart about the room. She knew something.

What, indeed, was going on?

"What's happened?" Her cousin Ashley stepped into the room next, tossing an apple between his hands.

"Someone's attacked the family. Again." Uncle Alec ran a frustrated hand through his hair, collapsed back in his chair. "This is getting utterly old."

But Lizzie wasn't watching her uncle. She watched her cousin, the same expression of understanding spreading over his features. And then most telling, his eyes drifted to his sister. Madeline shook her head discreetly. Had no one been watching—and as the attention in the room was most certainly directed to Austin comforting his wife, it was likely the case—it would have been missed, but Lizzie was paying attention, and she saw Ashley's corresponding frown.

"How do you mean attacked?" Ashley stepped forward.

Austin looked up from where he'd been soothing her clearly agitated sister. "He attempted to kidnap the boys, we assume, and when Emily stopped him, he tried drowning them in the Serpentine."

Ashley blinked. "Emily? Our sister, Emily?"

Jane nodded. "The very one."

"This doesn't make any sense at all," Sarah said, turning about the room. "Why would Emily do such a thing?"

"I think the real question is when was it that Emily became capable of doing such a thing." Austin's statement silenced the rest of the room, stricken into thought as they pondered that very thing.

Only Lizzie knew too well how Emily had become what she was now. Lizzie had witnessed it, reveled in it, and quite honestly, cheered her cousin on in her mad quest to become some sort of heroine of a modern day fable.

It was several seconds before she realized all eyes in the room had turned to her.

It wasn't a secret she had taught Emily how to fence or kept a regular sparring schedule with her cousin. It was no secret at all that she was likely the only member of the family to know what Emily was about these days.

She folded her hands in her lap. "I shall never tell," she said and was rewarded with a laugh from her grandmother.

She eyed the older woman, but she only laughed harder. "You sound just like your mother."

"What is there to tell?" Her aunt Sarah edged her way closer, her head bent, her eyes boring into Lizzie.

Madeline of all people saved her. "Mother, I think there's something else that should be said first."

Sarah stopped in her threatening progression and turned to her daughter. "More?"

Madeline exchanged a glance with Ashley who stepped up to Alec's desk as if stepping before a judge.

"There was an incident in the park earlier this week. An odd gentleman approached me and wagered I couldn't outrun him through the park."

He said this to the duke, his father, but it was Aunt Sarah who spun about, lecture at the ready. "You were racing through the park?"

Lady Jane spoke up. "Did you win the wager?"

Ashley's gaze narrowed, preparing for the scolding he knew would be coming. Knew, because Lizzie anticipated it as well, pitched eagerly forward in her chair, waiting for what would happen next.

"Well, that's just it. Madeline was in the park that day." He swallowed, looked at his sister. "I didn't realize she was on the path but when we approached, the man, the one who had dared me to race him, sent his horse into mine, and I lost control." Another swallow.

Oh God, this was going to be something awful.

"I nearly ran over Madeline."

Her aunt Sarah said nothing, and Lizzie sent up a small prayer for her cousin's safety. Silence from Aunt Sarah was far worse than a barrage.

Uncle Alec sank into his chair, scrubbed both hands over his face.

"When is this ever going to end," he murmured behind his hands.

Lizzie's mind raced. If Ashley and Madeline and Jane's boys had all been targeted then—

Something really was wrong. Jane was right about that.

Conflicted emotions warred within her. Knowing now that her siblings and Jane's boys were targeted, the need to reveal all she knew pulsed within her. She couldn't keep the secret from her family. Secrets were dangerous.

But her desire to protect Emily was strong. To allow her the redemption she so desperately sought, the redemption she somehow thought would save her from past sins, sins for which she'd already been forgiven.

But Emily had spoken the truth. She'd not forgiven herself for it, and until then, she'd remain exiled from the family who loved her.

This had to end.

Lizzie stood slowly, clearing her throat. "There's something you should know," she said when she had everyone's attention.

Seven pairs of eyes watched her expectantly, and for the first time in her life, she trembled, sent up a prayer that one day her cousin would forgive her. For she wanted nothing more than to have her cousin back. To have her family whole again. And without their help, Lizzie feared her cousin would be lost forever, a victim of this mysterious gentleman who had waged war against the Blacks.

There was only one way around it, and that was to get it out all at once.

"Emily overheard two gentlemen plotting the murder of Professor Xavier Mesmer in Barnaby's Books on Marlborough, and she intercepted the professor's ship at the docks and was forced to save him from two thugs bent on killing the professor at that moment. She's been protecting the professor the past week as he attends a conference on the Ottoman affair at Kensington Palace."

"How has she gone to Kensington Palace unseen?" Jane voiced the question with obvious disbelief.

"She wears a disguise."

Jane sucked in a breath. "That's why Xavier covered her with his coat like that. He was trying to shield her identity."

"The professor? He's here? You've seen him?" Aunt Sarah asked, and Jane and Austin nodded in acknowledgment.

Uncle Alec peered at Lizzie between his fingers, his hands still cupped over his face. "You're certain about this?"

"She asked me to alert the family if she...if she..." The words were much harder to say than she would have thought. "If she ended up dead."

Austin wrapped an arm around his wife. "We need Samuel."

* * *

"SHE OVERHEARD someone plotting the murder of Professor Xavier Mesmer whilst in Barnaby Books on Marlborough, and she took it upon herself to save him." Samuel perched on the edge of a chair in the Lofton library.

"And she's truly posing as a secretary? In disguise? How enthralling." Penelope's fingers wrapped tightly around the pencil she used to scratch notes into a small notebook she carried with her.

Samuel and Penelope had come quickly when a message was sent to Stryden Place, their London residence, and as the nature of the message was rather cryptic and yet titillating at the same time, they had arrived with Lizzie's parents as well. Nathan and Eleanora Black stayed at Stryden Place when they were in town for the season, arguing it was most convenient for the family, but Lizzie knew it was so they could spend more time with the other grandchildren. While Jane had had two boys, Samuel had somehow managed three girls, Nellie, Mary, and Pippa. They were hoping for a boy on that last one to name after the Earl of Wickshire, but as once more, the babe appeared a girl, they allowed the earl to pick the name. Pippa was incredibly suitable for the child who contained no small amount of pep.

All three of them had run off with Madeline to play with their cousins, and that left Lofton library a very somber place indeed.

Lizzie eyed her brother and sister-in-law now. "Two someones," she corrected. "She overheard two gentlemen in Barnaby's discussing the professor's murder."

"And she decided to save him herself." Samuel crossed his arms over his chest.

"Yes, that's exactly what she's done." Lizzie gestured around her to the gathered family. "Are you at all surprised?"

Every one of the older generations in the room worked for the War Office at some point while her brother was employed by the Metropolitan Police. It wouldn't be unlike any of them to have done exactly what Emily had, and she wouldn't allow Samuel to suggest otherwise.

He ran a hand over his face. "No, I suppose you're right."

He returned his gaze to her. "And then she—" He swallowed, gesturing with a weak roll of his hand.

"Met the professor's ship at the dock and carried him to safety when two thugs set upon him at his disembarkment."

Samuel grimaced. "Yes, I guess I had that right then."

"How did she do it though?" Penelope piped up. "Can you give us an example of her strategy?" She pantomimed what could only have been the thrusting of a sword.

"I wasn't witness to the display, I'm afraid." Lizzie suppressed a smile at her sister-in-law's obvious glee regarding the subject.

"But you did train her to be readily armed for such an endeavor?"

Lizzie turned about to face her uncle. "Oh, I only taught her the swordplay. She learned the rest on her own."

"The rest?" Penelope again, eager like a flower toward the sun.

"What rest?" Aunt Sarah asked, now stepping forward, concern knitted in the crinkles around her eyes.

"Uh..." Sometimes she forgot that not everyone saw Emily on a regular basis. It really would be so much better if her cousin simply rejoined the family. Her heart pinched at the thought, looking about her at all the change.

Soon Emily's siblings would be marrying, having children, extending the legacy of the Black family, and Emily would miss it all. That same pinching struck her heart, and she had to swallow.

Emily needed her right now, and she couldn't let sentimentality get the better of her.

"Emily is skilled at swordplay, yes, but she's also acquired a degree of agility and strength. I can't lay claim to those," she finished with a shrug.

"Agility and strength?" Uncle Alec asked from where he slouched in his chair behind the desk.

"You mean she's good at fighting?" This from Lizzie's own mother, drawing a smile to Lizzie's face. Leave it to her mum to ask the direct question.

Lizzie smiled harder. "Yes, Emily is a brilliant fighter. She's very nimble on her feet, and she always keeps her eyes ahead of her opponent's next move. It's really beautiful to watch."

"Are we still speaking of my daughter, Emily?" Uncle Alec shoved both hands into his hair. "The Emily I know wouldn't fight over anything lest it involved the prospect of marrying a duke."

"Well, that's just it." Lizzie made her way over to her uncle. "Emily's always had the fight within her. She's just spent it on other things. But now..." She let the sentence trail away as she thought about Emily. The debutante had slipped from her cousin's shoulders so easily, it was like a false skin, a molting snake only to reveal its true, lustrous scales beneath. "Now she's ready to strike for all the true reasons."

Her uncle regarded her, his mouth screwed up in question. "You mean she doesn't get upset over gowns now?"

Lizzie laughed softly. It was so odd speaking of Emily like this, and more, she hadn't realized how odd her family may think Emily had become.

"She hardly wears gowns now. It's easier to train in trousers."

Penelope shot out of her seat. "Trousers? Emily trains in trousers?"

"And the gowns she does wear are easily modified into trousers at a moment's notice," Austin said from across the room where he poured tea for Lizzie's still shaken sister.

"What?" Penelope blurted out with no grace whatsoever.

Austin's face lit with a grin. "Oh yes. She came stampeding across the lawn of the park, and her skirts simply fell away. It was like some kind of absurd magic trick."

"My daughter dropped her skirts in the middle of Hyde Park?"

Lizzie had never seen her uncle Alec express such strong emotion, but now she feared he might render the desk in half.

"She was wearing trousers underneath." Aunt Sarah attempted to calm her husband.

"I should say that's far more practical," Lady Jane thumped her cane on the ground. "But that's not the point. Someone attempted to drown the boys. We must get to the bottom of this."

"Lady Jane is right. We must focus." Samuel stood and paced the length of the room. "Two unknown persons were overheard plotting the murder of Professor Xavier Mesmer in Barnaby's Books, and Emily stopped the initial attempt on the professor's life when he reached the docks here in London."

He looked at her, and Lizzie nodded for him to continue.

"Emily has since been playing the role of secretary—"

"In disguise," Penelope interjected.

"In disguise," Samuel said with a nod to his wife. "In the hopes of uncovering the potential killer at the convention of delegates at Kensington Palace."

Once more he looked to Lizzie as if to confirm his summary of events.

"Yes, that's about it," she agreed.

"From there we have the incident in the park today with the boys," Samuel went on.

"Don't forget the bit about the horse race in the park." While spoken with authority, Ashley's face was painted in doubt as he slid a glance to his still fuming mother.

Samuel stopped, crossed his arms over his chest. "Yes, there is that bit. How strange though." He studied Ashley.

"And you'd never seen the gentleman before. The one who initiated the wager?"

Ashley shook his head. "Never."

"Can you describe him?" Penelope asked.

Ashley rubbed his hands together in contemplation. "Well, I suppose he wasn't very tall. He was shorter than me sitting atop his horse. He was rather thin, and I wondered if he was malnourished from illness or simply old age. He wore a hat pulled low over his face, and he seemed to shun the sunlight." Ashley shrugged. "I simply believed him to be of advanced age, but now I wonder if he was trying to hide his face."

"I'm afraid that may be the case," Samuel said, scratching at the back of his neck.

"Do you think they could all be related?" Lizzie's father spoke for the first time from where he'd settled into a chair next to her mother at the table at which they'd been playing cards.

Samuel dropped his hand, his body going dangerously still. "I think you can follow the natural assumption if they are related."

It was uncle Alec who answered. "If the same man is after the boys, Ashley and Madeline, and the professor, there's only one common denominator."

"Lord Crawley." Lady Jane spoke the words like they presented a foul taste in her mouth, and she spat them forth with great dislike.

"But Crawley is dead." Though the statement was one they were all thinking, Penelope said it with the objective- ness of a writer cataloging a turn of events, which was likely for the best.

Although Lizzie had escaped most of the danger herself when Crawley had first set his sights on her family, the same could not be said for the rest of them, and even with the passage of time, the scars still rose to the surface on occasion.

But it was hard not to appreciate those things that may not have happened without Lord Crawley's interference. Samuel and Penelope and the girls. Austin and Jane and the boys. It was hard to separate the good from the bad, and most of the time, life was just a mottled gray, and it was up to the viewer to find the good bits. At least, that was how Lizzie had come to think of it.

"That's the intelligence we received," Uncle Alec said, but the tone of his voice could be identified as far away as Westminster.

The fact that they would never be sure.

The news had come from deep within the Italian operatives stations on the European peninsula, and it had been murky at best. Lord Crawley was presumed dead from a wasting illness some three or four years ago. He hadn't been seen since, but as the Italian peninsula was largely in flux politically speaking, the War Office had never been able to ascertain solid proof.

"Who was the man on the job in Naples then?" Nathan asked.

"A chap by the name of Bennington. His family's been in it since before the colonial uprising."

Lady Jane made a noise of confirmation. "Benningtons have been at the War Office forever. Surely the man was quite capable of his job."

"Crawleys had been at the War Office for ages," Penelope muttered, but it was enough to capture everyone's attention.

"She's right, you know." Lizzie moved across the room to stand behind her sister-in-law. "Crawleys had been at the office forever. What if this Bennington fellow got it wrong?"

"Then Crawley could very well be behind these attacks," Sarah surmised.

Nathan stood, strode across the room with his hands at his hips. "I don't like this. It's far too many assumptions on far too little evidence. We're chasing at ghosts at best."

Sarah nodded. "He's right. We can't make these kinds of conclusions without more evidence."

"And in the meantime, he checks us off one by one like some damn list of revenge?" Alec asked, once more threatening the desk he was using as a rest for his tight fists.

"We'll be careful," Sarah answered. "It's not like this hasn't happened before. We know what to do."

"And then what? We investigate?"

Lizzie felt a lick of guilt scrape the back of her neck. "Um…" she began but when everyone's eyes turned to her, she felt the weight of the entire Black family at once, and that was an uncomfortably formidable thing, indeed. "There may be more."

"More?" Lady Jane's brow wrinkled in surprise.

Lizzie wiped her palms against her skirts. She was not one to be cowed, but her family was quite extraordinary.

"Emily is investigating the delegates at the convention. Each and everyone of them. She planned to follow them, but she said something about one of them. Saying she'd uncovered something, but that it wasn't favorable." She shrugged. "She never did get to tell me the story, but I think there's bits about this whole thing we don't know. Only Emily knows."

Alec's head sank as his hands finally gave up their fists to spread in defeat across the surface of the desk.

"Then I'll get Emily to talk to us." Sarah said it as if she were going to the milliner's to pick out new ribbon.

Lizzie was quick to shake her head. "She won't see you. She thinks she must do this herself."

"What for?" Penelope, beautiful Penelope, was never one to sit on grace.

Lizzie's gaze drifted to Jane though. "She thinks she must make up for past misdeeds."

"What poppycock."

"Nonsense."

"Is she mad?"

The room erupted in a blathering of denial, and Lizzie was forced to put up both of her hands to get the family to settle.

"Be that as it may—" She looked to each of them. "Nonsense, poppycock, or madness, she still believes she has a wrong to be righted, and she will not accept our aid."

"It's not accepting aid," Samuel scoffed. "It's aiding *us* in an investigation."

"And there is no wrong to be righted," Jane shot to her feet, shrugging off her husband's comforting arm. "She's family."

Lizzie loved watching how her sister had bloomed once life had driven her from the safety of her routines in her family's beloved bosom.

"Be that as it may, she neither wants help nor forgiveness." Lizzie shrugged again. "I've already tried."

Samuel regarded her for several moments before saying, "I may have a way of speaking with her." And he strode from the room.

Penelope watched him go but didn't retreat herself. Instead she turned to the rest of them. "What happens now? Are we to hide until the man is rooted out?"

Alec stood straight, looking more the duke than he ever had. "Of course not," he said. "We close ranks on the bastard."

CHAPTER 10

"You cannot make an assumption like that," Xavier said as Emily squished her way into the drawing room of 34 Whitaker.

"It's not an assumption." She set the soggy bundle that was her wig and hat on the floor. "It's a conclusion I've deduced from the evidence."

"What evidence?" His voice was riddled with incredulity.

"A smell, I'm afraid." She turned, fisted hands to hips. "I suppose I ought to get out of these wet clothes."

Her sodden trousers had become unspeakably chafing during the bouncing carriage ride, and she wanted nothing more than to strip utterly bare and soak in a warm tub. The Serpentine was not the freshest of swimming holes, and her skin crawled, itching to be cleansed.

She needn't ring for Mrs. Merriweather as the woman stepped promptly into the drawing room.

"I've seen to a bath for you, my lady. It shall be ready forthwith." She nodded once to Emily before turning a scowl to Xavier.

Emily couldn't really blame her. The woman was, after

all, merely being protective. It was nice to have someone looking after you. A deeply buried, secret part of her clenched at the thought, and she pushed it away.

Xavier returned his attention to her once he finished exchanging lethal glances with Mrs. Merriweather. "A smell?"

"Yes, it would appear so." She made to pace across the room, the movement entirely involuntarily as the first grind of wet wool between her thighs had her stopping abruptly. "It's a unique odor, one that clung to the gentleman in the bookshop. The tall gent who left before I could get a clean look at him." She pointed as if the Serpentine lay directly beyond the walls of Number 34. "The gentleman today had the same unique odor."

Xavier leaned against the door jamb, his coat fisted in one hand in slouchy defiance of her deductive powers. But it wasn't defiance she noted at all. Instead, her eyes were drawn to his bicep, pronouncedly outlined against the lawn of his shirt because of how he clutched his coat.

She had never thought of the professor before in a carnal way. That was, before before, when she was a debutante of London high society. But now there was no way of avoiding it. Her stomach clenched at the sight of him holding his coat, and her mind flashed back to the afternoon in the park when he'd grabbed hold of a speeding rider, strong enough to pull himself atop the horse and disable the man.

Fear slithered its careful way through her resolve.

This wasn't supposed to happen at all. She was simply to save the professor from his potential murder, redeem herself for a past wrong.

But this.

This was unexpected, unwanted, and...irresistible.

She swallowed.

"And you are identifying my potential killer by an odor?"

Well, that was odd. His voice had never before made her stomach clench like that.

But before, she'd never been able to recall the feel of his kiss, the strength in his hands as he'd pulled her toward him.

This was all going terribly wrong.

"Lord Pemberly did as much." The words came out strangled and rather pitched too high. She swallowed again. "In the case of the mole at the War Office. He identified the attacker based on the smell of roses."

She twirled a loose thread from her cuff between her fingers, wrapping it around only to unwind it. She did it several times before she realized it and stopped immediately.

What was wrong with her?

She'd never experienced this...before. Again, when she was a debutante, she'd been courted by any number of gentleman, the sons of dukes and earls and marquesses.

This was an *American professor*. He should hardly be evoking such a response from her, and yet...he did. Her eyes traveled the length of him, pitched there as he was against the door. His long frame, his strong hands—no, not his hands again—his disheveled hair and darkened jaw.

Oh. No.

She turned around abruptly, her eyes searching for something that would warrant her attention anywhere but on the man standing behind her.

Her eyes fell to the post left on the desk and before she could stop herself, she muttered, "That Brownlow woman is insufferable." She snatched up the invitation and tossed it in the wastebasket. "I will not attend your ball, my lady, no matter how many invitations you send." Slamming the post in the rubbish bin did wonders to help her focus.

Until.

"He identified a man from the smell of a rose?"

Her fingers trembled as she reached for the stack of journals on her desk, and she quickly pulled them back before he could hear the rustle of paper in her shaking hands.

"Mmm," she said distractedly. "The man had created a hybrid of roses in memory of his sister. Lord Pemberly was able to identify it on the man." She glanced over her shoulder. "Lord Pemberly is an accomplished gardener you know."

"I didn't actually." One side of his mouth tipped up in a grin. "And now you think you've done the same with whomever it is that wants me dead?"

That grin pierced her chest as it had never done before. Why had she let him kiss her? Why had she kissed him, come to that? Why had she allowed him to get this close? How stupid had she been.

The other night when she'd let things go so far, that should have been warning enough, but now? Now her heart was involved, and there was nothing worse than that.

She turned back to her desk, but its contents only swam before her eyes, her brain unable to focus on any of it. She had to do something about this. She had to stay focused on her plan or this would never work.

She would just hurt someone again, and she could never hurt Xavier. He was the one person with whom she could never fall in love.

The thought had her chest tightening, and tears threatened the backs of her eyes.

She had endured an unexpected ordeal that day. Seeing Jane after six years. Seeing the boys for the first time. Saving them from drowning. God, *Jane*. It was like no time had passed at all, and there she was, kneeling in front of Emily and saying her name, only her name. No cries of recrimination. No demands for apologies. Nothing.

Only Emily's name as if saying the very word would bring Emily back to them.

She wanted to shake the image from her mind, sweep it

away completely but she couldn't. It sat there, refusing to budge, and with every second, it dug deeper into her defenses.

That was all. That was why her emotions teetered so close to the surface. That was why she was suddenly so aware of Xavier as a...man. She drew a deep breath, forcing her resolve to harden.

Six years was a long time. She wasn't about to give up now on her determination to stay far away from her family, to stay far away from everything she cared about, so as not to hurt them ever again.

She had worked too hard to do anything else.

And Xavier.

She turned back to him, allowed herself to study him.

He was the only person with whom she could never *ever* let herself fall in love, and yet, he was the only man she *could* ever love.

Pain, hot and dividing, rampaged through her chest, but she was used to it now. Isolation meant a certain amount of rendering, separating of oneself from others. She could endure the pain, if only for a little longer.

Xavier would be going back to America when this was over. Surely, he would. And then an entire ocean would stand between her and this man.

Comforted by the thought, she said, "Yes, indeed. It's been bothering me since that day in the bookshop." She wrinkled her nose as if she smelled it now. "It's an usually cloying scent, unique, something that I must have smelled at one time because it struck a bell somewhere in my mind."

"It couldn't just be a cologne or something you smelled in a ballroom once?"

She shook her head, casting her memory back to that moment in the bookshop when the aroma had first reached her. It had pierced her with the deadly agility of a knife, striking deep within her memory. No, it wasn't something so careless as an element of odor one smelled in any of the ball-rooms of London.

It was something far more personal than that. Something she'd tried to banish from her mind.

Which was exactly the problem.

Xavier straightened, came toward her. "Perhaps some snuff or tobacco. A rare blend perhaps that is not regularly used."

"Maybe," she said, but she didn't believe it.

He was very close now when she looked up, but the emotions that had threatened to bubble out only moments before were safely banked. She had only to remember he would be leaving once this was all over, and she would be safely isolated again.

And everyone else would be safe from her.

She shook her head and moved away from him, not caring about the chafing the damp trousers caused her legs. The memory of the smell itched inside her skull, and she had to move.

Wet wool and camphor.

"But the issue of the smell aside, its existence suggests much larger implications." She reached the other side of the room, turned back.

"Meaning this man is after more than just me."

"And if he's after my—" The word family, so unfamiliar now, got stuck in her throat. "He's after Evanshire and his family as well as you would mean—"

"There must be a connection between all of us."

She looked up. "And the only connection between my family and you is—"

"Lord Crawley." He said the name as one would refer to dog excrement.

"Which would have a great deal larger implication than

the simple assassination of you."

He cocked up one side of his mouth. "Thank you for letting me know just exactly what you think of me."

She blinked at him. "Well, don't take it personally. I'm not the one with the grand plot of murder."

He tossed his coat on the sofa and walked to the other side of the room by the dormant fireplace. She kept whiskey stocked there on a small corner of the shelves largely taken up by books, and he went there now, pouring two glasses. When he approached her, she was careful not to allow her fingers to touch his on the glass he offered her.

She took a small sip, letting the magical heat of the liquor lick at the coldness that seemed to have enveloped her. Where was Mrs. Merriweather with that bath? She hadn't realized just how cold she'd become.

"Are we certain Lord Crawley is dead?"

She regarded him as she considered and realized she'd never had occasion to question the validity of any intelligence from the War Office. Having grown up mired in its inner workings, she had come to accept War Office business as a matter of course. It was strange to question it, to think of it in a different light.

"The War Office said the evidence of Lord Crawley's death was positive and unquestionable. It was delivered by one of their best agents." She shook her head. "I can't remember his name now, but it was someone whose name I trusted implicitly. His family has been in the War Office since you Americans decided to rebel."

He wrinkled his nose at that. "That accusation is unwarranted, don't you think?" He grasped the edge of his waistcoat as if haughtily gripping the lapels of his coat, but as he wasn't wearing one, the pose he struck was rather humorous.

She laughed, the sound startling her as just moments before she'd been roiled with dangerous emotions. The laugh died on her lips though as she caught his gaze, so steady, so full, so entirely caught up with her.

She finished the rest of her drink in one swallow, discarding the glass on the stack of books at her feet.

"There is no possible way for it to be Lord Crawley. We must think about something else. Entertaining such a thought will only distract us from the true criminal. We can't waste precious time like that." She forced her eyes to his. "I can't let anything happen to you."

She'd meant the words as a statement of fact to argue her point, but his eyes turned dark, stormy, at her words. He stepped forward and with his free hand, cupped her cheek, so gently, so softly, she wondered if she imagined it.

"But don't you see?" He breathed. "I can't let anything happen to *you*."

The air caught in her throat when her chest seized, and she choked. The blood thundered through her veins, and she didn't know how he didn't feel it through his fingertips. The fingertips that still grazed her cheek, caressed her skin, worshipped her with a whisper of touch.

She felt her body betray her, lean into his touch, accept what he offered.

But like dipping her toe in water she was startled to find was cold, she jerked away, stepping back toward the door.

"I'm sure Mrs. Merriweather has that bath ready now. Excuse me." She would not allow herself to run from the room, but once she was out of sight, she let the tears come.

* * *

SHE LEFT the house after midnight. She hadn't even attempted sleep. What would have been the point?

Never in the six years of her exile had she felt the gnawing of anxiety in her stomach, the clawing of regret along her insides. She had triumphed in her exclusion, found solace in her isolation, peace in knowing she would never hurt anyone again.

She'd never thought about what it would mean for *her*.

To be honest, her future hadn't mattered then. The only thing of import was what she had *done*, not what she could *do*. But that was all different now because of Xavier. He had her thinking about a future she could never have. Instead of finding the overwhelming sense of calm when she thought of her future as a recluse, she now only saw loneliness and boredom. A future she had once seen filled with study and exercise, she now saw empty of…

Love.

She pushed her legs harder, eating up the pavement with every stride. She was soon winding her way through the very heart of Mayfair, and it was several blocks before she realized she was headed in the wrong direction. She stopped, startled, peering about her in the darkness. Instead of heading toward the park, she'd turned inward to the center of Mayfair.

Toward home.

For the second time in so few hours, the air caught in her lungs and made her choke. How had she done it? How had she walked so far from her normal path? She looked about her, the townhouses of London's elite slumbering in nighttime peace. Here and there a single window pane glowed from the light of a comforting candle or fire. There was no sound of horse or carriage, the hour having grown considerably late and most of the ton would have returned to their beds, drunk from the champagne of whatever ball, soiree, musicale, or opera they had attended.

But not Emily.

Emily was awake, alert, and not at all drunk. She was far too aware of her feelings, tumultuous as they were, and wished for the briefest of moments for the intoxicating void of a drunken stupor.

She'd never been drunk before, had never cared for it, but standing there in the darkest part of the night, the reminder of her past and her traitorous thoughts staring down on her from all around, she very much wished for blissful nothingness.

It was likely because of this she didn't hear the carriage approach.

Her assailant was on her before she could pull her dagger from its hidden sheath inside the band of her trousers. She was tugging her arm free when the attacker got his arms about her, caging her attacking arm within his strong grasp.

He laughed, a sound so familiar it had her freezing in an instant.

"Instead of killing me, might I talk you into conversing with me?" Samuel asked, the laughter echoing in his words.

"If you wished to speak to me, why the theatrics?" She pushed against his arm, but he didn't move.

"In case we have any onlookers." She heard a rustle as if he were peering about them. "The old guard of Mayfair do enjoy a good spectacle." He leaned closer. "It's a good cover to have you appear to be apprehended by a member of the Metropolitan Police."

She sighed. "I do hate the obligation of keeping up appearances." She wiggled her arms. "If you must then. Apprehend me, sir."

"Come along with me, man!" Samuel raised his voice to a considerable level, and she ducked to protect her poor ears. "We'll not have you skulking about these streets anymore. Good people live here, you know!"

He picked her up bodily, and she wondered when her cousin had grown into a such a man. What else had she missed living in the cloud of societal trappings?

He dropped her unceremoniously onto the carriage bench, rapped at the ceiling, and slammed the door to just as the conveyance rolled into motion.

She tugged her mask from her face with a scoff. "Good people? Isn't that really too much?" She pointed out the window at a passing townhouse. "Lord Philips cheats his staff of their wages."

Samuel pushed the hat back on his head so she could make out his features, which were currently screwed up in a grin. "Spectacle, Emily. Spectacle." He leaned forward, his expression sobering. "I need to talk to you about Jane."

Her hand went to the door before she could stop it. The impulse to flee, to stop herself from hurting anyone, was powerful, but just as powerful was the sound of Xavier's voice, asking her to seek the assistance of her family.

She hesitated, just a moment, but it was enough.

Samuel went on. "I think you realize this thing is bigger than just the professor."

She snatched her hand back from the door only to pound it in a fist against her knee. "Lizzie squealed."

"Lizzie cares about you."

I can't let anything happen to you.

The sound of Xavier's voice spun out of the recesses of her mind, and she was forced to look away to regain some semblance of control. When she felt she could, she looked back at her cousin.

"What did she tell you?" It was difficult to force the words between her clenched teeth, but she knew she couldn't be angry with Lizzie. She was only doing what Emily herself had asked her to do.

Tell the family if something should happen to Emily. Lizzie had likely heard about the incident at the Serpentine and done what she'd thought best.

Damn her stupid caring family.

"Everything," Samuel said and then shot up two placating hands as she lunged for the door again. "Everything she felt she could. She said I must ask you for the rest of the tale."

Emily was torn, almost physically so, between the need to flee and the desire to wallow in the complete, perfect understanding Lizzie had of Emily's wish to remain isolated.

She didn't deserve such family. She'd already proven as much.

Reluctantly, Emily sat back. "There isn't much more than what Lizzie knows. I overheard the plotting of Professor Mesmer's murder whilst in Barnaby's Books. It all mostly unraveled from there."

"And you saved the professor on the docks?"

She shrugged, her shoulders brushing against the fine leather of the bench. "Yes, of course. What else was I to do?"

"Alert the family?" Samuel's question hung like a ghost between them, a ghost neither of them was brave enough to confront.

She decided to ignore the question. "I brought the professor safely to my home where I learned he was in the country to participate in the convention regarding the Ottoman affair."

"At Kensington Palace? Who requested he appear on the council?"

She blinked. She hadn't thought to ask that question when first confronted with the dilemma facing Xavier. Samuel was rather good at this. "His colleague at the Royal Astronomical Society. He asked that Mesmer join the convention as the professor finds himself engaged in the pursuit of peace between foreign powers."

Samuel watched her carefully. "Mesmer has a quest for peace?"

She adjusted on the bench, not wishing to admit her

cousin excelled at scrutinizing a person. No criminal stood a chance against him.

"Yes, well, it would seem Mesmer has parted ways with his telescope technology for the time being to pursue other, more tranquil endeavors." The words lurched from her mouth, and even she could feel their duplicity.

She recalled the expression Xavier wore as he emerged from Kensington Palace when he'd learned the truth of his friend's betrayal, luring him to England with a chance to uphold peace only to entice him to return to his telescope technology. She could even be so bold as to suggest she often wore a similar expression every time Lizzie mentioned Jane was in town.

"Interesting development," Samuel muttered.

She shoved the matter aside. It had already been too long of a day, and her emotions were wrought to their very end. She had no more to give on the subject, and finding a killer was far more worthy of what little energy remained to her.

"Yes, it is. As it were, Mesmer is serving on the convention, and I naturally thought that a good place to start the investigation into whom would seek his murder."

"And?"

She shook her head. "Nothing. We had planned to follow each of the delegates outside of the conference to ascertain their comings and goings beyond the convention, but—" She licked her lips. "Well, the one chance we had at it ended in the Serpentine."

"That was only today?" Samuel blinked in confusion.

"Yes, today. We've had several other missteps and challenges along the way."

"Such as?"

The carriage turned a corner, and she wondered where they may be going.

"A rider attempted to run down Xavier in the park."

Samuel leaned forward, his elbows to his knees. "A rider wagered Ashley to a race in the park, which nearly resulted in injuring Madeline."

Emily's back straightened instantly. "What? When did this happen?"

He waved a hand at her. "Just last week, but that's hardly the point. The similarities between the two are too hard to ignore."

She leaned forward, coming within breathing distance of her cousin. "The welfare of my little brother and sister are hardly inconsequential, Samuel. I should be notified of such occurrences."

The words rang in the air between them, now a flurry of ghosts pulsating in the space there. She leaned back as if snatching back the words with physical movement.

"Is Xavier all right?" Samuel asked, breaking the tension.

She regarded him. "Yes, he—" She licked her lips again. "He jumped the rider and brought him to a stop."

It was Samuel's turn to regard her. "He jumped a moving rider?"

"Yes."

"A rider attempting to run him over?"

"Yes."

"Doesn't he walk with a cane?"

The question sent an enticing image of Xavier leaning against the door jamb in nothing but shirt sleeves sailing through her mind. She swallowed. "He has incredible strength for a man with a disadvantage such as he has."

Samuel crossed his arms. "I suppose that might be the case. Were you able to question this rider?"

She nodded. "Yes, and it's rather muddy, I'm afraid. Poor chap with the name of Campbell, Judge Campbell's son. He was blackmailed into going after Mesmer."

"Blackmailed? With what?"

"I fear it may have something to do with that War Office business a few years ago, but if it should, how does whoever is blackmailing him know of it?"

"Unless he once worked for the Office."

Silence descended on the carriage as each of them thought about the ramifications of such a thing. If the man did work for the War Office as suggested by his knowledge of Judge Campbell, it would be just another piece of the puzzle leading back to Lord Crawley.

Samuel cleared his throat. "Is that all Lizzie was not privy to?"

Emily's face heated, and she hoped Samuel couldn't see her in the dark. There was plenty that had occurred in the past few weeks that involved the professor, plenty about which to feel guilt.

"I'm afraid that's all. The inroads we made at the conference proved fruitless. It was only our encounter with Campbell and the man at the Serpentine today that led to anything." She hesitated, but the question forced its way out. "Are Jane's sons all right?"

Samuel's features softened in the darkness. "They were asleep when I left Lofton House."

"Lofton House?"

Samuel nodded. "Your father has asked the family to gather."

She couldn't help the smile that pushed at the corners of her lips. "Just like old times."

Samuel laughed. "If your family is involved in espionage and criminal investigations."

She joined in his laugh, the sound releasing some tension from her body. "I suppose that's true."

Samuel rapped on the top of the carriage once more, and the conveyance turned sharply before coming to a stop.

"Thank you for talking with me, Emily. I hope if you uncover anything in the future you will let us know."

She looked to the door, no longer feeling the need to escape.

"Do you plan to pursue this as well?"

"Of course. It's my duty."

She grinned. "You were always one to uphold your duty."

He looked down, rubbed his hands against his thighs. "That's what happens when you're the first born."

"I know." She spoke the words softly, and he looked up at her, his gaze knowing.

She knew exactly the pressures of the first born even if she were not born a boy.

"I suppose you do," he whispered.

She reached for the door and stopped, turned back. "There is just one other thing."

"Yes?"

She recalled Xavier's reaction and pressed on anyway. "It's a smell."

Samuel tilted his head. "A smell?"

"Yes, a peculiar smell. One I've most certainly smelled before but is rather unique. I've been trying to recall what it is since I first smelled it on the tall gentleman in the book-shop. I smelled it again when I disarmed the attacker at the Serpentine."

"What kind of smell is it?"

She shook her head, more at her own thoughts than at the question. "It's like wet wool and camphor of all things, but I simply can't place where I know it from or why."

"But I guess it connects the two halves of this puzzle, doesn't it?"

She met his gaze, smiling softly. "I suppose it does."

She opened the door and descended to find herself not far from 34 Whitaker.

"I trust you can see yourself home."

"Would I be a Black if I couldn't?"

The words stabbed at her at the same time they brought her a faint sense of comfort.

"You will always be a Black, Emily. No matter how hard you try not to be."

He closed the door, and the carriage sprang into motion, rolling away down the street and into the darkness of the London night.

CHAPTER 11

*A*fter giving herself a stern talking to, she was prepared to encounter Xavier at the breakfast table and lay out the plan she had formulated after hearing what information her cousin Samuel had to share.

She hadn't been able to sleep anyway, and she sat up in her drawing room, reviewing each of the profiles she had assembled on the delegates of the conference. It was on the return walk to 34 Whitaker after Samuel had deposited her in Mayfair that she realized she'd missed a very important point.

Campbell had been blackmailed into going after them. Who was to say someone else wasn't susceptible to blackmail? Someone with access to Xavier, like a delegate of the conference?

She had devised a plan to route out that very thing and had carefully plotted her argument by the time she stepped into the breakfast room.

To find it empty.

The sideboard was stocked with steaming dishes of eggs

and bacon and sausages, but all of it lay untouched. She checked the time on the clock in the corner, thinking perhaps in her zest for her new plan, she'd forgotten the time and Xavier had already departed for the conference. Without her.

The zing of trepidation was real and harsh as fear gripped her heart at the thought of Xavier being at the conference unprotected. He didn't know about her siblings. He didn't know about the new blackmail angle. He could be walking into a trap.

She sprang into the hallway, pulling up her skirts in both hands to run the length of the hall to the servants stairs at the back. Her skirts caught on the door handles as she tried to pry open the door to the stairs, and she cursed gowns for the insensible garment they were. Seconds later she was in the kitchen startling a busy Mrs. Merriweather.

"Has the professor left?" she blurted out without preamble.

Mrs. Merriweather studied her over the rim of a pot she was scrubbing clean.

"The professor?" Mrs. Merriweather returned the pot to the sink and reached for a towel on which to dry her hands. "I'm afraid I haven't seen the professor this morning. He's not breaking his fast?"

Emily shook her head and ran to the mews door, flinging it open only to see the carriage and a startled Jackson blinking back at her.

"Did you take the professor to the conference this morning?" The words were rushed and falling over each other.

"No, my lady. I haven't seen the professor this morning." He wiped his hands on a rag he pulled from his pocket as he straightened away from the wheel he'd been greasing. "Are we leaving earlier than usual, my lady?"

She shook her head, made a placating gesture with her hands. "No, no, not at all. Thank you, Jackson."

She turned and bolted back through the kitchen without bothering to shut the door to the mews. She flew up the stairs to the main floor, tearing through each room as she came to them. If neither Mrs. Merriweather nor Jackson had seen him, then—

Then what?

Had he fled? Had he gone on foot to the conference? Hailed a hack once he reached a main thoroughfare?

She stopped when a sickening thought thudded like a dropped anvil in the pit of her stomach.

What if he had gone to her family for help?

She put a hand against the wall beside her, her fingers pressing into the silk wallpaper.

No.

He wouldn't do that to her. He wouldn't betray her like that. If anyone were to understand her determination to redeem herself, to put right what she had wronged, to make amends—no, it wasn't any of that.

It was far worse.

She couldn't *hurt* them again. Not any of them.

He couldn't have gone to them.

Her lips were trembling but not from tears. Rage, hurt, fear, disbelief surged through her until she trembled all over.

She made herself turn around, go up the stairs to the upper floors. She would need to change into a disguise if she were to go out and find him, if she were to go near her family's home again. One last whisper of hope shot through her mind. She'd check his rooms when she went up. Perhaps he had simply overslept. Maybe that was all. She was overreacting, being silly.

But the constant pressure she'd put on herself for the past

six years would not relent now, and her mind kept spinning to the darkest conclusions.

Her thoughts were so jumbled she didn't hear the noise at first. She had almost reached the other end of the house before she noticed it.

Thwack. Thwack.

She paused, her senses prickling.

It was a steady thumping noise, growing louder and more even, punctuated by—

Grunting?

She swung around, her eyes traveling the length of the hall and to the other side of the stairs where the guest quarters were. As it had taken a murder attempt for her to host a guest in the six years she'd resided at 34 Whitaker, she'd no use for the extensive guest quarters, so she'd converted the rooms to her needs.

And that sound, that sound she knew only too well.

Emotion drained from her, pooling at her feet on the carpet as she took a wobbly step forward. And then another.

The noise grew louder as she made her way across the house. She stopped outside the door where she knew the noise emanated from and stood there. Just listening. Conjuring in her mind the image that would greet her.

Slowly, oh so achingly slowly, she brought her head around the doorjamb.

And there it was.

Xavier. Dressed only in trousers, naked to the waist, sweat glistening down the rippling muscles of his back, his hair falling in a sweaty cascade over his brow, framing a face like granite, so focused was it on pummeling the punching bag suspended before him. His arms were defined yet not bulking, making him sleek and unassuming. He attacked the bag with a skilled precision, muscles rippling as they expanded and contracted.

The fire began to burn low in her stomach, and she called it what it was.

Desire.

Unadulterated, pure desire for him, Xavier, the only man to ever touch her heart.

She closed her eyes against the sight, but the fire still pulsed within her. She had prepared to meet him over eggs, prepared to endure the proximity, the forced closeness their situation would entail. She was not prepared for this. To be subjected to his maleness in such a carnal way.

Standing there in the corridor she could admit it.

She wanted him.

And she could never have him.

She forced her eyes open, squared her shoulders, and stepped into the room.

"What are you doing?" The words came out more crisply than she had intended, but she liked the effect. She couldn't let him know how much he affected her, and a cool front was a good way to disguise it.

He stopped, his gloved hand missing the bag on the final swing as he turned to look at her.

The smile that slowly crept over his features was enough to disarm her completely, but she straightened her back, steeled herself against it. She was a Black. She was designed to endure far worse.

"I must admit I like what you have done with this house." He stopped the swinging bag with the tap of one glove.

"Snooping about?" She had no qualms with such a thing, but making it sound as though she did kept the much needed barriers between them.

His smile turned into a grin. "Couldn't be helped." He raised a gloved hand to the floor above them. "After seeing what you had done to the sewing room, I knew you must have a space like this somewhere about. I must say it far exceeded my expectations."

She looked about the room, pride washing over her as it always did. The room had been the largest of the guest quarters, and she'd confiscated it for her exercise. She had a set of parallel bars installed as well as a series of punching bags based on the design she'd studied at Gentleman Jackson's. She had a set of Indian clubs as well and some dumbbells. It looked out of place against the hand-painted cherry blossom wallpaper and gilt trimmed scones, but the equipment was of far more use to her than another room with a four-poster bed that went unused.

She allowed herself a small smile of pride. "Thank you. It suits my needs."

He pulled at the bindings of his glove with his teeth, loosening it to slip his hand free so he could gesture to the parallel bars. "Might I ask what you use those for?"

She eyed the bars. "Agility. You may have noticed I sometimes find myself in situations where I must act quickly and lightly."

"You make a habit of climbing shipping crates?"

She crossed her arms over her chest. "Not particularly, but the necessity does come up now and again. I like to plan for every possible consequence."

He slipped the other glove from his hands. "Indeed." He set the gloves on the shelves that once housed a spectacular collection of porcelain shepherd figurines but which now contained three sets of gloves.

"And those?" He pointed to the Indian clubs.

"It's a form of weight training from India." She straightened and went over to the clubs, hefting one in her hand. "They're weighted in the cylinder portion at the base there, but the handle allows one to get a firm enough grip to—" She spread her feet into a fighting stance and raised the club as she would her epee. "Maneuver with it."

She didn't want to desire his approval so much, but when his eyes widened at her stance, she warmed in response.

"I'll say," he muttered. "You train regularly with these then."

She lowered the club, brought her legs comfortably together. "Yes, of course." She set the club back with the others. "You never know when you might have need for such skills." She gave him a sidelong glance, and he laughed in response.

"I'm terribly sorry my arrival has caused such a disturbance in your life."

She straightened to look at him fully. "No disturbance at all. I was actually quite glad to see you."

The words left her mouth in a waterfall, unable to be stopped even if she wished it so. She watched them fall between them like one watched a pitcher of milk about to be upended. There was a sense of the inevitable and an equal sense of the inability to do anything about it.

But Xavier being the gentleman he was, he let the words go. Almost. He smiled a smile that spoke of all the things she'd been running away from since he arrived, but he did nothing else.

Instead he said, "I was glad to see you as well."

The words were spoken so softly with such sincerity, a lump formed in her throat as the air constricted in her chest.

No, she had to remember why she was here. Nothing could come of this thing that was happening between them. Nothing *could* happen. She just couldn't allow it.

She had to stay on task so she said, "That's actually why I've come to find you this morning."

The smile slipped from his face, and he bent down. She realized he was retrieving his shirt, which he used to wipe the sweat from his face—and his sculpted chest with its dusting of hair she wanted nothing more than to run her fingers through, feel the muscle underneath, the beat of his heart, the heat of his—

"I hope you're not here to convince me to return to the conference today."

His words startled her, and she forced her eyes to his face. "You were thinking of not going?"

He tossed the shirt aside. "What would be the point?"

His tone was filled with hurt and disappointment, and she reached for him before she could think better of it. "Oh, Xavier, I'm so sorry."

Heat blasted through her fingertips, her bare skin touching his, and both of them looked to the place where she touched him. She snatched her hand back.

"I'm sorry you made this journey for nothing."

The grin returned to his face. "I didn't say the trip was for naught."

The lump sprang back into her thought. She paced away, ripping her gaze from his if only to focus.

"Well, then, I would hope you would help me with our investigation."

The sigh was quite clear from where she'd made it to the other side of the room. "Emily, I think—"

"I met my cousin Samuel last evening. It appears there were other attempts on my family. Ashley and Madeline specifically."

He stood rigid, his eyes locked on her. "Attempts?"

"A mysterious gentleman wagered Ashley to a race in Hyde Park and then bumped his horse and caused Ashley to steer into Madeline. They're both safe, thank God, but it means—"

"He's after all of us."

She waited a moment. She knew he would make the

connection, and she watched his expression sink into disbelief.

"But the only connection between your family and me is —" He licked his lips, clearly hung up on the word.

She had no such issue with the epitaph. "Lord Crawley." She employed the disdain she'd harbored for six years in her tone.

"But he's dead."

She held up a finger. "We think he's dead. The intelligence said as much, but I never saw his dead body."

He winced. "Is that necessary?"

"In this family, it is."

He tilted his head. "I thought you'd left your family."

The words were said gently, but they made their intended mark. She ignored him.

"That's not the point today, however. We've missed an important clue in the case."

"Which is?"

She smiled. "Blackmail."

He blinked. "Blackmail? You mean the Campbell chap?"

She took a step toward him, placed a hand on one of the parallel bars. "Campbell was blackmailed into doing what he did. What is there to say others won't be manipulated in the same way?"

He put his hands to his hips, drawing her eyes to study how narrow they were, how delineated, how his trousers clung—

God, she needed to get this conversation over with and get him back into some decent clothes.

"But you made profiles on all the delegates at the conference if that's where this is headed."

She nodded. "I did make profiles using public knowledge. At the time, I didn't yet know if it would be pertinent to obtain the knowledge only kept in dark places."

He straightened, easing his body toward her in a way that was provocatively protective. "Dark places? What are you saying, Lady Black?"

"I'm saying we must visit a brothel."

* * *

HE THOUGHT of himself as a steady academic. A man familiar with experimentation and keen on unexpected outcomes. Somehow Emily continued to catch him off his guard.

"I beg your pardon."

"A brothel." She nodded as if this would explain everything.

"I'm going to need a great deal more detail." He held up a finger when she opened her mouth. "And I would also like a better understanding of just how it was you engaged in a conversation with your cousin Samuel. As far as I know, we both retired early last night. Am I to believe you're engaged in some nocturnal proclivities?"

Although she watched him, he knew she had turned inward, deciding what she should say and how to best to say it. He knew of her desire to remain isolated from her family, her need to keep them from danger. So how was it that she'd so casually mentioned Samuel Black's name? How had she held a conversation related to their situation with the man?

And most importantly when?

He had gone to bed the previous evening as soon as she'd excused herself to the bath Mrs. Merriweather had run. Not that he'd slept. He'd spent the first few hours thumbing through a text on water filtration from a professor at a university in the southern states. Not much of it had caught his interest, and he wasn't sure which it was that drew his attention more—Emily or Lord Avery's intentions.

He could admit he hadn't given up his research easily. He

173

was on the brink of discovering a compact lens of immense capabilities. The applications were endless. But Bobby...

He just couldn't continue. Not with knowing the price that had been paid for what he had discovered so far. He'd left it all behind.

To have his friend beckon him from across an ocean under the guise of peace was...infuriating, degrading... unwanted. For although he wished to remain upset with his friend, there was a part of him that niggled at his conscience. He couldn't remain upset because Lord Avery was right.

Lord Avery was right, and Xavier knew it. He'd only been in denial these past six years with his insipid water filtration experiments. There was still so much more that could have been done with his lens work. So much more Bobby himself had imagined.

While he couldn't bring himself to touch his research after Bobby's death, something greater haunted him now. The fact that he'd never finished it. He'd never completed what he and Bobby had begun, and this more than anything haunted him now.

How had Lord Avery known?

He waited while Emily gathered herself, chose what she would tell him.

While he didn't doubt she would tell him the truth, he knew she couched things in a way she thought he would find more acceptable. If he considered how it was she chose to live her life now, he couldn't blame her for such reticence. But it bothered him. She should trust him implicitly, so why didn't she understand that?

He picked up his shirt again, scrubbed it over his face and along the back of his neck.

"I have a tendency to take walks in the evening to clear my head. My cousin Samuel had an opportunity to become familiar with this habit, and last night, he took advantage of it to convey the information he held regarding our situation."

"I think I should dislike how you keep referring to my possible murder as the situation."

She frowned. "What else would you have me call it?"

"I wish it weren't happening at all." He tossed the shirt back down. "So last night Samuel met with you?"

"Encountered me," she clarified with an upheld hand. "I had no plans of meeting him."

He crossed his arms over his chest. "I feel you're ensuring to make that distinction clear."

"You know how I feel about my family, Xavier." The words were whispered, hushed with feeling.

"I know, and I disagree, but that's of no matter here. What did Samuel say that has led you to blackmail?"

"It was the wager." She turned about, started pacing as she had a habit of doing. "I should have considered the fact that if our mystery gentleman were bold enough to blackmail one fellow, it would stand to reason he could blackmail another."

"Why a man?"

She stopped in her pacing. "I'm sorry?"

"Why must he blackmail a man?" He gestured to the room about them, hoping to encompass her current choices in life. "It stands to reason a woman would be just as capable of the feat."

She nodded. "You're right. I stand corrected." She nodded in acknowledgment before continuing her trek around the space. "Be that as it may, I realized I hadn't considered any of the delegates possible victims for blackmail." She looked at him. "I was only considering them as suspects in their own right."

"So your concern is that one of them may be bought?"

She turned, her fingers gripping the cuffs of her gown. "Everyone has a price. I learned that from my father."

This had him raising an eyebrow. "You learned that from your father?"

She nodded. "From his work at the War Office. He would always say trust went only so far as the sum for which it could be bought."

"What a terrible idea."

"Terribly true, I'm afraid."

He moved his shoulder against the ache his morning exercise had caused. "And so now you realize we must study the delegates for possible weaknesses?" He shrugged. "But I have no plans to return to the conference."

"Be that as it may, our mystery gentleman doesn't know that, which means he may still try to blackmail one of the attendees."

"That's all well and good, but you've failed to address my first question. My requirement for more details regarding your desire to visit a brothel."

She waved him off. "That part is simple. We must go to Lady Vivian Garwood."

"Lady Vivian Garwood?"

"She's the mistress of a house frequented by some of Mayfair's most elite gentlemen. And some women, actually." She moved across the room. "Lady Garwood is in a position to acquire information not readily known to genteel society."

"That stands to reason, I would imagine. So this Vivian Garwood. A lady, truly?"

She waved a hand at that. "Of course not. It's just an epitaph she conjured for business. Gentlemen like to think they're doing nothing more than paying a social call, you know."

"That's all well and good, but you're not going."

She gave him a frown that went on forever. "I hardly think you're in a position to tell me what I can and cannot do."

"I think that's part of our problem actually." He took a step toward her, his gaze focused on the way her lips parted on a breath of air as he approached. "I think you misunderstand exactly what the situation is between *us*, Emily."

"Situation?" Her eyes were wide, her lips parted just the smallest of degrees, but God bless her, she didn't retreat.

"We can't continue ignoring the fact that we're attracted to each other." He stated it plainly because he knew she was too sensible for any frippery.

The tiny space between her lips disappeared, and her eyes narrowed. "You cannot begin to understand how I feel, Professor Mesmer."

He laughed. "I beg to differ on that point, Lady Black."

"Is that so?"

"The evidence stands to the contrary, I'm afraid, and as a man of science, I can hardly ignore evidence."

He didn't wait for a response. He bent his head, sealed his lips to hers. She tasted of coffee and something salty like hard bread. And for the first time, she stepped away from his kiss. She backed herself into the parallel bars, knocking them loudly against one another as she bent awkwardly under the one she'd run into. He eyed her.

"For someone so independent, you have a remarkable talent for running away."

Her eyes widened again. "I do not run away."

He gestured to her awkward stance, bent under the parallel bar she still stood against. "What would you call this?"

"It's not running away."

He reached out, took her arms, and pulled her forward until she could stand properly in front of him.

"I think you need to tell me what it is that's going on in here," he said as he touched a single finger to her temple, ran that finger along the side of her cheek and under her chin until he could lift her gaze to his.

"I can't be with you." The words were stated as plainly as he had addressed their mutual attraction.

"Why not?"

"Because I simply can't."

He withdrew his hand. "Is it because I'm a lowly American professor and you're a fashionable lady of British society?"

She wrinkled her nose. "I thought you knew me better than that."

"I do, but I enjoy rattling your cage. So what is it then?"

Her eyes grew distant as if she were watching something else, something she held within her mind that she played back to herself over and over again. He shook her, his hands tightening on her arms because he knew exactly of what she thought.

"Emily, you need to stop blaming yourself for that day."

Her eyes flashed back to the present in an instant. "How can you say that? I've made you a cripple."

"A cripple? Would a cripple be able to do this?" He swept his arms around her before she could protest, and he bent her back, spilling over her to catch her lips in a hot, firm kiss.

He cradled her, his arms the only thing suspending her above the floor. She pushed at his shoulders, but it was more in shock than rejection because as soon as he deepened the kiss, her hands smoothed until finally they gripped his shoulders, pulled herself against him. He kissed her soundly, thoroughly, ceaselessly. When he thought she'd sustained enough, he rose, drawing her back to her feet and releasing her completely.

He stepped back, enjoying the sight of her attempting to regain her composure.

Her chest heaved as she pulled in air, but she managed to point a single, accusing finger at him. "You use a cane."

"I use a cane mostly for protection. I can't rely on the leg, and it affords me a greater advantage to carry a weapon with me."

The accusing finger wavered. "You don't need the cane to walk."

"Not usually. It helps when I'm tired or I've taxed myself with sport."

The finger fell. "Sport?"

"I enjoy a good row."

"Water sport?"

He nodded.

"I had no idea."

He reached out, and she let him draw her close.

"If you didn't spend so much time running away from me, you may just learn some things about me you like."

He'd meant it as a jest, a way to ease the startled tension wrought across her features, but instead, she stiffened, pushed against his chest.

"You don't understand, Xavier," she whispered, pushing harder.

He didn't let her go. "Help me to understand."

She looked up at him, her beautiful eyes so round, so wounded, so hurt by a past she couldn't change.

"You're the one person I can't let myself love."

His heart thudded in his chest as he drank in the sight of her. The anguish that had erupted in her eyes at her words, the sadness that threatened to spill over.

"Emily." He could only whisper her name as he folded her into his arms, cupped the back of her head, drew her close until she rested against him. "Emily, Emily." He kept saying her name over and over, his own anguish keeping him from articulating more.

The past hung around them like an impenetrable fog as they stood in the middle of that room at 34 Whitaker, embracing each other because what had happened wouldn't let them do anything else. In the quiet, in the perfectness of holding her, Xavier knew he had to give her the one thing she desired if he had any hope of freeing her from that past.

He turned his head, nestled his lips in the lavender scent of her hair before he finally said, "I've always wanted to visit a London brothel."

CHAPTER 12

"*D*o I dare ask how you became acquainted with Lady Vivian Garwood?"

They sat in the carriage the following evening outside of Lady Garwood's house on Caraway as a well appointed coach drew to a stop at the front stoop.

Emily leaned forward to get a better look at the occupant who alighted, so she didn't face him when she replied, "She's Mrs. Merriweather's daughter."

"Jesus." The oath was thick with shock and quite involuntary. He held up a hand and quickly apologized. "I'm sorry. I wasn't expecting that answer."

She blinked at him. "I'm terribly sorry. I thought I had already mentioned that."

He leaned forward, elbows to knees as he pointed out the window at Lady Garwood's house. "Does Mrs. Merriweather know?"

"Of course she knows. She gave Vivian the funds to get her set up in business."

He regarded her, the after effects of shock holding his eyes wide. "Gave her the funds?"

She nodded in the direction of Vivian's house. "It's the way of the world, I'm afraid, and Lady Garwood takes exceptional care of the women who come to her. They're often destitute, on the edge of complete and utter destruction, and Vivian takes them in, ensures they can earn a living when the rest of the world is against them. Is it so terrible that she tries to make better a situation that is inevitable in the world that is so unfair to the female sex?"

He leaned back, a hollow feeling in his gut. "I suppose it's not. But..."

She smiled, understanding. "Vivian has never engaged in the trade herself. She's too smart for that. But you may ask yourself how a respected housekeeper would come to have a daughter, and you may begin to understand Vivian's motivation to help women who find themselves the victims of circumstance."

The hollow feeling grew, and he had to swallow against it. "I'm sorry," he said.

She tilted her head. "For what? All of male society?"

He shrugged helplessly.

She placed a hand on his knee. "You can't apologize for established attitudes. It will take time to right the wrongs we see, but we will get there."

"We?"

She tossed him a grin. "What do you think I've been doing these past six years if not defying expectations?"

He returned her grin with a small smile of his own, the hollow feeling subsiding. "I suppose just that." He nodded out the window now. "How are we to get inside? I suppose we're not introducing ourselves at the front door."

"Hardly." She went to the opposite door and alighted, looking up into the carriage expectantly. "We go around back. Back doors are always where the interesting bits happen."

She waited for him to follow before she took off down the block. She waved a hand up to Jackson, and the man pulled away, slipping into traffic as if he were just another carriage carrying another member of the ton. Gripping his cane securely, Xavier took off after her.

They made the alley that ran between the row of townhouses just as the sun slipped below the roofline, the landscape about them falling into indescribable darkness. The space between the townhouses here was not as generous as that on Whitaker, and he found himself darting around open garden gates and rubbish strewn along the way until finally Emily ducked into the mews behind the house they had been watching from the street.

She glanced back at him, a curious expression on her face, and he wondered what she could be thinking, but then she swept up to the back door and rapped three times. The door opened the smallest of degrees.

"The rain is coming on these days," came a guttural whisper from within.

"Dis rain ain't nothing like what them Yanks 'ave."

While her low brow accent was remarkable, he couldn't help but clear his throat behind her.

Once more she looked curiously back at him and whispered, "I didn't make up the secret code."

This was not a comforting fact.

The door opened with a hushed swish revealing a bear of a man dressed in unrelenting black. His hair was unkempt and long, pulled back with a twist of leather. His beard was short and rough, obviously trimmed with a pair of shears likely by the wearer himself. A gold hoop earring glinted from his right ear, and his dark brown eyes hovered watchfully from the small space between hair and beard.

"Hello, Trelawney," Emily said brightly.

The bear let out an uninterpretable sigh but stepped aside

and with a grunt allowed her entrance, but his hand shot up like an arrow from a bow when Xavier stepped up to the door.

"He's with me," she said gently, placing a hand on the arm that barricaded the door.

He grunted again and once more stepped away.

Xavier nodded in greeting. "Good day, sir," he said as he passed the man.

Emily was several feet along the rear corridor when he caught up to her with a hand to her elbow. She paused, turning her head in question.

"Does that man have an earring?" he whispered.

She nodded, her ear brushing his cheek as he was so close. "He was a buccaneer for a time. Suffered a bad mutiny and gave up the sea. He still wears the earring though for good luck."

He straightened, peering back the way they had come. "If he suffered through a mutiny, I don't know how much luck the earring brought."

She smiled knowingly and pressed on.

They were in some sort of rear corridor of a townhome, and he expected they would spill out in the kitchens. But something was different about this space. There were extra rooms along the way including one with a heavy door and bulky lock that rested expectedly on a forged hinge. He stared at it in wonder as they passed it, keeping his cane close as he followed Emily.

They finally broke through into the kitchens he had anticipated and were met with a wall of steam and yeasty aromas. A woman he presumed was the cook raised a hand in greeting before returning the same hand into a fist that pounded a ball of dough on the table before her.

Emily didn't stop as she crossed the room and went up a flight of worn, wooden stairs he thought might be the rear servants' stairs, but again they were the slightest bit different. At the top there was a vestibule of sorts with a footman standing guard.

The young man was hardly a man at all and was really more of a boy, but he smiled immediately and gave a bow. "I shall let the lady know you are here, Lady Black."

Emily returned a slight curtsy. "Thank you, Thomas."

The young man turned and opened the door behind him. Xavier hesitated, but Emily gestured for him to follow. The door closed with a soft click once they were inside.

Xavier looked back at the closed door and then at Emily.

"Lady Garwood employs children?"

Emily's smile was soft. "Viv caught Thomas trying to lift her purse in Covent Garden. She gave him a job instead."

"Ah." He didn't look at her when he replied as he was too busy taking in his surroundings.

They were in some sort of drawing room. The walls were all hung in silk wallpaper with an Oriental influence, reds, golds, and jades. Thick tapestries adorned the windows in waterfalls of satins and gold tassels. On the far side, adjacent to the red brick fireplace with a carved mahogany mantle of Chinese dragons, sat an immense walnut desk with intricate scroll work across the top and giant lion's paws for legs. The rest of the room was littered with plush furniture, most of which allowed for the sitter to achieve a horizontal position. He swallowed nervously and eyed Emily.

She was stripping off her gloves and gave a tentative smile. "Something the matter?"

He shifted uncomfortably. "I've never been in a brothel before."

"Did you have some expectations of what you might see here?"

He crossed his arms over his chest, his black cane coming about at an angle as he did so. "Well if I did, they most certainly wouldn't have measured up to this." He pointed to the desk with its dichotomy of feminine intricacies and natural predator. "Is that to be a warning?"

"It's more of a suggestion, I think."

He pivoted at the voice, having not heard the swish of a door or the fall of a single footstep against the hardwood of the floor. He wasn't sure what to expect from the madam of a house of ill repute, but this certainly wasn't it.

She looked like someone's mother.

She was small in stature with soft brown hair tied back in a simple knot low on her neck. Her features were plain and even, her skin white and unmottled. She wore a modest gown of pale blue and walked with an upright carriage and determined steps.

But there was something about her soft eyes and gentle smile that had him yearning toward her like a child to his mother's arms.

Her smile was pleasant as she turned to Emily, hands outstretched in greeting.

"To what do I owe the pleasure of a visit from the Lady Black?"

Emily squeezed Lady Garwood's hands. "I'm afraid it's business. Might be of the nasty sort."

Lady Garwood's frown was modest like the rest of her. "Then I suppose you must tell me who your gentleman friend is."

Emily made the introductions. "Professor Xavier Mesmer, this is Lady Vivian Garwood."

Xavier made a neat bow. "It's a pleasure to meet you, Lady Garwood."

She laughed just as softly. "No need for the proprieties here. Viv is fine." She sent a sidelong glance to Emily. "This wouldn't be *the* professor, is it?"

He stilled at the discreet question, Viv's knowing grin.

What exactly had she meant by that? He quickly looked to Emily to find the damn woman blushing.

"Yes, it is." He'd never heard Emily say anything so weakly in his acquaintance with her.

His gaze traveled between the two women, and he realized with a jolt they must be friends and Emily had spoken to Viv about him at some point. Selfishly, he wondered what she had said about him, if it were good or bad or worst of all, indifferent. But his heart started thumping again at the thought, at knowing Emily had someone other than her family in which to confide. Especially after she had isolated herself from said family to such an extreme degree.

"Well then," Viv said, licking her lips as she turned back to him. "It is indeed a pleasure. So let's hear what it is that's brought you to my home under such auspicious circumstances."

"I'm afraid it pertains to your book."

Viv's face closed immediately, the softness evaporating from her features.

"In six years, you've never once asked about my book, darling. This must be serious."

Emily looked at Xavier when she said, "I'm afraid it is. Someone has made attempts on the professor's life as well as those of some of my family members." She paused, and he found he leaned forward in anticipation. "There is concern the culprit is Lord Crawley."

"Oh, Emily," the words were whispered, the pain evident in how Viv reached automatically for Emily's arm, placed a hand softly on it.

Emily must have told her about Lord Crawley at some point as well.

"But isn't he dead?" Viv asked.

Again, Emily looked at him when she replied. "There's a

concern the intelligence passed through regarding his death was inaccurate.

Viv's face hardened. "What do you need from me?"

"We would like some information on three gentlemen who may have frequented your establishment."

Viv considered her. "And they are?"

"The Duke of Chichester, the Duke of Milton, and Baron Fitzwilliam Heathmore."

Viv's eyes widened. "That's a remarkable list. Two dukes and a baron?" She laughed in her throat. "Why these three in particular?"

Xavier spoke up at this. "I was asked to be a part of a peace convention at Kensington Palace. These gentlemen are also delegates. We believe they may be susceptible to blackmail and could be pressured into doing me bodily harm."

Viv's frown was sincere, the concern brimming in her eyes. "That's just awful."

"We're hoping you may have evidence of cause for blackmail on any of these three men," Emily said.

"I can tell you the Duke of Chichester is no worry. I'm assuming you're speaking of the Ottoman crisis?" Viv directed this to him, so he nodded in acknowledgment.

Viv made a dismissing gesture with her hand. "Chichester is a weak minded fool. His only priority is his shipping concerns in the Mediterranean. The worst offense he's ever committed is not lifting his little pinky when sipping tea."

She crossed the room to a black lacquered curio cabinet nestled in the corner between two Chinese guardian lion statues. She pulled open the front of the cabinet revealing a neat stack of uninteresting linens. She reached under them and pressed on the floor panel of the cabinet. A distinct pop was followed by the floor panel lifting up, revealing a worn red leather ledger underneath. Viv withdrew the book and made her way to her unique desk, placing the book squarely upon its surface.

"The Baron Heathmore though. I'm afraid the poor man has the unfortunate circumstance of enjoying the sexual pleasures of other men. While we do not disparage such proclivities here, it's enough to consider giving in to blackmail to keep it from being exposed to society's strict rigors."

She flipped the book open, ran a single finger down a line of names. She stopped, her expression growing serious. "The Duke of Milton though." She looked up from under her eyelashes, her gaze wary. "The duke has been accused of murder."

* * *

THE WORD RESOUNDED through the room much as it had in Barnaby's Books the first time she'd heard it uttered in connection with Xavier.

She glanced at him now, remembering how she'd watched him follow her through the alley between the houses only minutes earlier. How the guilt had not been as great as it once was when she thought of what she'd done to him. Seeing him in her exercise room, stripped to expose the obvious definition of muscle, she began to doubt her resolve to remain isolated, to keep her distance to avoid hurting anyone else,

Because Xavier was strong and capable, despite what she'd done.

She pushed the niggle of doubt away as she had to focus.

"Murder?" It was Xavier who repeated the word.

Viv's finger followed the trail of Milton's name in her book.

"It was four years ago. He was accused of murdering his mistress."

"Gwendolyn Rivier." The name hurtled out of the darkness until it tripped from her lips unaware. Emily looked at Xavier. "It was in all the papers. Rivier was found dead in the townhouse Milton had secured for her. She was—" She had to draw a breath to release the word. "She had been bludgeoned to death. Milton was accused of committing a crime of passion."

Viv shook her head, her finger deeper into the notes she'd clearly stenciled into the book in her neat, fine handwriting. "But it never stuck. Milton was cleared of all charges, and the crime remains unsolved." Viv finally looked up. "He's frequented three of my ladies, and all of them have had the same reports. He's a gentleman and all that is supposed to entail. Any one of them would accept him as a client again."

Xavier stepped closer. "But then why would he bludgeon his mistress? Fit of rage? Momentary lapse of judgment?"

"Do you recall why it was he was never tried for the murder?" Viv asked the question of Emily.

She shook her head. "Everything went quiet so quickly. It was as if the police were given evidence contradicting the matter, and they didn't wish to look foolish in the public eye. My cousin Samuel is always saying perception is the biggest challenge for the police."

"Do your notes indicate Milton ever mentioned his mistress?" Xavier asked.

Viv bent back to her book, her head already shaking. "The entry is brief. That's likely because Milton didn't seem a threat. I only added the mention of the murder accusation when it came out." She looked up. "There's nothing incriminating in here. He was a right regular gentleman."

Xavier rocked back on his heels, palming the head of his walking stick. "But the baron's proclivities would be cause for blackmail. Do you think perhaps we shouldn't negate that for the sensational crime of murder?"

Emily ran a finger along the intricate scrollwork of the desk, her mind jumbling one thought after another. "Something doesn't sit right." She studied her companions. "Why would a duke be accused of murder in the first place unless there was truly evidence he did it?"

Viv straightened. "You're right. An accusation against a member of the aristocracy, a duke no less, would not have been taken lightly."

"Especially by the newly formed Metropolitan Police." Emily glanced at Xavier. "I don't like it."

Xavier opened his mouth, but no sound emerged as the room was engulfed in an explosion of banging.

Emily winced at the sudden commotion, her hand coming up to shield her ears until she realized the banging had been followed by shouting.

"Police! This is a raid!"

Emily swung her gaze to Viv, who rolled her eyes and sighed in frustration.

"It's simply routine. I've paid my fee to the inspector for this month to be left alone. They just do this for show." She slammed her book shut, scooped it up to hurry it back to its hiding place. "They really mustn't be so dramatic about it."

It was a moment before Emily realized Xavier had taken her arm.

"We should get out of here," he whispered down to her.

She nodded and looked to Viv who was already waving her off. "Go out the side door there. It will take you to the private drawing rooms. They never go in there. You'll be able to get out the front without detection."

She went to move but Xavier pulled back on her arm. "Why not go back the way we came?"

Viv stalled at the door. "The police watch the rear entrance. I'm protected, but not the patrons. They enjoy catching a juicy politician if they can." Viv's frown was

191

sardonic. She gave a quick nod in farewell. "Do please let me know what you find." And with that, she left, calling out for the police to stop their shouting.

Emily tried moving again, but again, Xavier stopped her.

"I still don't like this." His face was tight with concern.

"Viv said it's just a regular raid. We need only get out without being seen."

He shook his head. "I don't know. The raid happening when we happen to be in attendance."

Emily watched the door where Viv had disappeared. "Do you think someone is after you?"

"Or you." The two words were spoken with deadly calm.

"What do you suggest?"

"I don't like it, but I think we should separate."

She wrinkled her nose. "Whatever for?"

He was already moving to the door they had entered through, the one that led down to the kitchens. "Whoever it is won't get both of us, and the other can go for help."

She hated it when he was practical. "I suppose that makes sense. You're to go that way then?"

He nodded, one hand on the door knob. "What do the London police want with an American professor?"

Hated it when he was practical. "We'll meet at the carriage."

He gave one quick nod and went to slip through the door, but something made him stop. He watched her, and she wished she could interpret his gaze. It was heavy, filled with something unspoken, something that weighed on him. She felt it ripple up her skin like a caress.

"I'll be all right," she heard herself say when he still hadn't moved.

He didn't say anything, but his expression softened, became more resigned, and he disappeared through the door.

She wasted no time in moving to the third door. Carefully, she opened it the smallest of degrees. The room beyond looked much like the one she was in. The decor held Oriental themes covered in a haze of smoke from the opium pipes lying discarded about the room in various smoking stands.

She slipped inside and coughed, choking on the remaining opium fumes. She waved a hand in front of her, darted her gaze side to side as she moved through the room. The house had gone eerily silent around her, and she kept her senses alert. There were footsteps above her, some shuffling, and a door banged. She reached the archway that led into the front parlor, eased her head around the frame to peer into the room.

It lay in much the same state of sudden departure as the drawing room, but now she could hear voices from the front hall. They were soft and echoing as if the occupants were farther up the stairway she knew was there. She didn't hesitate. She darted into the room, her eyes focused on the front door she could just glimpse through the opposite archway.

That was why she didn't see him.

He was on her before she could react, his arms sweeping around her middle like a vise, pulling her back against his bulky, gluttonous frame. A blast of opium smoke surrounded her as her attacker let out a throttling laugh. She couldn't see. She couldn't breathe. She fought, but the opium smoke had filled her lungs. Nausea swamped her, her mind clouded, her fingers fumbled as her fists fell open.

Failure roared at her like a beast in the night.

She had trained for this. She was prepared. She was ready. She could…

Do nothing.

The opium.

She couldn't see. She couldn't breathe. Her limbs…she couldn't *feel* them. She had to get her arms up, bring her elbows down on the arms that captured her.

But she couldn't do it.

He squeezed her harder, gyrated his hips against her backside, laughed riotously. Through the murky haze, she realized it wasn't a policeman. She hadn't been caught.

She'd been...trapped.

"Ah, and where do you think you're going, pretty darling?" The same thick, throaty laugh.

Her stomach reeled.

"Where has that whore Garwood been hiding you?" He nuzzled his slick, sweaty nose against her neck.

The bile rose in her throat. She had to fight back. She had to raise her arms up—

Another blast of opium smoke hit her. Her legs disappeared. The man laughed uproariously.

"Oh, darling, you pretty little thing. You're just a little thing, aren't you?" His hands were moving. He no longer gripped her like a rag doll. Instead he cupped her, caressed her, ran his hands where no one had a right to put them.

Her mind screamed against the haze, clawed at her awareness, begged her to wake up. To. Fight. Back.

Why hadn't someone come into the room? Where was Viv? The police? Anyone?

Oh God, Xavier.

No.

Her eyes drifted shut as the man's hands dipped into her bodice, ripped the neckline of her gown as his fat fingers kneaded her delicate flesh. She cringed against the intrusion, winced at the pain.

No, this wasn't her. She wasn't this person any longer. She was no longer the naive debutante, tricked and fooled by the men who surrounded her. The men who held all the power because society dictated it so.

"Ah, what a sweet thing." He shoved his hips against her, his erection a clear bump against her backside through the layers of clothing that separated them. "I'm going to enjoy pounding my cock into your tight, virgin flesh, aren't I?"

No.

No.

Her fingers scrambled, failing to catch hold. They were limp, useless. She was helpless.

No.

No.

Not again.

The man laughed at her feeble attempts, coughing opium smoke into her face. She turned her head, struggled to find a clear breath of air. If only he would stop. If only she could breathe. She needed to get the drug out of her lungs. Out of her mind. Out of—

"How about we just take a look see, you virgin whore?"

He was pulling up her skirts. The garment scraped up her legs, and then his hand was there, on her inner thigh, stroking the silk of her stockings. His hips gyrated spasmodically against her.

"Oh, you're a fine one, you naughty gel. You're going to like it when I pound my cock into you. Perhaps I'll even give it to you in the back side. You'd like that, wouldn't you?"

She couldn't stop the sick from erupting into the back of her mouth. She tried to swallow, choked on the acid in her throat.

No.

No.

No.

Her attacker only laughed until—

"Perhaps we should see how you like it."

Xavier.

Oh God, Xavier. No. She didn't want him to see. She didn't want to hurt him again.

But then her attacker was gone. There was a crack, and

she knew Xavier had wielded his walking stick, his words in the exercise room ringing back in the foggy voids of her mind. There was another thump, and then a thunderous, splintering crash. Her cheek met carpet, lint sticking to her lips as she struggled to draw a clean breath.

And then hands. More hands.

She jumped, but no. It was Xavier. She knew those hands. Knew their touch. She reeled toward him, reached through the fog, her hands searching for safety. He was there, his arms around her, lifting her.

No, he needed a hand for his walking stick. He couldn't carry her.

"Shhh," he hushed her for she must have protested out loud. "Let someone else save you for once."

The words rattled through her, and for once, she did what she was told, letting consciousness slip away.

CHAPTER 13

I t was after midnight when she finally woke.

He sat in the chair beside her bed, unmoving. Mrs. Merriweather had brought him a pot of Emily's special tea hours ago, but he'd drunk none of it. He sat there, his legs pushed out as his old wound throbbed. He didn't notice it, or if he did, he welcomed the pain. Anything to distract him from what he was feeling.

Hopelessness.

That was the word. In the darkness of her bedchamber, he felt the hopelessness surround him, overtake him. It clawed at his skin and filled his throat. He wanted to rub it from his eyes and shake it from his person, but he couldn't do either of those things.

He watched her in fitful slumber. Mrs. Merriweather had sent for a doctor, but he'd already known she would be fine. It was only the effects of opium on one not used to such an intoxicating substance. She'd wake with a wallop of a headache and little else.

But not him.

He had seen what that man was trying to do to her. He'd seen the way her hands had uselessly scraped at her captor. He'd heard the man's words. Seen her legs go out from under her when the opium became too much.

For all her bravado, a single drug had been her demise.

And it wrenched his heart, twisted his gut, and had him charging hopelessly into despair.

If he hadn't changed his mind, if something had niggled at him that he shouldn't leave her alone in a brothel, he never would have turned back. He never would have been there when—

He swallowed, pushed his throbbing leg against the carpet until the pain throbbed differently, newly.

He'd almost lost her.

The thought ravaged his mind, over and over, unending. But it wasn't the facts of the incident in the brothel. It was the meaning behind it that plagued him.

What if he wasn't there for the next encounter? What if she was rendered helpless then? What if...

The questions spun over and over like wool on the wheel. He couldn't make it stop, and as he watched her, resolutions danced about in his thoughts. Resolutions he knew she would never abide by.

She would never give up this life. She would never give up this ridiculous fight she was so hell bent to win. But she was only playing against herself, and that was a game she *couldn't* win. Why didn't she realize that?

She didn't need to prove herself to anyone. He had forgiven her. Hell, he'd never blamed her in the first place. Her family...he couldn't speak to her family's thoughts, but if Lizzie's treatment of her cousin were any indication, he would think the Blacks had forgiven her as well.

So why must she keep going?

Why had she not forgiven herself?

That was the real question, and he knew the answer to it could be influenced by no one but her. And she was not open to renegotiating it.

She came awake for the last time with a moan, deep in her throat, rattling out until it spilled from her lips. Her head came off the pillow, her shoulders lifting, her body tensed for a fight.

"Easy now. You're all right." The words lacked feeling, and their dullness surprised him. He had had hours to let his frustration boil, and now it had seeped into his words.

He leaned forward, elbows to knees, squeezed his hands together and willed himself to be fair. He wanted to tear her limb from limb, force her to understand this quest was madness.

But he couldn't do that. If simple reasoning hadn't worked with her, force would get him nowhere.

"What's happened?" The words came out thick and garbled.

He rose, picked up the now cold tea Mrs. Merriweather had left, and poured some in a cup. He sat on the edge of the bed, helped her to a sitting position before pressing the rim of the cup to her lips. She sipped, sputtered, tried again. She drank the entire cup down, taking it between both of her hands. When she finished, her head dropped back into the pillows, her golden hair fanning out around her.

She looked so beautiful then. So innocent. Mrs. Merriweather had gotten her into a nightdress, and its pearl white collar framed her unlined face.

She was far too young to have encountered the things she had and to carry the guilt she did.

He drew a deep breath, bone deep weariness penetrating his every effort. "Emily—"

"We need to find Milton. Do you think he's still attending the conference?"

Her eyes were wide, face flushed. Tendrils of matted hair framed her face. But it was what was in her eyes that disturbed him, had him pausing.

They burned with the same fire, the same intensity, the same drive within her for redemption.

"Emily, I think—"

She shoved at the covers that cocooned her. "We can use surprise to our advantage. He'll have had no indication he's under suspicion and—"

He put his hands over hers on the blankets, stilling her mad movements.

"Emily." He said her name sharply, concisely, and finally his tone carried through to her. She stilled, her gaze watchful, her lips slightly parted. "Emily, it's the middle of the night."

She looked about her as if a clock would appear to confirm his statement. "Middle of the night? That can't be. We just left Viv's, and—"

"Emily, you've been asleep for several hours. Mrs. Merriweather sent for the doctor. You've been drugged with opium. You need to rest."

She shoved at the blankets once more. "No, that can't be right. I'm perfectly fine. We need to—"

"Emily." He'd never been one to shout, never been one to raise his voice, but at her frantic maneuvers to escape the safety of her bed, something inside of him snapped. "Emily, you must stop or you will get yourself killed."

She froze as if his words had been a physical blow.

"Excuse me?" She whispered the words, but her eyes didn't match their softness.

He didn't want to fight with her. He didn't want to

persuade her from her ridiculous quest. He wanted her to see reason for herself.

"Emily—"

"Quit saying my name and say something useful."

The forcefulness of her words stung, and he drew back, gathered himself.

"You could have been killed."

"So could you have been."

The retort was quick and emotionless, calm with logic. Her eyes flamed with an intensity he was becoming familiar with, but there was something else there now. Desperation.

"I cannot allow you—" He knew the moment he'd misspoken. As soon as the word tripped from between his lips.

She didn't hesitate. She shoved his hands away, pulled her legs from under the covers, and gained her feet. But she wasn't strong enough yet, and she faltered, her bare feet slipping on the carpet. He reached for her, coming to his feet to hold her, but she shoved him away.

She spun, pushing the hair from her face at the same time. Her expression was cold.

"You will not *allow* me to do anything."

He held up both hands, placating. "I misspoke. I apologize."

"You did not misspeak. You wish to control my actions. You wish to stop me from earning my redemption."

He crossed his arms over his chest now, the need to placate vanishing at the first sight of her resistance. "Yes." His admission seemed to startle her, but he pressed on. "Yes, I do wish to keep you out of danger. I do wish to protect you. I do wish to keep you safe. What is so catastrophically wrong with that?"

"It's none of your business to take care of me." Her

nostrils flared, and she gripped the skirts of her nightdress in her fists.

"It is my business. The moment you decided to defend my life it became my business."

"That is not at all logical. I'm saving you."

"And who is supposed to save you, Emily?"

The question rendered her silent. She pinched her lower lip between her teeth, regarded him with brooding eyes.

"I don't require saving." She moved, turned away from him, and he knew she was going to dress, to go after the Duke of Milton.

The spark ignited inside of him so quickly he hadn't fully realized it was aflame. But he grabbed her, all gentleness aside, wrenched her around so she collided with his chest. She bounced lightly against him with the force of his embrace, and she peered up at him, her eyes wide now with...

Surprise and even more, curiosity.

"And neither do I." He flung the words at her, their meaning slaying the point of her ridiculous quest.

Her muscles were taut under his hands, her palms pressed to his chest. And then all at once, like air leaving a bellows, it was gone, and she deflated against him. Her expression melted, the fierceness devoured by something else.

Helplessness.

"But I *must* save you. Can't you see that?"

"Why?" The single word was whispered as he could no longer find the fight to drive it forward.

She was so lost in his arms, searching his face for a clue he didn't know how to give her.

"You don't know what it's like." Her eyes shone now but not with tears. Perhaps weariness from the burden she'd carried for so long. "You don't know what it's like knowing you've ruined a man's life. Ruined it. And you would do anything to ease the burden of that. Anything to no longer bear the guilt."

Her words ended him, his chest constricting, his gut wrenching. He hadn't known. He hadn't fathomed she carried such guilt with her. That she blamed herself entirely for the course his life had taken.

"But that's not true. None of it is true." It couldn't be. He couldn't have caused her this much pain. "Emily, I am fine. My life was not ruined by what happened."

She pulled against his grip, not in an attempt to escape, but rather as a way to emphasize her words. "It is not at all the same. You've abandoned your research. You've given up your whole life to work for peace."

"That's not because of you." The words rushed to be said. "Bobby—" The name died on his lips, and for a terrible moment, he wondered.

He wondered why he was doing this.

Bobby was dead, and Emily carried a burden she should never have been forced to carry. And his research. Avery wanted him to continue his research. To help people.

Because he was distracted, she was able to slip from his arms. She was two paces away when he awoke from his troubled thoughts, saw her escaping.

"You can't do this, Emily. Not alone."

She turned only her head. "Will you have me ask for the help of the family I betrayed?" Her voice shook with her unshed tears. "I can't do that, Xavier. I must prove myself. I must show them—"

"Show them what? That you're just like them? Prove it by going to them for help."

She shook her head, but her trembling lips said she wanted to believe that and just couldn't. "I can't." Her argument had been reduced to those two small words.

He reached a hand toward her, and she turned back to the door, fleeing.

"Emily, I can't let you do this." Again, he'd spoken the words he knew would upset her, but instead of reprimanding him, this time she spun about, her nightdress floating about her, her hair falling across her shoulders in agitation.

"Why, Xavier?" Why must you stop me?"

"Because I love you." He nearly shouted the words.

"And because I love you I must do this!" she shouted back.

The energy in the room drained in an instant. They stood regarding one another. She blinked at him, her soft lips falling open. His chest thundered with the pace of his beating heart.

"I love you," she finally whispered after the silence nearly drowned him. "That's why I must do this."

She walked away slowly now, her feet padding across the carpet until she slipped into the adjacent dressing room, shutting the door behind her with a resounding click.

It was to the empty room that he whispered, "And because I love you, I must betray you."

He left the room, and for the first time in six years, he felt all of his broken parts.

* * *

IT TOOK her three days to get a lead on the Duke of Milton.

She'd gone round to his townhouse in Mayfair, but the servants were not pliable to a quid. The back door had been shut in her face, or rather the face of three different costumes in the duration of two days. It made her uneasy that Milton's servants should be so loyal. Either the man really was a murderer and his servants were scared into silence by it, or the man was truly innocent, a pillar of the community and revered by his staff.

The evidence was not solid enough for her to move forward on a conclusion, so she'd tried a different tact.

His club.

The duke, like many of his peers, had selected White's for his patronage, and she found relief when the man finally frequented the place because she had any number of contacts inside.

All of whom had been incredibly unhelpful.

The duke largely kept to himself, was polite and courteous to the staff, and tipped generously. There was nothing of note on which they could comment.

It was only through sheer luck she'd gotten the lead in the first place.

She'd been sitting atop her carriage, next to Jackson on the bench, outside of Milton's home. She was dressed as a tiger to avoid suspicion, and any passerby would have believed them waiting for their mistress who would presumably be in one of the homes visiting.

That was how she'd seen the messenger boy scamper up the steps. She watched him deliver a message, a *verbal* message, retrace his steps back to the pavement, and take off to the corner. Jackson set the carriage into motion without a word from her, and they soon found the lad on the adjoining street, his arms swinging madly, chest puffed out as if he'd landed a big one.

She jumped from the bench, landing directly in front of the lad's parading steps, and proudly displayed a guinea to his knowledgeable eye. The lad had talked immediately.

Thank God for corruptible youth.

The boy had delivered a message that Milton was to meet his friend at The Rusty Anvil in Bloomsbury at half nine that next evening.

His friend.

That was who the gentleman contained in the message

was referred to. She tried prying it out of the boy who the sender of the message was, but he only shrugged. He'd been given the message from a footman and hadn't a clue as to who the true sender was. He'd also been approached on the street, so he couldn't say from what house the footman had come.

But The Rusty Anvil had been clue enough.

So it was that she sat in The Rusty Anvil the following evening after three days of avoiding Xavier.

Her thoughts thudded, tripping over one another as she forced her attention back to the pub around her.

But she couldn't stop the sound of his voice from ricocheting through her head.

Because I love you.

That was entirely what she should never have let happen. The one person she could not allow to love her...did. The one person she couldn't love...she did. It was all wrong. It was all—

She had to finish this. Maybe then things could be different. Maybe she could let herself love him. Maybe she could see her family again.

Maybe she wouldn't be so alone.

A roar of laughter from the neighboring table brought her attention back to the present.

She sat at a table in the corner, her hands wrapped firmly around a tankard of ale. She had chosen the lad's costume as it gave her the greatest freedom of movement, and she wasn't sure what it was she might encounter. She kept her hat pulled low over her features as she noted all of the pub's exits.

It was a rather fine establishment as it was in Bloomsbury and frequented by the nobler gentry of London. She spotted a few titled gentleman she recalled from her short-lived season. With a shock she realized they were likely married by now, had started families of their own.

The tide of loneliness swamped her once more, but she shoved it away. There was work to be done.

Milton had entered the pub some minutes ago. He was a man of later middling years, gray of hair, and soft of body although more from age than neglect. He was of average height and had a tendency to walk on the balls of his feet as if he were always in a hurry.

He'd taken a seat opposite the door and nursed his own tankard of ale. A few of the other patrons had greeted him with casual understanding, and the bar wench was met with a congenial smile and polite nod, no wandering hands or stolen caresses like some of the other patrons.

It occurred to her then that she'd be unable to see the face of the person Milton was to meet as his back would be to her. She didn't let this bother her, but instead, studied the room for a way to get around Milton's table.

She'd worked out a rather circuitous route when the door to the pub opened again, admitting another well to do gentleman judging by the quality of his clothes. His outer garments were all black, and he moved too quickly for her to see his face or more of his person than that. He greeted Milton with a hearty handshake and took the seat across from him.

He received a tankard of ale but left it untouched at his elbow. He spoke earnestly to Milton who only nodded in response. It was several minutes before Milton offered a reply, but she could make out neither the words nor the shape of his lips. The two huddled together as if their conversation were of particular delicateness, and she pushed to her feet, mapping out the steps she had planned in her head to make it about the room.

She was nearly to the bar when the conversation between

the two gentlemen turned animated, Milton's face twisting with apprehension, his head shaking in denial. His companion's hand fisted on the table, nearly knocking into the tankard of ale. She had to get closer, faster.

She pushed aside a gentleman who was sharing a raunchy story of a whore in a brothel he'd visited in Paris, and this brought her to the edge of the two men's table. She was careful to keep back, keep her movements casual and loose so as not to draw attention.

She was almost there when it happened.

A gentleman at the table beside her suddenly stood, pushing back his chair with a cringing scrap along the stone floor. He was slender and bent from age, the knuckles of his hands standing out prominently in their swollen state. He wore a high collar that shielded his face at the angle at which she observed him, and his copious sideburns blocked even more.

But it needn't matter.

It was the smell that gave him away.

Like wet wool and camphor.

Wet wool and camphor…

The smell hung in the air like a tangible thing. She need only reach out, touch it, and she would connect it with the memory that hung just out of reach.

She pivoted, her hand going to the dagger at her belt under her greatcoat, at the same time the man pulled his other hand from his pocket. The warm light of the pub glinted off the metallic barrel of the pistol, the smell of gunpowder mixing with the distinct aroma of their villain.

The pistol came up, its barrel aimed with deadly accuracy at Milton. Her hand rose, the dagger slipping from its sheath, her body turning. The man cocked the pistol with a single, arthritic thumb. Her hand came about, the dagger cutting through the air.

It was then Milton became aware of his potential death. She saw it the instant it registered, his body going up, out of his seat. She expected him to feint away, duck out of danger. But he didn't.

Instead he threw himself over his companion, knocking him to the stony ground.

She couldn't stop to ponder that because by then her dagger had finished its arc, but a man behind her at the bar suddenly moved, jostled her, and shoved her off her target. The blade missed, sliced through the weak flesh of the villain's upper arm. The man cried out in pain, the sound guttural and hoarse.

The pistol exploded at the same instant, the shot going astray as the man had lost his grip on the weapon. It clattered to the ground, the man's opposite hand going to the wound that spurted blood on his upper arm. She didn't stop. She brought the dagger up, ready to strike again when someone caught her upraised arm.

She kept going though, closing her eyes in concentration, pushing to shake her captor's grip. The force of her struggle knocked her into their villain.

Wet wool and camphor.

Wet wool and camphor.

Like a runaway horse and carriage, the smell connected with memory, exploding through the dark recesses of her mind. Her eyes flew open in time see the villain hobble out the door of the pub.

Lord Crawley.

She saw Lord Crawley scamper out the pub door, blood from the wound she had rendered trailing down his arm.

The room came about her in a rush. Men were on their feet, shouting, brandishing tankards of ale. Someone still gripped her, and a voice.

Someone was speaking to her.

Saying her name.

"Emily!"

She blinked, forced her thoughts into some kind of order when all she wanted to do was go after Crawley.

But who would know her name?

She turned unwillingly to her captor, drank in the face that met her eyes. So familiar a face. So handsome a face.

One she hadn't seen in six years.

"Father?" The word came out tremulous and weak.

"Emily!" He was nearly shouting, much as Xavier had that day in her bedchamber. "Emily, are you all right?"

She shook her head. Why did he care if she was all right?

"I'm fine." She turned to the door. "I must go after him. I must—"

"You need to come home." Her father's eyes, green eyes just like hers, sparked with a fire, a yearning so strong she wanted to lean into it.

Because she wanted to go home.

More than anything.

But Crawley was still out there.

She wrenched her arm free as Milton gained his feet behind her father.

It was then she realized her mistake. Milton wasn't a murderer. Milton was an agent for the War Office, and that was why he was meeting her father at The Rusty Anvil. That was why the charge of murder had been dropped without ceremony. That was why the two halves of Milton's character didn't match.

He was hiding a secret identity just like so many members of her family.

Milton had dove to save her father, and when the danger had passed, her father had stood, found his daughter standing before him, and tried to gain her attention. It was a blur speeding through her mind, and she wanted time to figure it all out.

She couldn't wait though. She had to go. Crawley already had a head start.

"I can't," she whispered. "Not yet."

She bolted for the door, eclipsing the startled men and vaulting upturned chairs. She broke free into the falling London night only to find the street empty. A trail of blood lay to her right, and she took up the chase. Her eyes darted to the trail and back up to her surroundings. This part of Bloomsbury bordered on a residential area, and the farther she went the farther she drew into it. Shops and pubs turned to townhouses and churches until the trail suddenly stopped five blocks later, the last drop of blood sitting indelicately on the curb.

He'd boarded a carriage.

She spun around, taking in the vehicles that passed her, but she'd been too late. She shouldn't have stopped to speak to her father. She shouldn't have hesitated.

She cursed herself for her momentary weakness, at letting herself wallow in the words she wanted to hear.

You need to come home.

Her insides twisted as she stood there on the corner of the street, her gaze sweeping back and forth, unable to register what she was seeing.

Lord Crawley was alive, and he was out for revenge. The Blacks had stopped him once before, and now he was out to make amends.

You need to come home.

The Blacks had stopped him once before.

Not for the first time that night her thoughts screeched to a sudden halt in her mind as the world seemed to right itself.

The Blacks had stopped him once before.

Xavier was right. Her father was right. It wasn't that she couldn't do it alone. It was that she didn't have to.

She'd been wrong this entire time. So swept up in her need for redemption, she'd missed the truth staring her in the face. She didn't have to avenge her family by herself. She only had to prove herself a worthy part of it.

Her legs were moving before she realized what she was about, pumping as they drove her through Bloomsbury, skirting Marylebone as she made her way into Mayfair. She ran, her arms flying, her heart pumping, her sabre bumping her leg as she bolted through the streets.

She reached Lofton House before she realized it, and suddenly, her legs gave up, bringing her to a teetering halt on the edge of the pavement at the cross street. She stared down the street at her childhood home, sitting in quiet slumber as night fell around it.

Seeing it again had her already roiling emotions turning over on themselves, and she stared at the building for several seconds. She had almost mustered the courage to approach when a hack passed her, its cumbersome carriage lumbering past with a great clack. She leaned forward in anticipation, thinking her father may have taken a hack to The Rusty Anvil for cover.

But it wasn't her father that stepped from the carriage.

It was Xavier.

He strode up the front steps of Lofton House and disappeared through the already opening door as if they expected him.

Betrayal surged through her, complete and deafening. She reeled against it, her heart stuttering, her stomach upheaving.

He knew what this meant to her. He knew she wanted to prove herself.

And yet he had gone to her family against her explicit

wishes. While she had only just realized the errors of her intentions, he didn't know that. He had chosen to betray her.

The thought rocked her. She blinked against a sudden rush of...not tears but an insensible haze.

But it needn't matter because at that exact moment, a crested carriage pulled along side her and two gentlemen jumped from the bench. They had the hood over her head and her hands bound before she could do anything at all. They loaded her into the carriage without a fight for she had none left to give, and in utter darkness, she rocked into the unknown.

CHAPTER 14

*W*hen they finally ripped the hood from her head, the last thing she expected to see was Lord Avery offering her a cup of tea.

"I'm terribly sorry, but we wanted to ensure the utmost discretion. I couldn't very well invite a lady of your station to take tea in the home of a bachelor and holding an audience at the Office would draw far too much suspicion, and we really must have the element of surprise on our side for this mission," he said when her eyes had finally adjusted. "Do you prefer milk in your tea?"

She was in a wood-paneled room, which markedly resembled a study with the swirling colors of the Aubusson rug beneath her feet, the heavy green drapes drawn over the windows, and the gilt framed portraits of men she did not recognize, men she could only assume were Avery's ancestors. Only a few lanterns were lit about the room, but through their soft glow she could make out exquisite trappings. She could only assume this was the marquess' own home.

Her captors had been largely silent except for the occasional apology when they'd jostled her from the carriage and into the building where she now found herself, but she sat unbound, her arms having been released with the cutting swoosh of what she presumed was a knife.

But they hadn't harmed her, and now Avery offered her tea.

She eyed him speculatively. "What is going on?"

"Ah," Avery pronounced, setting the tea cup at the table at her elbow. "You will likely have questions."

"Several," she uttered dryly.

Avery took a seat opposite her own and leaned forward, his hands intertwined and dropped casually between his open knees. His posture spoke of assurance, ease, and trust-worthiness.

"I should begin with the most important one. That of my identity."

"If we're revealing identities, I'm going to need a great deal more time." She tossed him a mocking grin.

He laughed. "I should think so. You've established quite a career for yourself. The War Office is impressed."

Her eyes narrowed. "You're the head agent at the Office now, aren't you?"

Avery jostled his hands up and down. "I knew it wouldn't take you long to deduce that. I thank you for not making me explain it all. It saves time."

"Time for what?" She regarded the tea at her elbow, deciding finally to just pick it up and draw a much needed sip. Between the altercation with Crawley at the Anvil, the resulting chase through Bloomsbury and into Mayfair, and her subsequent abduction, she was entirely parched.

"To discuss what it is you're going to do about Crawley."

Her eyes flew to the older man over the rim of her tea cup.

"You know about him?"

"My agent on the matter sent through his intelligence this evening confirming the man's identity." Avery reached for his own cup of tea, sipped softly.

"I would think we shouldn't have been fooled by Crawley's attempt to disguise his voice." She thought now of the odd voice that had plagued both she and Campbell and was irked at her inability to see through the farce.

Avery raised his cup in acknowledgment. "I had my best agent press Bennington for the truth. It seems our man had been blackmailed into passing along falsified information."

"It seems Crawley has a few too many secrets up his sleeve, and he's using them all to exact his revenge."

Avery lowered his tea cup. "It would seem so."

"You're agent is sure Bennington was lying?"

Avery's grin was playful. "As I said, I put my best agent on it."

"The last time we thought it was the best agent, Crawley turned out to still be alive."

Avery's expression turned thoughtful. "This time my best agent is your father."

She was about finished with shocks for the evening. "But my father retired from service when he assumed the title."

Avery held up a single finger. "Your father stepped back when he acquired the title, but his duty to the Crown would not allow him to give it up entirely. I kept him abreast of current events, and when the present situation became apparent, he stepped up to lead the mission."

"So if your best agent is on it, why the need to kidnap me?"

Avery's brows drew together, his expression growing serious. "I'm afraid it's come to my attention it's time for me to activate a letter of recommendation that was left in my care." He gestured to Emily's disguise. "Evidence stands that it is well past time."

His words confused her, and a sense of trepidation tripped across her skin.

"Letter of recommendation? Those are bestowed upon the War Office by fellow agents in recommendation for a new recruit."

"Yes, that's right." Avery once more intertwined his hands. "It seems someone submitted a letter of recommendation for you."

The confusion grew, but soon she forced a befuddled laugh. "I'm terribly sorry, Lord Avery, but you must ignore whatever attempts my father has made—"

"The letter isn't from your father."

The words stopped her own with the effectiveness of a cannonball through a brick wall.

If her father hadn't submitted a letter, then who had?

Avery stood up, pushing his hands against his thighs. He walked over to the walnut desk that stood in shrouded darkness at the opposite end of the room. He picked up a single leaf of parchment and returned, extending it toward her.

She didn't reach for it though.

"If you act on this letter, you're asking me to become an agent of the War Office." She looked up at him. "Why?"

He withdrew the parchment as he said, "Lord Crawley's grip in London has too many tentacles. I need someone with unusually high skill in subterfuge to make the catch using any means necessary."

"Make the catch? Will Crawley be tried for treason? His crimes were committed so long ago, and there isn't evidence to how wide spread they were."

"There is evidence enough to convict but…" Avery let the sentence trail off.

"But if capture is not possible…" Emily joined in, not finishing her sentence.

Avery gave a small shrug. "Then capture is not possible. As an agent, you would be authorized to use necessary force."

Necessary force.

He was saying she could kill Crawley, and the law couldn't touch her. Her stomach came up into her throat. Too many times tonight her world had upended itself, and she grew wearier with every shock.

In all these years, she'd never considered killing Crawley. Never considered it because in her mind, he was already dead.

She considered the parchment once more.

"You think I have the skill to take this mission?"

Avery extended the parchment. "I have it on good authority that you do."

Reluctantly, she reached for the parchment, felt it crinkle in age between her fingers. She drew it into the light of the lamp on the table at her elbow. Immediately her eyes were drawn to the signature at the bottom. A cry of despair lodged in her throat at the sight of it. Her eyes raced to the top and began at the beginning.

2 FEBRUARY 1833

DEAR SIRS:

I SUBMIT this letter of recommendation in the name of my granddaughter, Lady Emily Jane Black. While she is but sixteen years of age, I have already discovered the fortitude of her character, and it is this that will unquestionably be of great value to such a prestigious outfit as the War Office.

. . .

LADY EMILY PRESENTS herself before every problem with cunning strategy, thorough discipline, and stunning capability. Should her attention be directed to do good, I cannot say of what she might be capable, but it is sure to astound even the most well-trained agent of this esteemed office.

I CANNOT in good conscience allow my life to pass without declaring such truths, and I offer them to you with the full consideration of my own history in service thereto.

RESPECTFULLY SUBMITTED,
   Lofton

HIS GRACE RICHARD BLACK, the Duke of Lofton

SHE SWIPED the tears that threatened to spill down her cheeks and mar the letter from her grandfather. She swept her gaze upward, locking on Avery.

"Surely he submitted one for each of his grandchildren. There are so many of us."

Avery's eyes widened, and he resumed his seat opposite her. "In fact, he submitted but one." He pointed. "That one."

She looked back at the words her grandfather had penned so shortly before his death, but her eyes were too watery to read the words clearly now.

"It seems your grandfather recognized in you an ability others missed."

She brought her eyes back to Avery. "Ability?"

He gave a sheepish grin. "If I recall, you were a tenacious debutante. It was likely that which Richard identified as a necessary skill for an agent. Dedication and focus are often lost when distractions arise."

"I'm not proud of what I did as a debutante."

Avery leaned back in his chair, seeming to relax for the first time. "I had heard as much from your father. Some sort of self-imposed exile, was it?" He gestured to her current state. "I've also heard any number of stories from my agents lamenting the devilish antics of a certain lad." He grinned on one side of his mouth. "I should say congratulations are in order."

She glanced at the letter again, the tears having dried as she absorbed the reality of what her grandfather had done, what it meant in rewriting a history on which she had based her future.

Her grandfather believed in her enough to submit a letter to the War Office in her name. Over all of his other grand-children, including Samuel. Although by then, Samuel had made it clear his loyalties lay with the police force.

Still.

The world she had so carefully erected for herself began to crumble. As she sat there in Lord Avery's study, holding a piece of her history she had not known existed, the world began to undo itself, pieces shifting from the places she had put them to the places in which they were meant to be.

She set aside the letter, leaned forward in earnestness.

"You're asking me to join the War Office. That's a serious undertaking, and one I've never considered before. What would suggest I would accept such a request?"

Avery settled farther into his seat, intertwining his hands again. "I would think it would legitimize your quest at redemption."

She sat up. "Redemption?"

Avery raised a single brow. "Isn't that the reason for the way you've chosen to live your life currently?" He gestured with a hand as if to encompass her entire life. "By acting as an agent, such choices would be mandated by your position. It wouldn't be considered out of the ordinary for you to practice with—I had heard a rumor your weapon of choice is the sword. Is that correct?"

She nodded, her tongue suddenly growing thick in her mouth.

"We would need you to stay abreast of all current forms of self-defense as well as intelligence gathering." Again, he gave the all encompassing gesture with his hand. "You have already proven yourself capable in matters of disguise and deception. Although I must say I enjoyed your secretary's costume much more than this. It had such character, didn't it?" He paused, but he didn't seem to expect an answer. She could only smile in recognition of his knowledge in that it was her in that costume.

"What is there to prevent you from continuing such endeavors once you're an agent? I should think then it would be quite expected of you."

She had never considered her life as anything holding structure. She simply did as she pleased in the vein she had chosen, that of redemption if possible, but more often than not, simply preventing further destruction to her family.

A family who needed her now.

She squared her shoulders. "I want to be clear, Lord Avery. I am to become an agent of the Office based on this recommendation from my grandfather, and you are asking me to commit to the mission concerning Lord Crawley."

Avery leaned forward, his brow growing heavy, his eyes focused in a way they hadn't been until that moment.

"I'm asking you to make Crawley pay for the traitorous acts he has cast on this office."

Lord Avery was an affable man. In the days at the conference, he had been nothing but pleasant, jovial, inviting. He had taken care of the wishes of all the delegates and seen to their every comfort.

Now it appeared as though he could maim with a single glance.

She leaned forward, dropped her voice. "I'll accept your offer. On one condition."

* * *

"YOU WILL NOT DISCOVER her whereabouts by treading a hole in the carpet."

Xavier swung about at Mrs. Merriweather's pronouncement from the door of the drawing room.

He hadn't seen Emily in three days. The day he'd finally gone to the Black family. Mrs. Merriweather had said she'd gone out, and when she hadn't returned by nightfall, he thought the worst.

So he went to her family.

He knew she had been pursuing the Duke of Milton, had resisted betraying her until he had no choice, but when she hadn't returned that night...

His heart began its raging stampede every time he thought of it. They way the clock in the drawing room had announced every moment she hadn't returned, like some sick countdown to utter devastation. How the house had settled with creaks and moans as he'd waited, unable to move, unable to give up the watch.

It was enough to have driven him from the house.

And he'd gone to the Black family.

He'd known since that day in her bedchamber she had forced his hand, but it needn't matter. His love for her far outweighed anything else, and even though it ate him to not allow her this one thing, to not let her go through with her mad quest for redemption on her own terms, he had courage enough to admit how selfish he was.

He wanted to keep her safe. He wanted to keep her alive.

So he could marry her.

He wasn't sure when the thought had coalesced in his mind, but now it was a tangible thing. He might as well have it marked in his agenda for all he knew it would happen. He couldn't let her go. Not now. Not after everything.

But he damn well had to keep her alive so she could keep the appointment he had set for her.

And perhaps so he may ask for her hand.

It was a trivial matter with which he had not thought over much. In his mind, he was already at the altar, seeing her safely wed. To him.

But then the duke had returned that night. He'd already taken on the case after Emily had met with Samuel, and he'd been meeting his contact at some pub, the name of which he'd forgotten because it wasn't important.

The contact was the Duke of Milton himself, a fellow agent at the War Office, a fact which dissolved the duke of any criminal suspicion because Xavier had witnessed for himself situations where the Blacks had committed acts, which if their status as agents was unknown to the general public, would have been suspect.

But while Milton had been cleared, there were other important bits about that meeting.

Namely that Emily had fought their mysterious gentleman. And wounded him.

But the man had escaped. Xavier couldn't fault the Duke of Lofton for not apprehending the man. As the mystery gentleman had tried to take Lofton's life and Lofton had encountered his estranged daughter in an unusual costume and circumstance, Xavier could give him a by on this one.

But the retelling of the incident had only further fueled his anxiousness. He'd recounted all that he knew of the case to the Blacks when Lofton had managed to gather everyone. He'd promised to keep on the matter and to let Xavier know when anything developed.

That was *three* days ago.

Emily had not returned to 34 Whitaker, and he'd received neither a missive nor seen an advertisement in the papers suggesting the state of her well being. He'd had only one note from Lofton indicating there was something in progress with the War Office and to stay safely at 34 Whitaker.

There had been certain "developments."

That was what the missive had stated.

Developments.

He was ready to put a fist through any and all developments.

The fact that he had taken to pacing was indication of just such a thing, and Mrs. Merriweather was not so timid as to neglect to point it out.

The housekeeper had been rather attentive the past three days, her usual cool mein replaced with a coaxing, motherly demeanor. He wasn't sure which it was that had her warming to him. The part where he'd nearly gotten Emily run over by a horse or the part where she'd been drugged in a brothel.

If he had to choose, he would pick the bit where she got into a brawl in a pub.

But there was something different about Mrs. Merriweather. Her eyes were softer, her smiles inviting. He wondered, morosely maybe, if he'd passed some sort of test. Was it simply a matter of surviving in Emily's presence for more than a month? He could attest to the number of times his own life had been in danger in that time, and he could understand how being alive at the end of such a period could show evidence of his fortitude.

He eyed her now and her suspiciously cheery glow.

"I suppose I shan't," he finally said.

She gave a nod and said, "You've a visitor."

His spine straightened, and his hand came about on his walking stick to grip it like a club.

"It's Lord Avery. Shall I tell him you are not receiving guests?" Mrs. Merriweather asked at the sight of him preparing to do battle.

He relaxed his grip on his walking stick. He hadn't seen Avery since that day at the conference, and although he really hadn't thought about the man since, he had no desire to see him now.

But he had come all this way, and he had thought of the man as a friend once.

He gave a nod. "I'll see him."

"Shall I bring tea?"

"No." The word was colder and harsher than he'd meant it. He drew a breath, forced his muscles to unclench. "I don't believe the marquess shall be staying so long."

"Very good." She gave that confusing smile and turned away.

Lord Avery appeared some moments later. He hadn't bothered to doff his hat, and Xavier felt a rush of relief that this audience would likely be short.

"Ah, Mesmer, my good man," Avery began, his smile jovial and wide. "I've come to invite you to a ball."

"I beg your pardon?"

He had spent the few seconds waiting for Avery preparing all of his excuses to not continue their conversation regarding Xavier returning to this telescope research. But to hear this nonsensical statement threw him off balance.

"It's a masquerade ball actually. Quite fun. You'd enjoy it." Avery's smile grew wider, his teeth showing a display of mirth.

Xavier blinked at the man, considered whether or not his hearing was going or if he were suffering some sort of delusional fit.

"A masquerade ball?"

Avery came farther into the room, rubbing his hands together. "The Brownlow masquerade ball is the event of the season. You'll have a walloping good time."

A walloping good time?

Xavier closed his eyes, thinking when he reopened them perhaps this entire ludicrous situation might have passed. When he opened his eyes, Avery looked even more pleased.

"It's tomorrow evening. I trust you brought appropriate attire?"

Xavier hadn't the slightest idea what appropriate attire for a masquerade ball was.

"I beg your pardon, Avery, but did you say Brownlow?" He'd heard that name before. He scratched at the recesses of his memory to discover where.

"Yes, Brownlow. They hold the masquerade every season. It is really a must."

Brownlow. Hadn't Emily said something about the Brownlow affair? She'd been muttering, and he had just recently found himself once more in her acquaintance, and those early days were foggy at best.

But Brownlow…

He was sure he knew that from somewhere.

"What is appropriate attire for a masquerade?"

Avery pushed his lips together in thought, shook his head slightly as he gathered his words. "The usual formal attire, I would think. And a mask!" He added with a chuff of his hand. "You must wear a mask. Do you need me to procure one for you?"

Mere weeks before Avery had been attempting to persuade him to return to the research he'd abandoned, having lured him across an entire damned ocean under the ruse of a peace conference. And now the man had the gall to invite him to a masquerade ball?

"I'm not sure I'm following." Xavier crossed his arms over his chest. "You've brought me to London under false pretenses, and now you wish to take me dancing? I've been out of the astronomical circles of London for some time, Avery, but even this is a stretch."

Avery's eyes glinted with mirth if it were even possible for the man to become more engaged with his proposal of attending a masquerade ball.

"Yes, that's it precisely. You will love the masquerade. I promise. You may find what it is you seek there." The words were said so softly Xavier almost missed them.

"Pardon?" he asked quickly, the muscles at the back of his neck tightening. "What was that?"

Avery's features did not change. "Fun. You shall have fun at the masquerade, old friend."

"No, not that. The other bit. What I seek. What was that about?"

Avery laughed his usual exuberant laugh. "Ah, Mesmer, always reading into things. That's what I like about you. You never take an invitation at face value." This from the man who had tricked him onto a damned ship.

"Yes, but you said something. Something about seeking. I'm very much interested in that bit."

Avery extended both arms out to his side in a wide gesture of welcome. "Well, then come along and see what it is I mean." He reached forward, gripped Xavier's hand in his own and slapped him on the back. "I'll see you there then, eh? Tomorrow evening. Tally ho."

And the marquess was gone.

Xavier stood in the drawing room for several seconds

after the man had left, replaying the conversation over and over in his head.

No, Avery had most definitely said something. Something about finding what he sought.

But what did Xavier seek?

In London? Well, that could only be Emily.

Emily.

He marched from the room and down the hall, taking the servants' stairs to the kitchen at a near drop. He came into the kitchens in a bluster.

"Mrs. Merriweather." He hadn't realized how close the woman stood, but it spoke to her resilient nature when she merely raised an eyebrow at his outburst. "Where might one find a mask for a ball?"

CHAPTER 15

The Brownlow estate was a monstrous affair.

He peered up at it from where Jackson had dropped him at the front entrance. He was jostled at every turn by masked ladies and gentlemen pressing to get into the house as quickly as possible. The air was atwitter with laughter and amicable shouts of frivolity.

It did not suit his mood at all.

It was now four days since he had last seen Emily, and his temper was the worse for it.

But he'd taken Avery's words to heart, and now here he was, masked just as much as the rest of them. He palmed the head of his walking stick, enjoying the feel of the cold metal phoenix against his hand. Whatever the reason was for Avery's odd insistence that he attend tonight's affair, Xavier would be ready.

A pair of centaurs crashed into him, pushing him into the wrought iron gates that marked the entrance to the estate. This was followed by an Artemis he thought and perhaps a Persephone. He looked around for Hades for surely there wouldn't be a Persephone alone.

But he never got the chance to find her because just at that moment, the whispered words of the guests registered.

"They say she accepted the invitation."

"She'll be here tonight. Can you imagine? It's been so long since anyone has seen her."

"She's a spinster no less! The daughter of a duke. Such shame."

His heart thundered in his chest.

Were they speaking of Emily? Was Emily going to be in attendance? He had to know. He swirled around to find someone whispering these mysterious words, but they swam by him too quickly.

Instead he found Lord Avery.

In a toga.

Xavier blinked but Avery did not change shape or form. The toga was wrapped over Avery's billowing lawn shirt and black trousers tucked neatly into square shoes, but most impressive of all was the headpiece, an intricate wreath of grapes and vines.

"Mesmer!" Avery called out joyfully. "You came. I always knew you had it in you."

"Had what in me?"

Avery cuffed him on the shoulder. "Curiosity, old man."

Xavier touched his mask and indicated Avery's own bare face. "I thought this was to be a masquerade."

"Oh, it is," Avery said, placing both hands to his face. "But I'm afraid the mask didn't go with my costume." Here he scrubbed his hands along his bushy sideburns and gave a chortling laugh. "Shall we?"

He indicated for Xavier to proceed him, so he did, stepping into the flow of guests streaming to the front door. He tried once again to catch the excited whispers of the guests, but they were all moving too quickly now into the crush.

The interior of the Brownlow mansion was much like the

exterior. Its corridors were vast and overwhelming and through it all hung a peculiar Egyptian motif. He was pressed through the hallways toward the rumbling, concentrated sound of gaiety. The rumbling grew louder the farther they pressed into the mansion until they tumbled into the ball-room and the heart of the party.

The ball was…ridiculous.

Xavier's instincts to flee took hold, and it was only Avery's grip on his arm that kept him from running. This was what a crush must be. Bodies pressed up against one another, glasses of champagne passed over their heads, laughter rang in his ears until he could hardly hear the spin-ning of his own thoughts.

Avery led him to the far side of the room up against a display of ferns. The fauna provided a false sense of isolation, but it was enough to allow his ears to cease ringing.

Avery laughed. "I take it you've never been to a function quite like this."

Xavier eyed him. "I can safely say I have not had the pleasure."

Avery slapped him on the back before scooping up two flutes of champagne from a passing footman. "I can assure you it will be worth it." Avery handed him a flute. "Drink this. Trust me."

The last two words were spoken with the fleeting utter-ance in which the man had been speaking for the past two days. Xavier's gaze flew to the man as he downed the entire glass of alcohol. His friend's hand was steady on the glass though, and Xavier wondered how much his paranoia was affecting his thoughts.

Four days.

Four days was an eternity, and his mind was more than capable of conjuring all necessary evil ends to which Emily may have gone. He'd had no more word from the Blacks, and now his friend had appeared at Emily's home as if it were perfectly normal for the man to invite another man to a ball.

Something was going on.

Something Xavier was not privy to.

He gripped his walking stick and threw back his head, downing the champagne in one go.

"There's a good chap," Avery said, snatching back the flute. He flagged down a footman and deposited the flute, switching them for two full ones.

Again he handed the flute to Xavier.

"Sometimes these things can be a bit much. It's best to be ready if you know what I mean." Avery sipped the champagne now.

"Ready for what?" Xavier was tired of playing these games. If his friend would not tell him what was going on, he'd demand the answers himself.

Avery's perpetual smile dimmed, his features slipping into an expression of consternation. His eyes narrowed, and his jaw hardened. If Xavier hadn't watched it happen, he never would have guessed he still stood next to his friend.

"I'm sure there's no need for me to tell you you've fallen in with an interesting family here in London, Mesmer." The marquess' tone had lost its verve.

Xavier's eyes darted out over the crowd, his body suddenly alert.

"No, you must not tell me that for I most certainly already know."

Avery gave a short laugh. "Then I can assume you know of their history. What it is they hold as their legacy."

"Their special association with the government, you mean."

Another short laugh. "That is certainly one way of wording it."

The crowd shifted around them as the orchestra struck

up a waltz. The dance floor cleared as couples assembled for the next dance. The room was awash in the glow of a thousand chandeliers, and the entire space unfolded like a dream before him.

It was several bars into the waltz before Avery turned to him. "I've heard rumors you are quite capable with that walking stick of yours."

The statement was not unexpected.

Xavier set down the champagne flute on the tray of a passing footman, picked up his walking stick more firmly in his grasp.

"Quite," he replied even though a response was unnecessary.

Avery's eyes were hard now. "I have once more lured you to a place under false assumptions, but I suspect you already guessed as much. I shall ask for your forgiveness later except I believe this is where you may wish to be."

"What's going on, Avery?" Xavier's tone held an iron edge.

Avery finally met his gaze. "For a man determined to find peace, are you willing to fight for the thing you love most?"

An image of Emily sprouted in his mind at the words, unbidden and involuntary.

He gripped his walking stick. "Yes." Only the single word, bitten off through a tense jaw.

Avery nodded. "That's good. Because you may just need to match the actions to such a sentiment this eve." The man bowed ever so slightly. "I ask for your help tonight, Xavier. Stay alert."

And with that the marquess bowed his way into the crowd.

Xavier wasted no time in trying to keep his eye on his friend but instead turned his attention to the crowd. The guests were in full lather with the dancers swirling to the waltz, the others milling about awaiting a turn at the dance floor. Champagne was passed along with the gossip, and not a chance was missed for an illicit grab or knowing glance to be passed between rowdy patrons.

Xavier left the sanctuary of the ferns and waded into the crowd. He caught the attention of a gaggle of debutantes who twittered as he passed by. He spared them not a glance, keeping his eyes continuously moving about the crowd.

He spotted Lofton almost by accident.

The man stood a head taller than the gentlemen who surrounded him. He stood, seemingly engrossed in conversation with these men, but his costume made him difficult to lose in the crowd.

He wore a tunic of ancient armor, his head bare of ornament or mask. Alexander the Great if Xavier were forced to name the duke's chosen disguise.

He turned in Lofton's direction, but the gaggle of debutantes apparently had friends. They swarmed him, pulling at his arms and hands. He thought the behavior rather uncouth, especially for ladies of the ton, but he was beginning to understand at the Brownlow ball, the prosperities were set aside for a night of debauchery.

When he finally shed the debutantes, he found he'd been pushed off course and now stood at the edge of the dance floor, Lofton now standing along the perimeter to his right.

He made to step along the edge of the crowd where it would be easier to move when the first shot rang through the air.

While he had been expecting danger, he hadn't anticipated their mystery gentleman would be so vulgar as to put it on display like that. The crowd erupted in screams of terror, shouts of exclamation. He was standing far enough away to avoid being trampled, but then the oddest thing happened.

No one moved.

They couldn't move.

The ballroom was too packed. People couldn't get out the doors.

Another gun shot split the air. More screams.

Xavier was around the edge of the crowd, heading for Lofton, when Lord Crawley stepped from the crowd, a Pepper-box revolver aimed at the Duke of Lofton's head.

Xavier stopped, yanked the mask from his face to see more clearly.

Yes, it was Lord Crawley. He'd remember that craggy, sunken face anywhere. Emily was right. She had known the man's smell for she was the only one of them that had once been close enough to identify his odor.

Xavier's gaze flew to Lofton. The man had not moved. He had not lifted so much as his voice in retaliation. He stood at the edge of the dance floor, facing his executioner.

Xavier was too far away. He'd never make it in time. He—

"The Duke of Lofton," Crawley pronounced.

"Traitor," Lofton fired back, his lips slipping into a mocking grin.

The crowd drew a collective hiss of shock.

Crawley's mouth hardened. "I am no traitor, Lofton. I have done just what the damned War Office asked of me. Me and my family. And for what?" The words shot out, spittle falling with them as the revolver shook in Lofton's direction.

Crawley was coming undone.

Xavier looked about them. At the stunned crowd. At the opulence draped in sudden terror.

Crawley had snapped. He'd gone too far and now his vehemence was a pathetic, deadly show. He'd never get away with this, but that clearly wasn't his plan.

Crawley was prepared to die if it meant getting his revenge for the glory the Black family had stripped from his own family, the glory he thought rightly belonged to the Crawleys.

It had started when Crawley had simply tried to steal Xavier's telescope technology, sell it to the highest bidder, and run off into obscurity to enjoy the rest of his life on the funds such a sale would garner.

The Blacks had stopped him, and now he sought revenge at all costs.

Just like Emily.

The thought whispered through his mind, and his stomach reeled at the implications. He couldn't let this happen to Emily. He couldn't let her desire for revenge turn her into the mad shell of a human Crawley now was.

"To betray them?" Lofton quipped.

Crawley's revolver shook harder. "I would curse your name, Lofton, but there would be no point in it. Soon I shall have my revenge on all of you."

"All of us?" Lofton crossed his arms over his tunic-clad chest. His grin turned cocky. "That's not how I see it."

Crawley steadied his grip on the firearm, pulled back the hammer. "And why is that?"

If Xavier had not been watching so intently, he would have missed it. Standing opposite him along the rim of the crowd was Belladonna, the Roman goddess of war. She wore a gown of sparkling silver complete with saber at her waist and a brilliant military helmet concealing her features.

He should have known.

He should have known as soon as he saw the saber.

But he was too caught up in the aim of Crawley's revolver.

Belladonna moved just then, so gracefully one might have thought her dancing. She withdrew her saber, leaped forward, and swept the sword around the barrel of the gun, trapping Crawley's pistol within the intricate twists of the sword's handle.

Startled, Crawley squeezed the trigger. The shot went off,

but Belladonna pivoted with the grace of a ballerina, sweeping forward until she held the pistol aloft, trapped in the might of her saber. The bullet went astray, and the sound of breaking glass echoed in the distance.

She held Crawley captive. He refused to relinquish the pistol, and she held it firmly clasped with her saber, the muscles of her finely toned arm rippling above the edge of her evening glove and below the short sleeve of her costume.

That was when she removed her helmet, sweeping it from her head with her free hand.

Her long, golden hair fell about her shoulders, and she shook it back, revealing a proud smile so much like her father's.

But it was Lofton who answered Crawley. "Because my daughter is just as deadly in a gown as she is in trousers."

* * *

SIX YEARS WAS a long time to wait to make a man cry.

To be fair though, she hadn't thought it an option. She'd thought Crawley was dead.

But the satisfaction she gained now, watching him squirm, watching him pull with his weakened, aged might to free his pistol—

It had all been worth it.

Spittle sprang from his lips as he muttered oath after oath at her, yanking at his trapped revolver.

"You!" he shouted. "You whore!"

"It's lady actually," she replied cooly. "Lady Emily Black. I would call you out for such slander, but well…" She nodded to Crawley's current circumstance and gave a soft laugh. "I hardly think you're in a position to entertain a duel."

"Look what you have done!" Crawley continued to spit. "You've assaulted a weak old man who has done nothing."

She smiled, her eyes traveling down the length of the arm that struggled to maintain its grip on the revolver.

"You may have forgotten, weak old man," she threw his words back at him, "but four days ago I marked a would-be assassin in The Rusty Anvil in Bloomsbury. The man tried to kill my father, and I slashed his right arm with a dagger." She nodded at Crawley's shooting arm. "That wouldn't be blood dripping from your arm, would it? Had any recent encounters with a dagger?"

The crowd gave a collective gasp as they all must have observed the telltale drip of red cascading from Crawley's upper arm. The strain must have opened the wound, and his coat sleeve turned crimson with blood.

His pathetic smirk turned sinister. "You won't get away with this. It's your mistake to think I'd come here alone."

She laughed, the sound light and airy, even as the blood thundered at her temples.

"Oh, we didn't expect you'd come alone."

Crawley's expression turned to stone. "We?"

"The War Office," her father said from behind her. "Crawley, I'd like to introduce you to the Office's newest agent."

Crawley's eyes flashed frantically from her father back to her.

And Emily wanted nothing more than to see Xavier's face at this announcement. What did he think of her? What was he feeling? She'd seen him at the edge of the crowd, his body tensed as if to save her father when Crawley had attacked. Her heart had squeezed at the sight of it.

For four days she'd wanted to tell him, but she couldn't risk their plan. She couldn't put him in any more danger until she was sure they had their villain.

"It can't be true. She's...she's...she's a debutante!" Crawley finally managed.

"That was a long time ago," her father said. "You were loyal once." He gave a shrug. "It seems we all change."

"My men will be here any moment. Give up now, Lofton!" Crawley demanded.

"Your men?"

A ripple of exclamation passed through the crowd as it suddenly parted to Emily's right, her cousin Samuel stepping forth, a thug, bloody and beaten, hanging from his grasp.

"Do you mean this man?" Samuel tossed the thug on the ballroom floor.

The crowd screeched and shuffled back from the edge of the dance floor where the man had fallen as if avoiding the scurry of a mouse.

Crawley's face convulsed. "Samuel Black, you—"

"Detective Inspector for the Metropolitan Police. I'm sure that's what you meant to say."

The crowd parted again and Penelope stepped free. "And his wife." She crossed her arms under her bosom. "Novelist," she said with a triumphant grin.

Crawley let out an unnatural noise of anguish, his guttural scream of frustration ricocheting off the high ceilings of the room.

His scream was joined by others as another man fought his way through the crowd. He was filth and decay in human form and his sneer revealed a mouth dangerously empty of teeth. He catapulted himself onto the dance floor only to be met with the solid thwack of Xavier's walking stick.

The bloke went down with a thud, his head striking the floor so hard it bounced. Xavier twirled the walking stick before softly placing it on the ground. Leaning onto it, he crossed one ankle over the other, the epitome of gentlemanly decorum.

"Perhaps you've forgotten me, Crawley," he called across

the space. "Xavier Mesmer. Professor," he added with a wink at Penelope.

Crawley sputtered but only for a moment.

That was when her uncle Nathan and aunt Nora emerged from the crowd. Uncle Nathan deposited his man on the floor much as Samuel had done, but Nora held onto hers between excruciating pinched fingers about her man's ear.

The poor chap dropped to his knees on the dance floor, tears streaming down his face as Nora pinched harder.

"If you get this gown dirty, you'll have me to deal with, me boy. Do you understand?" She shook the man. "Does your mother know about your ill manners?"

The man cried, begged to be let go.

Nathan could only smile at his wife.

Finally, she looked up, her glare focused on Crawley. "Nora Black." She shook the man between her fingers. "Housekeeper."

Crawley's eyes flashed back to Emily.

"Enough." He coughed now, his arm weakening, the revolver sinking.

She didn't buy it.

For six years, she had known the drive of redemption, knew how hot the fire could burn.

He was not giving up now.

The crowd told them when the next pair arrived. More gasps of startled guests, and then there they were.

Emily allowed the smile to come to her features as Evanshire stepped free of the crowd, dropping another thug to the floor. Jane stepped free from behind him.

"Evanshire," Crawley growled. "And you." He didn't bother with Jane's name, but he didn't have to.

Jane fisted her hands at her hips. "Lady Jane Peregrine, the Marchioness of Evanshire. And I'm the most fearsome of all."

Crawley twitched a lip. "Oh?"

She leaned toward him, her eyes piercing. "Enraged mother," she seethed.

Crawley swallowed, returned his attention to Emily.

"So that's it then. You gave up. Finally went running home to your father." His words were wet with saliva.

She shook her head. "I didn't give up, or I wouldn't be the one with the upper hand right now, would I?"

He only sneered.

She wanted desperately to look at Xavier, but she couldn't risk removing her eyes from Crawley.

"I realized this revenge doesn't belong to me. Six years ago you violated the sanctity of my family. Every person here has a stake in seeing it avenged."

Finally, her mother stepped from the crowd. Sarah Black, the Duchess of Lofton, was resplendent in a golden gown as Hera. She held a staff in her hand, and she crossed her body with it, holding it with deadly assurance.

"All of us," Emily stated with finality.

Crawley's eyes swam about, attempting to take all of them in.

Emily strengthened her grip on her saber, raised it until Crawley gave a sharp cry of pain, his free hand clutching the spurting wound on his upper arm.

His smile was evil. "You think you're different, but you're not. You're just like me. Out for a revenge no matter the bloody cost."

She pushed on the revolver, and Crawley shattered in pain once more. But still, he refused to let go. He clawed at the revolver, pushed against the handle with the barrel, but the firearm wouldn't budge.

She made sure his eyes were on her when she said, "But we're nothing alike, Crawley. You seek revenge." She shook her head. "I sought redemption." She let her eyes flow over the people who stood beside her.

Her family.

When she'd delivered her condition to Avery, that her family be a part of the mission to stop Crawley, she hadn't known what to expect, but it wasn't this.

The instant response, the open arms, the welcoming words.

They hadn't hesitated. They'd merely stepped in as if she'd never been separated from them at all. It had been her cousin Jane who had devised the Belladonna costume to disguise Emily's identity without the hindering quality of a mask. Samuel and Evanshire had procured building schematics for the Brownlow mansion to plot how Crawley would disburse his men.

And it was her own father who had suggested Emily take point because she had the most knowledge of the case and could act with the best intelligence should the situation grow urgent.

And Xavier.

Samuel had suggested keeping him at bay. As an American, they couldn't promise him the protection of the War Office, and they couldn't be sure what Crawley would do. He was safer not being implicated in their plan.

He would be furious of it when he learned, but she loved him too much to risk his prosecution.

She let her eyes drift back to Crawley.

"One should never have a need to seek redemption from family because family means understanding. Family means love. No matter what."

It had been a hard lesson to learn, and one that still scared her. But Xavier had been right. She didn't need to do this alone. And she hadn't.

Crawley floundered, and his hand dove inside his jacket

before she could react. The knife flashed in the light of the chandelier, swiping at her torso, but she didn't bother to defend herself.

Lizzie plunged from the crowd, her epee striking the knife from Crawley's hand in mid-arc. The knife skidded with a clang across the floor as he cried out. Blood sprang from where Lizzie had sliced open the skin along his knuckles.

He glared at her, spit collecting in the corners of his mouth.

Lizzie held her epee at the ready. She hadn't bothered with propriety and sported her usual trousers and lawn shirt.

She grinned at Emily. "There will never be another season as good as this one, cousin. I'm so glad you came back."

Emily returned her cousin's smile with her own heartfelt one, but it became apparent that Crawley was finished.

He yanked at the revolver, reaching up with both hands to shake it free. Emily pivoted, allowing the revolver to drop from the handle.

Crawley was so stunned to have his revolver freed that he never saw the dagger she plunged into his heart.

CHAPTER 16

*C*rawley's dead body barely hit the floor before he had her in his arms.

Xavier crushed Emily to him, his arms dodging her deadly saber to draw her against him, to hold her, to feel her realness.

Chaos surrounded them as the polite ladies and debonair gentlemen of London's infamous *ton* shattered around them at the sight of one of their own committing murder. There were screams of horror, gasps of shock, shouts of confusion as people finally attempted to squeeze out the doors. Some stampeded, some shoved, and most everyone pushed to get away from the gruesome scene.

Bodies lay like the feathers of a burst pillow across the ballroom floor, but he didn't care. The thud of Emily's heart pounded against his chest, and he couldn't have cared for anything else in the world.

He pulled back long enough to push the hair from her face, drink in the sight of her eyes, and finally to crush his mouth to hers. Wonder of wonders, she kissed him back, her arms went about him, and she pulled him even closer.

He didn't know how long they stood there, embracing in the middle of the mayhem, but it didn't matter. He couldn't get enough of her.

He was the one to pull back first.

"I thought something had happened to you." He could barely get the words out as his lungs struggled for air. "I would never betray you if I didn't think something had happened, but you didn't come back that night, and I—"

She cupped his face, drew his forehead down to hers as she hushed him with her soft voice. "Stop. It's all right," she whispered. "Everything's all right now."

He gripped her wrists. "But you must know. I wouldn't have done that if I had had a choice."

She leaned back far enough to look him in the eyes. "When I saw you go into Lofton House, it shattered me. I didn't understand then what you had meant. About not doing this thing alone." Her smile was soft, tentative. "I understand now." She looked about at the carnage. "In case that wasn't clear."

He couldn't help the smile that came to his lips. "You saw me go to Lofton House?"

She frowned. "It's a very long story, but I owe you an apology first. I'm sorry we had to keep you in the dark. Samuel couldn't be sure what protection you would have as an American in case this went poorly." She moved her hands, gripped the lapels of his jacket. "I couldn't let anything happen to you." Tears strained her voice, and he gathered her close.

But—

"Where did your saber go?" he asked over her head.

"Oh!" She pulled back, swept down, and picked up the weapon from the clutter on the floor. "I didn't want to stab you." She smiled brightly and tucked the saber back into its sheath at her belt.

"Well, that's very kind of you. Now then. Where were we?"

He swept her into his arms and kissed the very life from her. Never before had he felt this rage of heat, this waterfall of sensation. From the feel of her, the taste of her, the smell of her—it swallowed him whole, and he wanted nothing more than to revel in the very existence of Lady Emily Black.

Until a distinctly irate throat cleared next to them.

Xavier sprang away from her, his eyes flying to the stoic expression of the Duke of Lofton, the father of the woman he was ravaging in the middle of a ballroom in Mayfair.

Lofton eyed him. "I would tell you to get your hands off my daughter, but she's clearly demonstrated she can take care of herself."

Xavier cleared his own throat and nodded sheepishly. "Yes, about that—"

"So if I shan't ask you that, I do think you must have a question for me." He moved as if to grip the lapels of his jacket when he must have realized he wasn't wearing a jacket, but instead sported a tunic of ancient armor. He settled for crossing his arms over his chest.

"Father—" Emily began.

But Xavier interrupted. "Your Grace, I should like to ask for your daughter's hand in marriage."

"What?" The word sang like a shot from Crawley's pistol as Emily peered up at him.

Lofton reached out, grabbed Xavier's hands, and forced a hearty shake. "Yes, absolutely. The deal is done. You can't give her back." He stepped back, his smile triumphant.

"Marriage? Did someone say marriage?" Lady Jane, the dowager duchess Lofton, stepped carefully over the debris left by the departing crowd.

"Who's getting married?" The current duchess stepped into their group, looking expectantly to her husband. "Oh, did he finally ask for her hand?" She clapped her hands together around her staff. "Oh good!" she said at her husband's nod. She laid a hand on Xavier's arm. "We've been waiting for so long."

Soon they were all crowded around them, Samuel and Penelope, Evanshire and Jane, Nora and Nathan, and Lizzie, smiling harder than any of them.

Xavier didn't miss the secret smile Emily shared with her cousin, her accomplice in much of the six years of Emily's exile.

Lady Jane peered about them. "Oh my," she breathed. "Do you know what this reminds me of?" She spun until she locked her gaze on Nora. "Do you remember the ball where Nathan shot the wrong man?"

Nora's smile was warm as she slipped under her husband's arm.

"How could I forget?" she said, peering up at the man who had been her husband for so many years.

Xavier watched them. The Black family. Young and old and in between as they gathered around the one they thought they had lost.

But when he tried to step back, Lady Jane looped her arm through his, holding him still.

She looked to her son, the duke. "You told him we won't take her back?"

Lofton nodded. "I've explained to him the perimeters. He's accepted."

He didn't recall accepting, but he wasn't going to argue.

Lady Jane smiled up at him. "Xavier, dear. May I call you Xavier now that you're a part of the family?"

He didn't even have time to nod before she went on.

She gestured to the disarray around them. "It was 1814. Do you remember what happened in 1814? Damned Napoleon." She shook her cane with frustration. "But we really mustn't be angry with him. He's the reason I have such beautiful daughters-in-law. Did you know that?"

Again, he didn't have time to answer.

"It is. And this one." She drew Nora over, slipping the woman under her arm. "This one was a housekeeper at that ball, and that's how she met Nathan. He shot the wrong man. Did you know that?" she whispered conspiratorially. "Quite an uproar."

"We have now all relived the fact that I shot the wrong man, Mother. Is there a point to this story?" Nathan pulled his wife back.

Lady Jane shooed him away. "Xavier is a part of the family now. There is so much history on which he must be educated."

Emily's laugh was deep beside him. "I don't recall agreeing to this plan," she said, and her voice rang with laughter.

But Xavier could only watch Lady Jane as she radiated with pride for this family she had created.

The old woman looked up at him, her face mapped with the passage of time, and in each line, he saw the history of which she spoke.

There, around her eyes were etched the lines of love, put there with every loving glance she gave to her husband, to each of her sons, to her first grand baby. And around her mouth, the lines spoke of the smiles at watching Young Jane take her first steps, at holding baby Richard in her arms for the first time, at whispering one last word of love as she buried the husband she would miss for the rest of her life.

He didn't know when Emily had slipped beneath his arm, but he looked at her now, studied her face, and imagined it one day covered in the lines that would tell their own story, and he tightened his arm around her as she smiled up at him, as he allowed the family Black to carry him away on the tales of their adventures.

* * *

ONE MONTH Later

HIS KNEE BOUNCED as he agitated his foot against the floor.

His wife put a hand to it, stilled the motion with her gentle touch.

"I won't do it."

"You haven't even heard what he's proposing."

"I don't need to hear it. I already know I won't like it."

"You can't make a judgment like that without at least hearing the man out."

"I just said. I don't need to hear it. I won't do it."

The outer door opened, and Lord Avery walked into his drawing room.

"Lady Emily and Professor Mesmer." He stopped, bowed. "Or should I say Mr. and Mrs. Mesmer?" His eyes twinkled with mirth.

Xavier stood beside her, his body rigid with apprehension. "Avery."

The two men hadn't spoken since the night of the Brownlow ball, and as she and Xavier were due to leave on a ship bound for America that afternoon, there was no more time to hold off this meeting.

She had married Xavier by special license the previous week, and it was decided it would be best if they took their wedding trip in America. It would allow time for the gossip to subside as Emily had killed a man in the middle of a ball after all. Such things didn't just die with the coming of the next season, and time out of the eye of society would help it disappear.

She felt a pang of guilt for chasing after the Duke of Milton now. This War Office business was tricky.

Avery approached his friend. Offered a hand. "I thank you for stopping in on your way to the docks. I'm sure you're eager to be off." He smiled at Emily. "And I'm sure your family will miss you once more."

Emily's return smile was quick. "We've had a lovely month together. Except for that business with Crawley. But other than that it's been wonderful to catch up." She slipped her hand into Xavier's as he returned to his seat beside her on the sofa. "And there was the wedding, of course."

"A beautiful affair. I'm so honored you included me." Avery face folded in joy.

While Xavier wasn't exactly pleased with Avery's deception to get him to London, he couldn't stay angry with the man. Without him, they wouldn't be wed now, and Emily knew that had swayed Avery into some good favor with Xavier.

But his friend had still lied to him.

"I'll make this brief," Avery said, his expression turning somber. "I never got to explain why it was I wished for you to carry on your telescope research." He held up a hand when Xavier made to interrupt, and Emily tightened her grip on his hand. He must listen. So much depended on it.

Avery went on. "I was hoping you would allow the British War Office to help develop some of your technology to protect our agents."

Xavier's hand twitched at the mention of the War Office, and he slid her a glance. She smiled softly. The fact that she was now an agent for the Crown was something they had discussed at length since the Brownlow ball.

She would need to stay in London to be close to headquarters, but she didn't wish for Xavier to leave his family. As he hadn't much left, and he'd been almost adopted by her grandmother, the decision was fairly easy to make. They would reside at 34 Whitaker, and Xavier's mother would come to live with them. Although, she held a suspicion a renovation would soon be underway, especially once they returned from their wedding trip.

If her suspicions were correct, she would need the nursery put back to rights not much after the new year. She couldn't help but smile with hope at the thought. And there was Xavier's mother who would need a suite of rooms as well.

"Agents? But I've already told you. My research won't be used for war."

Avery waved a hand. "It's precisely that. Our agents keep the wars from happening. I must keep them safe so they can prevent further atrocities. That is where I need your technology, Xavier."

"Your agents?" Xavier quipped. "Why do you keep referring to them as yours?"

Emily's face heated as Avery's gaze fell on her.

She shrugged. "I'm not to discuss War Office business with outsiders, am I?" She turned to her husband. "It would be a great deal less confusing if you just came on as a consultant."

Xavier turned quickly too Avery. "You're the new head agent at the Office, aren't you?"

Avery pushed his hands together. "I would be at that. I'm sorry to have to keep that fact from you, Xavier, but it's confidential as you must understand. If you were to join us in our fight for peace, I would be a great deal more forthcoming." His smile was wry.

"Fight for peace?" Xavier tilted his head in question.

Emily squeezed his hand again. "I know you've seen

enough instances of danger and intrigue when it comes to my family, but War Office work is largely about passing information. It's our duty to prevent the bigger conflicts." She watched his face, saw the message sink in. "You would be helping us keep peace in a world that grows ever more divided."

She watched his eyes change, and she could feel what he felt. The transformation of an idea long held that turned out to be misunderstood. Slowly, he turned back to Avery.

"I should like to think it over." His words were gruff, but he had to clear his throat before he finished them. "I will deliver my answer at the return of our wedding trip."

Avery stood, clapped his hands together. "Splendid! We will be delighted to have you on board. What you were doing with refracting lenses no one has attempted since—"

"I didn't agree yet." Xavier stood, both hands planted on his walking stick.

Avery waved him off. "Of course not! We'll see you upon your return. If you could revisit the hypothesis you made on condensing the lens to—"

"Still haven't agreed," Xavier cried, holding up his walking stick now.

Emily snatched his hand, pulled him toward the door. Avery bowed and waved them off.

"Good day, my lord," she called out. "We'll see you in a few months."

The only reply was Avery's uproarious laugh.

Hours later they stood on the deck of the *Caroline* as she pulled away from London. Emily had never left England, had never stepped on another shore. Exhilaration and fear shot through her, and she shivered.

But Xavier was there, and he gathered her into his arms.

"Do you know three months ago I detested the sight of London?" he murmured against her hair.

"And how do you feel about it now?"

He eased her back so he could look at her face. His smile was warm, genuine, and filled with a symphony of love.

"I'm going to miss it," he whispered.

She pulled him back into her embrace.

"We'll be back soon enough. For now, you must tell me about this exotic place called Cambridge."

His laugh was low and tickled her ear. She nestled closer and watched London slip away.

But the fear she felt for only an instant never returned because whenever she felt its pull, whenever the terror of the future, of the unknown into which they stepped consumed her, she remembered.

She always had her family, a family that included Xavier now, and her family would always be waiting.

Waiting for her to come home.

ABOUT THE AUTHOR

Jessie decided to be a writer because there were too many lives she wanted to live to just pick one.

Taking her history degree dangerously, Jessie tells the stories of courageous heroines, the men who dared to love them, and the world that tried to defeat them.

Jessie lives in New Hampshire where if she is not at her desk writing, she's probably letting the dog out. Again.

For more, visit her website at jessieclever.com.